SEEKERS
THE QUEST BEGINS

ERIN
HUNTER

HarperTrophy®
An Imprint of HarperCollinsPublishers

HarperTrophy® is a registered trademark of HarperCollins Publishers.

The Quest Begins
Copyright © 2008 by Working Partners Limited
· Series created by Working Partners Limited
All rights reserved. Printed in the United States of America. No part of this book may
be used or reproduced in any manner whatsoever without written permission except in
the case of brief quotations embodied in critical articles and reviews. For information
address HarperCollins Children's Books, a division of HarperCollins Publishers,
10 East 53rd Street, New York, NY 10022.

www.harpercollinschildrens.com

Library of Congress Cataloging-in-Publication Data
Hunter, Erin.
   The quest begins / Erin Hunter. — 1st ed.
     p.   cm. — (Seekers ; #1)
   Summary: Three young bears of different species—one black, one polar, and one
grizzly—travel on a perilous quest to the Northern Lights, escorting a shape-shifting
grizzly cub whose destiny will affect them all.
   ISBN 978-0-06-087124-6
   [1. Bears—Fiction. 2. Fantasy.] I. Title.
PZ7.H916625Qu 2008   2007049581
[Fic—dc22]   CIP
                                                               AC

Typography by Hilary Zarycky
❖
First Harper Trophy edition, 2009

11 12 13 LP/CW 10 9

With special thanks to Tui Sutherland

Seal
Rock

Walrus
Rock

Place of
Everlasting Ice

Ice Break

Place of the
Caribou
Flat-faces

LAST
GREAT
WILDERNESS

Place of
Fishing
Flat-faces

Snowgoose
Island

River

BLACKWATER
MOUNTAINS

Caribou
Valley

Bear
Rock

Great
Bear
Lake

Paw Print
Island

SMOKE MOUNTAINS

Big
River

The Claw Path

Place of
Metal Birds

SKY

RIDGE

TOKLO'S
BIRTHDEN

Bear
Snout
Mountain

Three
Lakes

SilverPath

LUSA'S
BEAR
BOWL

Great
Salmon
River

The Bears' Journey: Bear View

Lusa ———
Kallik —·—·—·—
Toklo ·············

Star

Island

Whale Rock

The Melting Sea

BURN-SKY
GATHERING
PLACE

BlackPath

The Bears' Journey: Human View

ELLESMERE
ISLAND

GREENLAND

BAFFIN ISLAND

Godthab

Iqaluit

Circle

Atlantic
Ocean

Hudson Bay

St. John's

Churchill   WAPUSK
NATIONAL
PARK

Lake
Winnipeg

Quebec

Trans-Canada   Highway   Montreal

Winnipeg

Ottawa

Boston

STATES

Toronto

St. Paul

New York

Minneapolis

CHAPTER ONE

Kallik

"*A long, long time ago, long* before bears walked the earth, a frozen sea shattered into pieces, scattering tiny bits of ice across the darkness of the sky. Each of those pieces of ice contains the spirit of a bear, and if you are good, and brave, and strong, one day your spirit will join them."

Kallik leaned against her mother's hind leg, listening to the story she had heard so many times before. Beside her, her brother, Taqqiq, stretched, batting at the snowy walls of the den with his paws. He was always restless when the weather trapped them inside.

"When you look carefully at the sky," Kallik's mother continued, "you can see a pattern of stars in the shape of the Great Bear, Silaluk. She is running around and around the Pathway Star."

"Why is she running?" Kallik chipped in. She knew the answer, but this was the part of the story where she always asked.

"Because it is snow-sky and she is hunting. With her quick and powerful claws, she hunts seal and beluga whale. She is the greatest of all hunters on the ice."

Kallik loved hearing about Silaluk's strength.

"But then the ice melts," Nisa said in a hushed voice. "And she can't hunt anymore. She gets hungrier and hungrier, but she has to keep running because three hunters pursue her: Robin, Chickadee, and Moose Bird. They chase her for many moons, all through the warm days, until the end of burn-sky. Then, as the warmth begins to leave the earth, they finally catch up to her.

"They gather around her and strike the fatal blow with their spears. The heart's blood of the Great Bear falls to the ground, and everywhere it falls the leaves on the trees turn red and yellow. Some of the blood falls on Robin's chest, and that is why the bird has a red breast."

"Does the Great Bear die?" breathed Taqqiq.

"She does," Nisa replied. Kallik shivered. Every time she heard this story it frightened her all over again. Her mother went on.

"But then snow-sky returns, bringing back the ice. Silaluk is reborn and the ice-hunt begins all over again, season after season."

Kallik snuggled into her mother's soft white fur. The walls of the den curved up and around them, making a sheltering cave of snow that Kallik could barely glimpse in the dark, although it was only a few pawlengths from her nose. Outside a fierce wind howled across the ice, sending tendrils of freezing air through the entrance tunnel into their den. Kallik was glad they didn't have to be out there tonight.

Inside the den, she and her brother were warm and safe. Kallik wondered if Silaluk had ever had a mother and brother, or a den where she could hide from the storms. If the Great Bear had a family to keep her safe, maybe she wouldn't have to run from the hunters. Kallik knew her mother would protect her from anything scary until she was big enough and strong enough and smart enough to protect herself.

Taqqiq batted at Kallik's nose with his large furry paw. "Kallik's scared," he teased. She could make out his eyes gleaming in the darkness.

"Am not!" Kallik protested.

"She thinks robins and chickadees are going to come after her," Taqqiq said with an amused rumble.

"No, I don't!" Kallik growled, digging her claws into the snow. "That's not why I'm scared!"

"Ha! You *are* scared! I knew it!"

Nisa nudged Kallik gently with her muzzle. "Why are you frightened, little one? You've heard the legend of the Great Bear many times before."

"I know," Kallik said. "It's just . . . it reminds me that soon snow-sky will be over, and the snow and ice will all melt away. And then we won't be able to hunt anymore, and we'll be hungry all the time. Right? Isn't that what happens during burn-sky?"

Kallik's mother sighed, her massive shoulders shifting under her snow-white pelt. "Oh, my little star," she murmured. "I didn't mean to worry you." She touched her black nose to Kallik's. "You haven't lived through a burn-sky yet, Kallik. It's not as terrible as it sounds. We'll find a way to survive, even if it means eating berries and grass for a little while."

"What is berries and grass?" Kallik asked.

Taqqiq wrinkled his muzzle. "Does it taste as good as seals?"

"No," Nisa said, "but berries and grass will keep you alive, which is the important thing. I'll show them to you when we reach land." She fell silent. For a few heartbeats, all Kallik could hear was the thin wail of the wind battering at the snowy walls.

She pressed closer to her mother, feeling the warmth radiating from her skin. "Are you sad?" she whispered.

Nisa touched Kallik with her muzzle again. "Don't be afraid," she said, a note of determination in her voice. "Remember the story of the Great Bear. No matter what happens, the ice will always return. And all the bears gather on the edge of the sea to meet it. Silaluk will always get back on her paws. She's a survivor, and so are we."

"I can survive anything!" Taqqiq boasted, puffing up his fur. "I'll fight a walrus! I'll swim across an ocean! I'll battle all the white bears we meet!"

"I'm sure you will, dear. But why don't you start by going to sleep?" Nisa suggested.

As Taqqiq circled and scuffled in the snow beside her, making himself comfortable, Kallik rested her chin on her mother's back and closed her eyes. Her mother was right; she didn't need to be afraid. As long as she was with her family, she'd always be safe and warm, like she was right now in their den.

Kallik woke to an eerie silence. Faint light filtered through the walls, casting pale blue and pink shadows on her mother and brother as they slept. At first she thought her ears must be full of snow, but when she shook her head, Nisa grunted in her sleep, and Kallik realized that it was quiet because the storm had finally passed.

"Hey," she said, poking her brother with her nose. "Hey, Taqqiq, wake up. The storm has stopped."

Taqqiq lifted his head with a bleary expression. The fur on one side of his muzzle was flattened, making him look lopsided.

Kallik barked with laughter. "Come on, you big, lazy seal," she said. "Let's go play outside."

"All right!" Taqqiq said, scrambling to his paws.

"Not without me watching you," their mother muttered with her eyes still closed. Kallik jumped. She'd thought Nisa was asleep.

"We won't go far," Kallik promised. "We'll stay right next to the den. Please can we go outside?"

Nisa huffed and the fur on her back quivered like a breeze was passing over it. "Let's all go out," she said. She pushed herself to her massive paws and turned around carefully in the small space, bundling her cubs to one side.

Sniffing cautiously, she nosed her way down the entrance tunnel, brushing away snow that the storm had piled up.

Kallik could see tension in her mother's hindquarters. "I don't know why she's so careful," she whispered to her brother. "Aren't white bears the biggest, scariest animals on the ice? Nothing would dare attack us!"

"Except maybe a bigger white bear, seal-brain!" Taqqiq retorted. "Maybe you haven't noticed how little you are."

Kallik bristled. "I may not be as big as you," she growled, "but I'm just as fierce!"

"Let's find out!" Taqqiq challenged as their mother finally padded out of the tunnel. He sprinted after her, sliding down the slope of the tunnel and scrambling out into the snow.

Kallik leaped to her paws and chased him. A clump of snow fell on her muzzle on her way out of the tunnel and she shook her head vigorously to get it off. The fresh, cold air tingled in her nostrils, full of the scent of fish and ice and faraway clouds. Kallik felt the last of her sleepiness melt away. The ice was where she belonged, not underground, buried alive. She batted a chunk of snow at Taqqiq, who dodged away with a yelp.

He chased her in a circle until she dove into the fresh snow, digging up clumps with her long claws and breathing in the sparkling whiteness. Nisa sat watching them, chuffing occasionally and sniffing the air with a wary expression.

"I'm coming for you," Taqqiq growled at Kallik, crouching low to the ground. "I'm a ferocious walrus, swimming through the water to get you." He pushed himself through the snow with his paws. Kallik braced herself to jump away, but before she could move, he leaped forward and bowled her over. They rolled through the snow, squalling excitedly, until Kallik managed to wriggle free.

"Ha!" she cried.

"Roar!" Taqqiq bellowed. "The walrus is really angry now!" He dug his paws into the snow, kicking a spray of white ice into their mother's face.

"Hey," Nisa growled. She cuffed Taqqiq lightly with her massive paw, knocking him to the ground. "That's enough snowballing around. It's time to find something to eat."

"Hooray, hooray!" Kallik yipped, jumping around her mother's legs. They hadn't eaten since before the storm, two sunrises ago, and her tummy was rumbling louder than Taqqiq's walrus roar.

The sun was hidden by trails of gray clouds that grew thicker as they walked across the ice, turning into rolls of fog that shrouded the world around them. The only sound Kallik could hear was the snow crunching under their paws. Once she thought she heard a bird calling from up in the sky, but when she looked up she couldn't see anything but drifting fog.

"Why is it so cloudy?" Taqqiq complained, stopping to rub his eyes with his paws.

"The fog is good for us," Nisa said, touching her nose to the ice. "It hides us as we hunt, so our prey won't see us coming."

"I like to see where I'm going," Taqqiq insisted. "I don't like walking in clouds. Everything's all blurry and wet."

"I don't mind the fog," Kallik said, breathing in the heavy, misty air.

"You can ride on my back," Nisa said to her son, nudging

him with her muzzle. Taqqiq rumbled happily and scrambled up, clutching at tufts of her snow-white fur to give himself a boost. He stretched out on her back, high above Kallik, and they started walking again.

Kallik liked finding the sharp, cool scent of the ice under the dense, watery smell of the fog. She liked the hint of oceans and fish and salt and faraway sand that drifted through the scents, reminding her of what was below the ice and what it connected to. She glanced up at her mother, who had her nose lifted and was sniffing the air, too. Kallik knew that her mother wasn't just drawing in the crisp, icy smells. Nisa was studying them, searching for a clue that would lead them to food.

"You should both do this, too," Nisa said. "Try to find any smell that stands out from the ice and snow."

Taqqiq just snuggled farther into her fur, but Kallik tried to imitate her mother, swinging her head back and forth as she sniffed. She had to learn everything she could from Nisa so she could take care of herself. At least she still had a long time before that day came—all of burn-sky and the next snow-sky as well.

"Some bears can follow scents for skylengths," Nisa said. "All the way to the edge of the sky and then the next edge and the next."

Kallik wished her nose were that powerful. Maybe it would be one day.

Nisa lifted her head and started trotting faster. Taqqiq dug his claws in to stay on her back. Soon Kallik saw what her mother was heading for—a hole in the ice. She knew what that meant. *Seals!*

Nisa put her nose close to the ice and sniffed all around the edge of the hole. Kallik followed closely, sniffing everywhere her mother sniffed. She was sure she could smell a faint trace of seal. This must be one of the breathing holes where a seal would surface to take a breath before hiding down in the freezing water again.

"Seals are so dumb," Taqqiq observed from his perch on Nisa's back. "If they can't breathe in the water, why do they live in it? Why don't they live on land, like white bears?"

"Perhaps because then it'd be much easier for bears like us to catch them and eat them!" Kallik guessed.

"*Shhhh.* Concentrate," Nisa said. "Can you smell the seal?"

"I think so," Kallik said. It was a furry, blubbery smell, thicker than the smell of fish. It made her mouth water.

"All right," Nisa said, crouching by the hole. "Taqqiq, come down and lie next to your sister." Taqqiq obeyed, sliding off her back and padding over to Kallik. "Be very quiet," Nisa instructed them. "Don't move, and don't make a sound."

Kallik and Taqqiq did as she said. They had done this several times before, so they knew what to do. The first time, Taqqiq had gotten bored and started yawning and fidgeting. Nisa had cuffed him and scolded him, explaining that his noise would scare away the only food they'd seen in days. By now the cubs were both nearly as good at staying quiet as their mother was.

Kallik watched the breathing hole, her ears pricked and her

nose keenly aware of every change in the air. A small wind blew drifts of snow across the ice, and the fog continued to roll around all three bears, making Kallik's fur feel wet and heavy.

After a while she began to get restless. She didn't know how her mother could stand to do nothing for such a long time, watching and watching in case the seal broke through the water. The chill of the ice below her was beginning to seep through Kallik's thick fur. She had to force herself not to shiver and send vibrations through the ice that might warn the seal they were there.

She stared past the tip of her nose at the ice around the breathing hole. The dark water below the surface lapped at the jagged edge. It was strange to think that that same dark water was only a muzzlelength below her, on the other side of the thick ice. The ice seemed so strong and solid, as if it went down forever. . . .

Strange shadows and shapes seemed to dance inside the ice, forming bubbles and whorls. It was odd—ice was white from far away but nearly clear up close and full of patterns. It almost seemed like things were living inside the ice. Right below her front paws, for instance, there was a large, dark bubble slowly moving from one side to the other. Kallik stared at it, wondering if it was the spirit of a white bear trapped in the ice. One that hadn't made it as far as the stars in the sky.

Taqqiq leaned over and peered at the bubble. "You know what Mother says," he whispered. "The shapes below the ice are dead bears. They're watching you . . . right . . . now."

"I'm not scared," Kallik insisted. "They're trapped inside the ice, aren't they? So they can't come out and hurt me."

"Not unless the ice melts," Taqqiq said, trying to sound menacing.

"Hush," Nisa growled, her eyes still fixed on the breathing hole. Taqqiq fell silent again, resting his head on his paws. Slowly his eyes began to droop, and soon he was asleep.

Kallik was feeling sleepy, too, but she wanted to stay awake to see the seal come out. And she didn't want to fall asleep so close to the spirit that was still moving below her feet. She flexed her paws, trying not to nod off.

Suddenly there was a splash, and Kallik saw a sleek gray head break through the surface of the water. She barely had time to notice the dark spots on its fur before Nisa was lunging headfirst into the hole. With a swift movement, she seized the seal and flipped it out of the water onto the ice. It writhed and flopped for a moment before her giant claw sliced into it, killing it with a single blow.

Kallik couldn't imagine ever being fast enough to catch a seal before it disappeared back under the ice again.

Nisa ripped open the seal and said the words of thanks to the ice spirits. Her cubs gathered around her to feed. Kallik inhaled the smell of freshly killed meat, the delicious fat and chewy skin. She dug her teeth into the prey and tore out a mouthful, realizing how hungry she had been.

Suddenly Nisa raised her head, her fur bristling. Kallik tensed and sniffed the air. A large male white bear was lumbering out of the fog toward them. His yellowish fur was matted with snow and his paws were as big as Kallik's head. He headed straight for their seal, hissing and rumbling.

Taqqiq bristled, but Nisa shoved him back with her paw. "Stay close to me," she warned. "Let's get out of here."

She turned to run, nudging her cubs ahead of her. Kallik sprinted as fast as she could, her heart pounding. What if the seal wasn't enough for the strange bear? What if he came after *her* next? As they raced up the slope, Kallik glanced back and saw that the bear wasn't chasing them. Instead, he was bent over the dead seal, tearing into it.

"It's not fair!" she wailed. "That was our seal!"

"I know," Nisa said with a sigh. Her paws seemed heavy as she slowed down to a walk.

"Why should that lazy bear get our meal, when you did all the work of catching it?" Kallik insisted.

"That bear needs to eat as much as we do," Nisa said. "When seals are scarce, you have to get used to fighting for every meal. You can't trust any other bears, my cubs. We must stick together, because we are the only ones who will look after one another."

Kallik and Taqqiq exchanged glances. Kallik knew she would do anything to take care of her mother and her brother. She hadn't seen many other bears, but when she had, they had been big and fierce and scary, just like the one that had stolen their seal. Maybe white bears weren't meant to have friends. Maybe the ice didn't allow it.

"We'll be all right if we stay together," Nisa promised.

"There's food to be found if you know where to look, and if you're patient enough to catch it. So don't get your head all matted with snow about it. I'll be here to look after you until you're strong enough to hunt on your own."

She swung her head around to the left. "Can you smell that?"

Kallik sniffed. She did smell something! But it wasn't seal . . . it was something else. Something fishier, but not exactly fish. She didn't recognize it.

"What do you think it is?" she asked Taqqiq. He was crouched down as if he was stalking something, and as she spoke, he leaped forward, pinning down a snowflake that had drifted to the ground. Kallik looked up and saw that it was snowing again. Her brother was happily batting at the snowflakes. It didn't look as if he'd even tried to sniff for what her mother had scented.

"Taqqiq, pay attention," Kallik said. "You'll have to hunt for yourself one day, too."

"All right, bossy paws," Taqqiq said, twitching his nose dramatically from side to side.

"Come along, quickly," Nisa said. "Try not to make too much noise." They followed their mother across the ice, padding as quietly as possible. The scent didn't seem to be moving away.

"Is it staying still?" Kallik asked. "Does that mean it doesn't know we're coming?"

"One way to throw off your prey is to hide your scent," Nisa said. "Like this—follow me." She led them to a channel of melted water in the ice and they swam across one by one.

"Blech, now my fur's all wet," Taqqiq complained, shaking himself as they climbed out the other side.

"That should make it harder to smell us coming," Nisa said.

"And that big, old bear back there won't be able to follow our trail, either, right?" Kallik said.

"Hopefully," Nisa said, touching Kallik's muzzle with hers.

As they got closer, the fishy scent got stronger, and Kallik could smell salt and blood and faraway ocean scents mingled with it. Soon she saw a dark shape lying on the ice. At first she thought it must be a giant seal, from the way the flippers were splayed out, but then she saw that it was the carcass of a whale. Huge chunks had been torn off it, and there were large bite marks and claw slashes in its side. The snow around it was covered in blood.

"It's a gray whale," Nisa explained. "Another bear must have killed it and dragged it onto the ice."

Kallik stared at the carcass in awe. It must have been a very strong bear to overpower something so big and pull it all the way out of the water. Even with the large bites taken out of it, there was still plenty for the three of them to eat. Hungrily, she stretched out her muzzle and tugged a piece of meat free.

Nisa nudged her, making her drop the meat. "Don't forget to express gratitude to the spirits of the ice," Kallik's mother said gently. "You must always remember that you are part of a bigger world." She bowed her head and touched her nose to the ice. "We thank you, spirits of the ice, for guiding us to this meal," she murmured. Kallik imitated her mother, whispering

the same words, and Taqqiq followed. Then, with happy rum-
bles, they began to eat.

The fog had rolled away by the time night fell, and the stars
shone brightly in a clear sky. Kallik sprawled on the ice, her
full belly keeping her warm. Next to her were her mother and
brother. Not a hint of a breeze stirred the fur on their shoulders; for once, the wind had died down and the sea far
beneath the ice was silent.

"Mother?" Kallik asked. "Please tell me again about the
spirits under the ice."

Taqqiq gave a little huff of laughter, but Nisa touched her
nose to her daughter's side with a serious expression.

"When a white bear dies," she said, "its spirit sinks into the
ice, lower and lower, until all you can see is a shadow under
the ice. But you shouldn't be frightened of them, little star.
The spirits are there to guide you. If you are a good bear, they
will always be there to take care of you and help you find food
or shelter."

"I'd rather *you* took care of me," Kallik said with a shiver.

"I'll take care of you, too," her mother promised.

"What about the ice spots in the sky?" Kallik said, pointing
her muzzle upward. "Aren't those the spirits of bears, too?"

"When the ice melts," Nisa explained, "the bear spirits
escape and drift up to the sky on the snow-winds, light as
snowflakes, where they become stars. Those spirits are watching you, too, only from farther away."

"What about that star over there?" Taqqiq asked. "The one

that's really bright. I've even seen it in the daytime, once, and it never moves like the others do."

"That's the Pathway Star," Nisa said.

"Why is it called the Pathway Star?" Taqqiq prompted.

"Because if you follow it," Nisa said solemnly, "it will lead you to a place far, far away where the ice never melts."

"Never?" Kallik gasped. "You mean there's no burn-sky? We could hunt all the time?"

"No burn-sky, no melting ice, no eating berries or living on the land," Nisa said. "The bear spirits dance for joy across the sky, all in different colors."

"Why don't we go there?" Taqqiq asked. "If it's so wonderful?" Kallik nodded. She felt a tingling in her paws, as if she could run all the way to this place where they would be safe forever.

"It is a long way away," Nisa rumbled. "Much too far for us to travel." Her black eyes stared into the distance, silvery glints of the moon swimming in their depths. "But perhaps we may have to make the journey . . . one day."

"Really? When?" Kallik demanded, but her mother rested her head on her paws and fell silent. She obviously didn't want to answer any more questions. Kallik curled into a ball in the curve of her mother's side and watched the ice shimmering under the moon until she fell asleep. In her dreams, bear spirits rose from the ice and began to dance, their paws light as fur as they romped and slid across the frozen landscape.

* * *

A strange creaking noise woke Kallik the next morning. It sounded like a bear yawning loudly, or the wind howling from underwater, but the air was still, and the noise came from the ice, not the sky. Her mother was already awake, padding in a circle around them with her nose lifted.

Kallik scrambled to her paws and shook herself. Her coat felt heavy with moisture, and the air was damp and soft instead of crisp and clear like it had been the night before. She turned to her brother, who was lying on the ice beside her, apparently still asleep. She nudged him with her muzzle.

"Walrus attack!" Taqqiq bellowed, suddenly leaping to his paws and knocking her over. Nisa spun around with a snarl, but stopped when she saw that her cubs were just playing.

"Quiet," she growled. "Taqqiq, stop acting like a wild goose. There is no time for playing. We have to get moving." She started across the ice without looking back. Kallik and Taqqiq scrambled to catch up. Nisa's grouchiness made Kallik nervous. Why would she scold them for playing now, when she'd let them roll around having fun the day before?

The creaking began again as they traveled across the ice. Nisa paused and swung her head around to listen. It seemed like the sound of the ice groaning and yawning underpaw was getting louder. Kallik could tell that her mother knew what this sound was—and that it meant something very bad.

Suddenly there was a loud crack and a horrible sucking noise, and Kallik felt the ground tilt below her. She was thrown off her paws and found herself sliding along ice that was no longer flat but sloped down steeply toward dark water. With a terrified squeal, Kallik scrabbled on the ice, her claws sliding helplessly on the slick surface.

A giant paw grabbed her and hauled her backward onto solid ice again. Kallik stumbled as Nisa bundled her away from the crack in the ice, where waves slapped hungrily against the new edge.

"Wow!" Taqqiq yelped. "The ice just snapped in two! Kallik, I thought you'd be swallowed up by the sea and we'd never see you again!"

Nisa hissed with frustration. Kallik peered around her mother's legs and saw that the ice in front of them had broken into two large chunks that were drifting apart on the sea.

"Already?" Nisa muttered. "But we've had no time at all on the ice! How are we supposed to survive on land if we can't hunt for long enough before?" She paced along the jagged edge of the ice, snarling at the waves that lapped at her paws.

"Mother?" Kallik whimpered. "What's happening? Is it . . . is it burn-sky?"

"It's too early for burn-sky," Nisa said. "But the ice-melt is coming earlier each season. We have less and less time to hunt." She chuffed angrily. "It can't go on like this."

"What do we do?" Kallik asked. "What's going to happen to us if the ice melts too soon?"

Nisa just growled, pawing the edge of the ice.

"Should we move to land?" Taqqiq asked. "Isn't that what we're supposed to do when the ice melts?"

"No," Nisa said, lifting her muzzle. "We must continue to

hunt, or else we shall not survive the long, hungry months of burn-sky."

"But—" Kallik started, glancing at the surging water and broken ice before them. What if the ice all melted before they could get to the land?

"We must go on," Nisa insisted. "We cannot go to the land yet—or we will all die."

She moved off across the ice, and Taqqiq followed her. Kallik paused for a moment on the jagged edge, the dark water lapping at her paws. She stared at the broken chunk of ice floating across the water from her. How far was it to land? Was there enough ice left for them to get there? And if there wasn't . . . what would happen to them?

CHAPTER TWO

Lusa

"*And over there you can see* Lusa, our youngest black bear, who is five months old. She was born right here in the zoo. Black bears actually come in a lot of different colors like cinnamon or gray, but Lusa's name means 'black' in the Choctaw language, and if you look closely you won't find one speck of another color on her coat. That's her mother, Ashia, and her father, King.

"All North American bears are suffering from the changes in their environment. For the most part, black bears are doing better than white bears and grizzlies, but we have had to rescue some of them when they run into trouble. We found King, for instance, wandering at the edge of the forest. He would have starved to death if we hadn't brought him here. Lusa's never known any other place, and she feels safe around humans, so she is certainly better off living in the zoo with us."

Patches of snow covered the bare rocks and grassy ground

inside the Bear Bowl, but the smell of leaftime was in the air, and a few purple crocuses were already nudging their way through the dirt. Lusa stood on her hind legs and twitched her ears at the group of flat-faces on the upper ridge of the Bowl. Several flat-face cubs were leaning against the railing, pointing at her and chattering. They sounded like birds. She didn't understand most of what the zoo guide was saying, but she knew her name in the flat-face language. Her feeders called her Lusa when they brought her food, so she could tell when the guides were talking about her to the visiting flat-faces. The wind brought a whiff of their strange scent to her—a warm, milky smell covered over by sharp, almost flowery scents. Their high-pitched voices made her ears hurt, but she liked the sound of their laughter.

Dropping back down to her paws, she scrambled into the part of the Bowl where three tall trees grew next to a log that never rotted. Lusa called this the Forest. Raising herself onto her hind legs again, she batted her paws in the air, as if she were fighting a butterfly, to catch the attention of the flat-faces. When she was sure they were watching her, she jumped onto the log and ran along it, jumping down on all fours at the other end.

As she'd hoped, the flat-faces made the quick huffing sound that meant they were pleased, and the guide leaned over the rail to give her some fruit. Lusa had to stand on her back legs and stretch as high as she could to reach the pear.

"What you see Lusa doing here is similar to what bears like her would do in the wild—stretching up into the trees to reach food like fruit, nuts, berries, and honey," the guide chattered.

Lusa wrapped her paws around the piece of fruit and nibbled at it. Suddenly she felt a paw cuff her shoulder. She knew from its size that it wasn't one of the bigger bears, so she had a good chance of defending her pear. With a snort, she tucked her paw around the fruit and turned to face Yogi, the other cub in the Bowl.

Yogi was one season-circle old, but he hadn't been born here. He talked sometimes about another zoo, where his mother lived, but he didn't remember it very well. He was almost as black as Lusa, but he had a pale splash of white fur on his chest.

With a huffing sound, he lifted himself onto his hind legs so he towered over her. "Lusa, share!" he demanded. "Give me some!"

"No!" she said. "It's mine!" She stuffed the fruit in her mouth and ran away across the enclosure. The flat-faces up above chattered and giggled as Yogi chased her.

Lusa scrambled up onto the Mountains near the back of the Bowl. She was better than Yogi was at balancing on the four large boulders. He huffed and grunted as he climbed after her. With a playful snort, Lusa leaped off the last boulder and tumbled straight into her father, King, who was dozing in the sun.

"*Hrr*—what?" her father mumbled. Then Yogi came bounding off the rocks after Lusa and crashed into King as well. This brought the giant black bear to his paws with a roar.

"Get off!" he bellowed, swatting at them. "Go away!"

Yogi fled to the Fence at the far end of the Bowl. On the other side of the Fence, Lusa could see the old grizzly rolling on his back, muttering to himself. Chuffing with laughter, Lusa followed Yogi.

"How can you find that funny?" Yogi asked, his fur standing on end. "Your father is so scary!"

"Oh, he's a big furball," Lusa said. "His bluster is worse than his bite."

"You don't know that," Yogi pointed out. "He's never bitten you—yet!"

"He wouldn't!" Lusa protested. "He was just startled, that's all. You know he's a bit deaf. He probably didn't hear us coming." She was pleased to see that Yogi had forgotten about the fruit. She sat down and finished eating it, licking the juice off her paws with her long tongue.

"Well, I'm not going to bother him again," Yogi said. "I'm going to stay over here and watch the white bears through the Fence." Lusa was glad that the bears in the Bowl were kept apart from one another by the cold gray webs of the Fences. She liked being with other black bears, but she was a little bit afraid of the big brown grizzly and the massive white bears. They were much, much bigger than she was, and their deafening roars sometimes kept her awake at night.

"That sounds like a good idea to me." Lusa turned and saw her mother, Ashia, lumbering toward them. "You two should learn not to disturb King, especially when he's resting."

"We weren't *disturbing* him," Lusa objected.

"Just stay out of his way and don't cause trouble," Ashia scolded.

"I don't want to watch the white bears," Lusa said to Yogi. "They're boring. Let's go hide in the Caves."

They scampered off to the back corner of the Bowl, where a ledge of white stone hung over a rocky patch of ground hidden in shadow. Lusa and Yogi crowded into the shadows, each trying to keep their paws out of the sun. They crouched as low as they could get and held very still.

"*Shhh,*" Lusa whispered. "There's a grizzly crashing through the forest."

"It's coming after us," Yogi whispered. "It's going to chase us with its giant hooked claws."

"But if we stay very still, it won't know we're here," Lusa breathed.

"Whoever moves first loses," Yogi challenged.

"All right," Lusa said, pressing her muzzle to her paws. "I'm going to win."

They fell silent. Lusa willed every muscle in her body to stay perfectly still. She felt the wind tickling around her ears and nose. She could smell every other bear in her section of the Bowl: King dozing in the sun, Ashia snuffling around the bottom of the wall for anything the flat-faces had dropped, Stella scratching her side against one of the trees.

In the next enclosure, one of the giant white bears was swimming around and around in a circle, from one lump of stone to the next. Lusa had seen it do this for hours. The white bears were even less friendly than the grizzly, who lived on his own and didn't say much. Lusa didn't know their names. The white bears stayed on their island of gray stone or in the chilly water and ignored the bears on either side of them. Lusa was fine with that; they were nearly three times her mother's size, and she sometimes got the feeling that they'd be perfectly happy to have her for dinner instead of the slabs of meat the flat-faces threw over the wall.

Her nose was beginning to itch. Lost in thought about the white bears, she forgot about the competition and reached up to scratch it.

"Ha!" Yogi yelped, jumping to his paws. "You moved! I win!"

"Oh," Lusa said, feeling foolish. "Well, it doesn't matter anyway. If a grizzly spotted me, I would just run up a tree. I can climb much better than any old brown bear!"

"Let's ask Stella to tell us the story of the Bear Tree again," Yogi suggested, flicking his ears.

The two cubs bounded across to Stella. She was older than they were, but younger than King, and she had lots of excellent stories about bears out in the wild, even though she'd never lived there herself. She had come from another zoo, where the bears had told her many things about life outside of the Fences. Her fur was a reddish brown, not dark black like Lusa's or Yogi's.

"Stella, Stella!" the cubs called.

"Tell us the story of the bear that turned into the tallest tree in the forest," Yogi begged.

"Please?" Lusa added.

The older bear snorted and sat down, lifting her front paws and raising her muzzle in the air, as if sniffing the wind. "Can you smell the forest?" Stella murmured.

The cubs lifted their noses into the air, flaring their nostrils. A million scents flooded Lusa's nose. She could smell all the flat-faces pressing through the zoo. She could smell the mouthwatering scent of flat-face food, and the tangy, almost-flower scent of their brightly colored pelts. She could smell many unfamiliar animals as well. Even though she'd never met them, she knew they were alive from the way their scent changed as they moved around their dens. She wondered what they looked like, and whether they'd be friendly or scary. And she could smell green things growing, but she didn't know if that was the forest that Stella meant.

"Maybe," Yogi said. "I can smell something."

"With your nose, it could be anything," Lusa teased.

"A long time ago," Stella said, ignoring them, "this whole land was covered in forest, and bears roamed freely wherever they wanted to go."

"What happened to it?" Lusa asked. "Where did the forest go?"

"Well, the flat-faces came and changed the land," Stella said, "but there is still forest out there, a long way away—like where King was found."

"Tell us about the forest," Yogi asked. "What does it look like?"

"There are trees as far as you can see, reaching in every direction, farther than any bear can run in a day."

"Even a brown bear?" Lusa asked. She'd heard about how fast grizzlies could run, although the one next door mostly lay around grumbling.

"Even a brown bear," Stella said. "And inside every one of those trees is the spirit of a bear."

"Are there that many bears in the world?" Lusa breathed.

"There used to be," Stella said. "And one of them lived right here in the Bowl, long ago, before you were born."

"What happened to him?" Yogi asked.

"He grew old—very old," Stella said. "He was much older than King. His muzzle was grizzled with gray fur, and when he walked he creaked like the branches of a tree in the wind."

"What was his name?" Lusa asked.

Stella stopped and thought for a moment, scratching her ear with one paw. "His name was Old Bear," she said. Lusa wondered if she was making that up. "Anyway, one day we came out for our morning meal, and he was lying under his favorite tree. He used to sit in its branches all day long, but on this day, he was just lying there on the ground. We went over and poked him with our paws and our noses, but he didn't move. His scent had changed, too. He was dead."

Lusa and Yogi both shivered, shaking the chills out of their fur.

"The flat-faces came in and took him away, but we could feel his spirit was still here in the Bowl. It whooshed around us like the wind all that day, making our fur prickle and our claws sting like ice. And then, as the sun was sinking beyond the edge of the Bowl, we saw something new in the pattern of the bark on the tallest tree in the Forest."

"What was it?" Yogi asked, wide-eyed.

"It was the face of a bear," Stella said. "You can see it on the side that faces the Mountains. The spirit of Old Bear lives in that tree still."

Lusa and Yogi stared at the tallest tree in awe, wondering if Old Bear's spirit was staring back at them. Lusa thought she wouldn't like to be trapped in a tree. She'd rather have paws for running and a nose for smelling.

"Let's go look for the face," Lusa suggested, and Yogi bounded after her over to the trunk of the tree. They padded around it in a circle, staring at the knots in the trunk. Lusa stopped and lifted onto her hind legs, peering at the bark.

"I think I see it!" she cried. "I see a face!"

Yogi stood up beside her. He tilted his head. "I don't see anything," he rumbled.

"It's right *there*," Lusa insisted, waving her paw. "See, this is his eye, and this—" As she leaned forward to bat the small black spot that looked like a bear's nose, suddenly it moved!

"It's alive!" Lusa yelped, leaping back. "Old Bear is coming out of the tree!" She fled to the nearest boulder, her heart thumping wildly. But when she turned around, Yogi was rolling on the ground laughing.

"What's so funny?" Lusa demanded.

"It's a beetle," Yogi huffed. "You ran away from a beetle!"

"Oh." Lusa sat down and licked her paw. "I knew that."

Just then the bears heard a voice calling their names in the flat-face language. Two of the feeders had come to the edge of

the railing with the bears' evening meal. Yogi ran over immediately, grunting with pleasure, and the other bears followed.
King lumbered to his paws slowly and wandered over. He
always ate last, and Lusa knew, like the other bears, that she
should leave the least rotten fruit for him, since he was the
biggest and oldest bear in the Bowl.

Lusa picked through the berries, choosing the ones she
liked best. With a cooing sound, one of the feeders reached
down and scratched her back with a long stick. Lusa wriggled
happily, letting him get to all the parts that itched. She was
still full from the morning meal and didn't really care if she
ate or not tonight.

As the flat-faces moved on to the grizzly bear, Yogi found
a rotten apple and nudged it toward Lusa.

"Yuck," Lusa said, kicking it back to him. "No rotten apples
for me, thanks."

"Now, now," Stella said. "That's no way to show respect for
your food."

"Do we show respect for it by eating it?" Lusa asked cheek-
ily. She'd heard Stella's "respect" lectures before, but she found
it hard to believe there was any connection between noble
bear spirits and the chunks of broken fruit the flat-faces
tossed onto the ground for them.

"You should always treat anything from nature with
respect," Stella said, "even when you eat it. You never know
when it might have the spirit of a bear inside it."

"Oh, no!" Lusa cried, pretending to act horrified. "A bear
spirit! I don't want to eat any of those. I'll never be able to eat

apples again." She flounced back to the log. Stella and Yogi
laughed.

A few stars came out as the sun went down, but most of
them were hard to see in the orange glow from the flat-face
lights. King ambled back to the boulders, where he slept outside. The other bears preferred the dens of white stone at the
back of the Bowl, where they could be sure they wouldn't be
rained on suddenly in the middle of the night. King was the
only one who didn't like being indoors. Ashia had explained
to Lusa that he didn't like the walls' straight edges, or the feeling of being trapped, but Lusa didn't understand. Inside the
den it was quiet and warm. Out there, you could hear the
grizzly bear grunting and the white bears snoring and insects
buzzing around your ears all night long.

She rolled onto her back and looked up at the sky through
the clear, hard square in the roof. One bright star hung there,
always watching her, night after night. It was the only one she
could always see, and it never seemed to move.

"Stella?" Lusa asked. "Do you know anything about that
star?"

"That is the Bear Watcher," Stella murmured sleepily. "Like
us, it has found a good place and it stays there, never wandering."

"Tell us more," Yogi prompted. "Is it the spirit of a bear?"

"Don't be silly," Stella said. "Bear spirits live in the trees.
But my mother did once tell me the story of a little bear cub
in the sky."

"A bear cub in the sky?" Lusa echoed.

"Yes." Stella wrinkled her nose as if she was trying to remember. "She keeps the bright star in her tail, but there's a big brown bear who wants that star for his own. So he chases the little black bear around and around the sky . . . but he never gets the star, because black bears are too clever, even if they are smaller than other bears."

"So the little bear gets to keep the star," Lusa said, pleased. She was sure she could be fast and clever, too. Certainly more clever than Yogi or the fat brown bear next door.

Stella had fallen asleep, making drowsy buzzing noises through her nose. Yogi was licking his paws, digging his teeth in between his claws to get at the last sticky bits of fruit.

Lusa didn't feel tired. She scrambled to her paws again and padded outside, hoping she could see the little black bear and the big brown bear running around and around. She padded over to the Mountains and stood on the tallest boulder, craning her neck to look up at the night sky.

The only star she could see was the motionless bright one, twinkling down at her.

Lusa sat on her haunches and gazed up at it—the little bear watching the Bear Watcher.

CHAPTER THREE

Toklo

Toklo crouched in the long grass. All around him the trees waved softly, and he could feel the breeze ruffling his shaggy brown coat.

Toklo opened his mouth and breathed in the musky smell of prey. He twitched his ears at the sound of snapping pine needles and let his breathing slow down until it matched the sighing of the wind. Then, with lightning quickness, he charged, sinking his claws into rabbit flesh. The creature squirmed and flailed, trying to get away, but Toklo's long, razor-sharp claws pierced its fur and pinned it to the ground. With a fierce snarl, the grizzly bear cub sank his teeth into the rabbit's neck.

"Toklo! Toklo, MOVE!"

His mother's voice jerked Toklo's attention back to the real world. He let go of the log he'd been pretending was a rabbit and looked up.

A firebeast was charging straight at him!

Toklo scrambled backward as fast as he could, making it to the nearby grass just as the firebeast roared past, missing him by only a few pawlengths. Horrible black smoke filled the air as it shot by, spraying brown slush from the puddles over his fur.

"Blech!" Toklo spat, rubbing his face with his paws. The taste of the firebeast's fumes was all over his tongue and up his nose. For a moment he couldn't smell anything except the beast and burning.

"Toklo, you troublesome cub!" His mother lumbered over and cuffed him on the head, making his ears ring. "How many times have I told you to stay away from the BlackPath? You could have been killed!"

"I could have scared away the firebeast," Toklo muttered. "I've been working on my angry face, see?" He raised himself on his back legs and bellowed, baring his sharp teeth.

"*Nothing* scares the firebeasts," Oka snarled. "And you'll never be as big as they are, so don't even think about fighting them."

Toklo wished he could be that big. Then nobody would ever scold him or tell him what to do or make him eat dandelions. He'd been following his mother through the valley all day, and they had barely found anything to eat. Although the season of fishleap was almost here, drifts of snow still covered the ground around the mountains, looking from a distance like piles of white fur on the rocks. But here and there it was melting, revealing patches of dirt and feeble bits of grass where snowdrops and dandelions poked through.

"Why can't you be quiet and obedient like your brother?" Oka grumbled. She swung her head around to look at her younger son, huddled beneath a tree.

"Obedient?" Toklo scoffed. "You mean weak."

"Tobi's sick," Oka growled. "He needs food. Gather some dandelions for him, and eat some yourself instead of rolling into the BlackPath like a blind deer."

"I don't like dandelions," Toklo complained. "They're all smushed up and full of dirt and they taste like metal and smoke. Yuck!" He pawed at his nose, wishing he had a real rabbit.

"We can't afford to be picky," Oka said, digging through the snow with her giant claws. "Food is scarce enough. You have to eat whatever we can find, or you will starve to death."

Toklo snorted. Tobi ate whatever he was given, and he was doing much worse than Toklo, so Toklo thought being fussy was just fine. He couldn't understand what was wrong with Tobi. All he did was lie around looking sad and moaning.

Toklo dug up a few dandelion stems and padded over to his brother. The damp grass under the tree tickled his paws as he nudged Tobi's side.

"Come on, Tobi, eat these," Toklo said. "Or else you'll be too tired to keep walking—again—and Mother will probably blame me for not feeding you."

Tobi opened his dark brown eyes and gazed up at his brother. He pressed his front paws into the ground and lifted himself weakly up to a wobbly standing position. He leaned over and put his mouth around a dandelion, which he chewed as if it were a chunk of stone.

Toklo sighed. Tobi was useless and he had been his whole life, as far as Toklo could remember. He was too small and too tired to do anything fun. He couldn't hunt. He couldn't feed himself. He couldn't play-wrestle. He couldn't even walk faster than a caterpillar.

If it were just me and Mother, Toklo thought, forcing himself to eat one of the dandelions, *we could run right across the mountains and chase rabbits and eat anything we wanted.* His fur burned with resentment. Tobi got all the attention and all the praise, but he was nothing but a burden. Toklo was the one who would grow up to be a real bear. He was the one who would take care of them all once he was big enough.

Oka shambled over, sniffing the air and warily eyeing the BlackPath. Toklo could feel the rumble under their paws that meant that another firebeast was coming.

"Let's keep moving," she said. "I think we've dug up all the dandelions here."

Finally! Toklo woofed happily and broke into a run, galloping up the hill into the woods. There were much more interesting smells coming from up the mountain. In the valley where they'd always lived, the smells of the flat-faces and their firebeasts covered everything else.

"Toklo!" his mother said sharply. "Come back here. We're going this way."

The bear cub's shoulders slumped. "But, *Mother,*" he whined. "I want to go into the mountains and catch a goat. I'm sure I could if you let me try!"

"Tobi will never make it up that slope," Oka pointed out. "And it will be too cold in the mountains for him. We have to stay low until the snow melts, when it'll be easier for him to travel up there."

Toklo stood up on his back legs and pawed at his ears, trying to hide his frustration. It wasn't fair! Stupid Tobi. Every decision they made was all about him.

"Let's check the sides of the BlackPath," Oka said. "If we're lucky, one of the firebeasts might have abandoned some prey."

"Fine," Toklo said, sprinting ahead along the edge of the BlackPath. He liked the feeling of leading the others, of being the one who decided where to go, even if he wasn't really in charge. Oka followed, helping Tobi plod along beside her and nudging him forward every few steps with her muzzle. Toklo stayed in the shadow of the trees, keeping at least a bearslength away from the BlackPath. He'd never seen a firebeast leave the BlackPath before, but he thought they probably could if they wanted to.

The roaring and growling from the firebeasts started to hurt Toklo's ears, especially as more and more of them raced past. Toklo couldn't pick up any prey scents, and the sounds of the forest were completely drowned out. The rustling and pattering from under the snow, where mice and other tiny creatures lived, usually made his mouth water and his heart beat faster. Here, there was nothing to get him excited.

After a long time, Oka barked to catch his attention. He turned and saw what she had spotted: a deer carcass lying by the side of the BlackPath. He hadn't noticed it because it didn't smell like prey or like any kind of food.

But he followed his mother and helped her drag the dead deer off the BlackPath and back into the trees. He sank his teeth into the flesh with a shudder, feeling the frozen meat crunch in his jaws, and dug his paws into the ground to pull it backward. As soon as they were under the tree cover, he dropped the carcass and wiped his tongue with his paws.

"That is disgusting," he announced.

"We're lucky to find any meat at all," his mother said. "Here, Tobi, take a bite." Dutifully, the smaller cub tugged free a piece of ragged flesh and swallowed it.

Toklo tried to do the same. He bit into the deer's haunch, but it was hard to tear apart the frozen, dead meat, and once he did get a mouthful, he couldn't bring himself to swallow it. He spat out the meat and sat up.

"I can't!" he said, backing away from the carcass. "It's the most horrible, awful, disgusting, dreadful thing I've ever tasted in my whole life."

"Toklo!" Oka snapped. "Stop being so fussy! By the Great Water Spirits, are you a bear or a squirrel?"

"I'm a bear!" Toklo cried.

"Then eat like a bear!" Oka said. "Or don't eat at all; see if I care."

Toklo scratched crossly at the ground. This wasn't eating like a bear! This was eating like a scavenging wolverine. A real bear wouldn't eat the long-dead carcasses killed by something else. He'd be out there chasing goats and rabbits and anything else with a heartbeat, slaying them with his long claws, powerful paws, and fierce teeth. A real bear would go anywhere he pleased and he wouldn't have to drag a useless lump of fur like Tobi along behind him.

Well, Toklo was not going to eat this vile, stinking deer. Tobi could have the whole thing, not that he was strong enough to take more than two bites. Toklo sulked off to the nearest tree and sat behind it, rubbing his nose and making just enough grumbling noise so that his mother and brother could hear how upset he was.

Oka had only brought Toklo and Tobi out of their BirthDen two moons ago, and in that time they had wandered in circles up and down the valley, going from one feeding site to the next. At first it had seemed huge to Toklo, but now he felt bored and trapped, especially with the mountains surrounding them on all sides. They ate meat if they could find it, but mostly they had to make do with green plants, termites, and roots they could dig up with their long, straight claws.

Their mother always kept them close to the BlackPath of the firebeasts, which ran through the heart of their range. There was another path that crossed it higher up the valley, but that was a SilverPath, harder and shinier than the BlackPath, and the firebeasts that ran along it were much longer and larger than the regular firebeasts. Toklo's mother called them snakebeasts, because they ran back and forth along the narrow SilverPath like big roaring snakes, making strange, high-pitched whistling and hooting noises that sounded like giant birds. Toklo could remember the place where the two paths crossed. They had found a grain spill there, piles and piles of grain just lying on the ground for them to eat. He hated the noise along the SilverPath, but at least the grain had filled him up.

He perked his ears. A long, mournful sound wailed in the distance. He recognized it, and he knew if they followed it, it would lead them to the track-crossing place. "Mother!" he called, bounding to his paws and scrambling through the snow to her side. She looked at him wearily, pausing with her claws buried in the deer's neck.

"Do you remember the grain spill we found?" Toklo prompted. "I think we're close to where it was. I bet I could find it again."

"Toklo," Oka said, shaking her head, "the grain will be long gone by now."

"I know," Toklo argued, "but maybe there's been another spill. Maybe there's more to eat there. Shouldn't we at least look?" He was so sick of being told he was wrong, of having to live his life limited by Tobi's weakness. This was a good idea, and he was going to make his mother see that.

To his surprise, Oka looked at him thoughtfully, the long brown fur rippling across her shoulders. Then she bent her muzzle to Tobi, sniffed him once, and looked up at her older cub.

"All right, Toklo," she said. "Lead the way."

Toklo's heart swelled with pride as they climbed over a low ridge and spotted the SilverPath crossing in a dip below them.

He'd found it! All on his own, he had tracked his way back to a food source, just like a grown-up grizzly bear.

When they had still been under the snow in the BirthDen, Oka had told them stories about her life before she had cubs. She told them about one caribou that she had tracked through the deep earthsleep snow for three days until it was too exhausted to continue and she killed it. That prey had provided her with food for many days.

She also spoke of the places where rocks and snow charged down the mountains, roaring like bears. She would often dig for squirrels along these paths during fishleap season. Toklo's belly rumbled at the thought of fresh squirrel meat. He shook his head, trying not to think about it. Grain would be good enough for now.

He wished they could hunt in the mountains, but he knew better than to ask his mother again. He'd only get the same answer he always did: "Tobi isn't strong enough yet. Mothers with cubs have to make do as best they can. Only adult males are strong enough to eat wherever they want."

Toklo couldn't wait to be full grown. He'd kill so much prey, he'd be able to feed his mother and brother, too. He glanced back at Tobi, shambling along with a weaving, dizzy walk. Oka touched her muzzle gently to her younger cub's head, encouraging him forward. Why did she waste so much attention on him? Tobi would never be a great hunter. Not like Toklo.

The smell of the grain reached Toklo's nose, and he picked up speed, running down the slope ahead of the others. When he reached a pile of the tiny yellow seeds, he bent his head and began to eat without waiting for his mother and Tobi. His belly felt like an empty cave. He didn't care that the grain tasted dry and dustier than it had the last time they were here. At least it wasn't rotten deer that had been trampled by fire-beasts.

Tobi and Oka nosed around the pile, crunching through the scattered grain. Something rumbled under the ground, and Toklo leaned down to listen. The trembling shook his paws, and he stepped back, looking up to see one of the long snakebeasts charging along the SilverPath. The sound of its rattling paws hurt his ears, and as it went by it let out a long, mournful wail. Toklo buried his face in his paws, batting at his ears to clear out the ringing. As the noise was fading into the distance he heard something else—the snapping of branches under large paws. With a fierce grunt, Toklo spun around.

A huge male grizzly was walking toward them. It was twice Oka's size, with a jagged scar across its flank and a wild look in its eyes. It didn't speed up when it saw them, but it kept coming straight in their direction, as if it knew they couldn't fight him.

"Come on, Toklo!" Oka called. "It's time to go!" She was already halfway up the next slope, shoving Tobi along in front of her.

"But I was eating!" he protested, clawing at the dirt.

"Toklo! Now!"

He ran after her, across the SilverPath, which stung his paws with cold sharpness. They galloped up a slope flecked with snow until they reached the edge of the woods.

Toklo sat down and looked back at the crossing place. The male bear was helping himself to the pile of grain, scooping it into his mouth with his paws. Toklo seethed with fury. It was not fair that they should be driven off so easily. It wasn't fair that he was so much smaller than that bear. He'd come all this way and found the grain on his own. He should get to eat it all!

He wished Oka would stand up for them. Why didn't she challenge that bear down there and scare *him* off instead? Maybe if she fought a bit more and nagged a bit less, she wouldn't have to spend so much time worrying about finding their next meal.

He glanced over at her and saw that she was pacing back and forth, growling to herself and shaking her head. Toklo padded over to the snowbank where Tobi was huddled and sat down next to his brother. Oka looked pretty angry. Perhaps she really was thinking about going down there and fighting that bear. Toklo felt a prickle of excitement in his paws. He could help her fight! He'd be happy to use his claws for something more exciting than digging in the dirt.

Suddenly Oka rounded on them. "You're both skin and bones!" she spat. Toklo stared at her in astonishment. It wasn't *his* fault he was so thin.

"Skin and bones," she growled again. "Living on grain and dandelions. You need fresh meat!"

Toklo nearly blurted out, "That's what *I've* been saying!" but he thought better of it. Given the look in his mother's eyes, he could almost imagine her feeding him to his brother. *She prob-*

ably would one day, he thought bitterly. That way precious Tobi could live, at least.

Oka clawed at the snow, ripping up tufts of grass and flinging them in the air. An uneasy feeling crept through Toklo's fur. He didn't know why, but it frightened him to see her like this. What was she doing to the grass? She didn't expect him to eat it, did she?

Finally she stopped and looked at them again. With a heavy sigh, she sat down under a tree. "We must go over the mountains," she said quietly. Tobi and Toklo glanced at each other. This was strange enough that even Tobi was paying attention now.

"Over the mountains?" Toklo echoed. Where she had always said they couldn't go because Tobi wouldn't make it?

"There's a river over there," Oka explained. "A wide river, filled with salmon. That is what we should be eating, not grain and leaves. You'll starve if we stay here any longer."

Toklo shivered with excitement. He didn't know why his mother looked so worried. This sounded like the best idea she'd had in ages—a great adventure, a journey over the mountains, a chance to find out what a salmon looked like— *and* tasted like. Oka had told him about the plump, juicy fish that leaped out of the water into your mouth, begging to be eaten. At last his mother was making the right choice. And finally he would catch salmon like a real grizzly bear.

CHAPTER FOUR

Kallik

Kallik followed her mother away from the broken edge, back onto the ice, watching the bubbles and shadows swirling below the surface. The water gurgled behind her, and she wondered what happened to the spirits of the bears when the ice shattered instead of slowly melting. Were they washed into the sea to swim with the seals?

She wanted to ask her mother, but she could tell that it wasn't the right time. Nisa was tense and alert, testing the ice carefully as she walked on it, her nose low to the snow to sniff for signs of thawing. Even Taqqiq was quiet for once, walking behind Kallik without whining for a ride on Nisa's back or jumping at snowflakes.

They walked all day and saw no sign of seals. Nisa explained that it was harder to find breathing holes once the ice started to break up, because the seals could get to the air from anywhere in the water and didn't need the holes anymore.

Suddenly she paused. Kallik held her breath. Was the ice

breaking up here, too? Were they about to be plunged into the freezing water?

Nisa gave a grunt and broke into a run, speeding across the snow with her muzzle stretched out. Kallik and Taqqiq exchanged a puzzled glance and galloped after her. Nisa skidded to a halt at a small mound of snow and started sniffing it.

Kallik was disappointed. It was just a pile of snow. There was nothing to eat here.

Then Nisa reared up on her back legs and pounded on the snowbank with her front paws. She reared up again and again, smashing her massive forelegs into the snow. To Kallik's surprise, a pair of fluffy white seal cubs spilled out of the mound of snow. Nisa killed them quickly, and her cubs rushed over to say the words of thanks and then eat.

"That was a seal's BirthDen," Nisa explained, her muzzle dripping with blood. "They have to have their cubs on the ice, so they leave them buried in heaps of snow while they hunt for food in the water."

Kallik felt much better with juicy mouthfuls of seal fat in her. Suddenly it seemed like everything was going to be all right, even when burn-sky came. Her mother could look after them just like always.

Taqqiq batted at one of the seal flippers, sending it flying across the snow to Kallik's paws. Cheerfully she batted it back, and they chased it around for a while, feeling happy and full.

"Stop that!" Nisa called. "Show more respect for your prey, little ones. Remember it was given to us by the spirits of the ice."

As she spoke, two young male bears appeared over the nearest snowbank. They were at least a snow-sky and burn-sky old, more than twice the size of Kallik and Taqqiq. They bared their teeth and charged down the hill toward the dead seals.

Nisa raced over to her cubs. "Hurry!" she said. "They probably aren't the only bears who smelled this prey."

The three ran across the frozen landscape. At one point, Nisa lifted her head and roared a warning—another large bear was coming from the sunup direction. They switched course to avoid him. Alarm and excitement gave an extra burst of speed to Kallik's paws, but she wasn't really afraid. She knew she was safe with her mother and brother, and she loved the feel of the wind in her fur and the ice thudding below their paws. As long as she had her family, she could survive anything.

Kallik felt herself growing bigger and stronger the longer they stayed on the ice. The air felt warmer and warmer all the time, and each night when she looked for the Pathway Star she saw the moon changing shape—first getting bigger and fatter like a milk-fed seal cub and then shrinking down to a thin curl of hair floating in the sky.

One day, Nisa spotted a young seal lying on the ice, basking in the sun. She signaled the cubs to be quiet with a flick of her ears, and they crept forward on silent paws. Nisa nudged Taqqiq with her muzzle and pointed her nose toward the seal.

"Quietly," she whispered. "Like we practiced."

Taqqiq placed one paw cautiously in front of the other, sliding across the snow as silently as he could. Kallik stayed frozen, trying not to make a sound. Was her brother about to make his first catch?

The seal lifted its head and spotted the white bear cub sneaking up on it. With a startled bark, it pushed itself on its flippers toward its breathing hole in the ice. Kallik jumped to her paws. It was going to escape!

Taqqiq hurled himself forward, but he wasn't quite fast enough. Nisa bounded past him and sank her claws into the seal just as it hit the water. She dragged it back onto the ice and fastened her teeth in its neck, shaking it.

"Hooray!" Kallik called, scampering up to her. "You got it, Mother! That was amazing!"

Taqqiq shuffled his paws in the snow. "I nearly had it," he grumbled.

"You did really well," Kallik told him. "You got much closer than I could have."

"And you have plenty of time to learn," added Nisa. "You'll make great hunters one day, both of you."

After they ate the seal, Kallik stretched out on the ice, panting. The sun beat down, making her almost wish she could shed her thick fur and warm skin. She felt like every whisker on her head was burning. She tried to press herself closer to the ice to cool down. Next to her, Taqqiq and Nisa were doing the same, slumbering drowsily in the heat. If burn-sky was any hotter than this, she thought she would melt like a chunk of ice.

Kallik was glad when the sun finally sank below the edge of the sky. It was much cooler at night, with the ice spots twinkling in the darkness above them. The moon's light made the snow gleam, stretching for skylengths in every direction as far as a bear could see.

"Tomorrow we will leave the ice," Nisa said with a sigh.

Kallik rested her chin on her mother's leg. "Already?" she asked. "Can't we stay a bit longer?"

"It's too dangerous," Nisa murmured, her black eyes sad. "We must get to land before all the ice is gone."

"What is the land like?" Taqqiq asked. "Is the snow deeper there?"

"In some parts there is no snow at all," Nisa rumbled.

Kallik wondered what else there could be. "Then is it just water?"

"There's something called dirt, and stones and rocks and grass. Dirt is like brown snow, but it isn't cold, and it goes down and down forever, no matter how far you dig. And the grass is like green whiskers growing out of the ground, which you can eat if you have to."

"What is green?" Kallik asked.

Nisa paused, twitching her nose. "It is one of the colors in the sea," she answered finally. "Like blue, but different. You'll see."

"Are there other bears there?" Taqqiq asked. "And seals? And geese?"

"There are all kinds of animals you haven't seen yet," Nisa said. "Like foxes—they're even smaller than cubs, and they have sharp pointy noses and fur the color of fog. And there are beavers, who have large flat tails and big flat teeth. And caribou, big animals that travel in large groups. They have long skinny legs, and some of them have antlers."

"What's—" Kallik began.

"Antlers look like big claws growing out of their heads," Nisa said.

Kallik clamped her jaw shut, astonished and a little bit terrified. Animals with flat teeth? Animals with claws growing out of their heads? Whiskers growing out of the ground?

She didn't think she was going to like the land very much.

All night Kallik had strange dreams about odd-looking creatures and brown snow. She was relieved when her mother nudged them awake early, just as the first pale beams of sunlight began to ripple across the ice.

"We have to start now," Nisa said, her voice filled with urgency. "We must get to land as quickly as possible."

"But I'm hungry," Taqqiq complained. "I want more seal skin."

"We don't have time to hunt," Nisa said. She nudged both cubs to their paws with her muzzle and set off across the snow at such a rapid pace that they could barely keep up. Kallik could hear the ice creaking below her paws again, and in places it felt frighteningly thin and slippery. She stuck close to her mother, wondering what would happen to them if they didn't make it to land.

All at once Taqqiq let out a howl of terror. Kallik spun around and saw him vanish into a black river that had opened up under his feet. With a loud crack, the ice beside her snapped off as well, and her paws slid out from under her as the whole chunk she was on tilted sideways. She sank her claws in and managed to stay on as it bobbed upright, but with horror she saw Taqqiq's paws flailing in the dark water as he lifted his nose into the air with a terrified cry.

A jagged line like a claw scratch in the snow sliced along the surface in front of them, and the ice split in two, leaving Kallik floating on a small island in the middle of a tiny sea. She couldn't believe how quickly it had happened—one moment they were on solid ice, and the next they were floundering through dark ocean.

Nisa plunged into the water and dug her teeth into the loose skin at Taqqiq's neck. Shivering with fear, Kallik watched from her island as her mother paddled strongly to a large, free-floating chunk of ice and dragged Taqqiq up onto it. He lay panting for a moment, then shook his head, sending out a spray of sparkling water droplets.

"Come on, Kallik!" Nisa called. "Swim over to us!"

"You mean get in the water?" Kallik gulped. "On purpose?"

"You can do it!" her mother said encouragingly. "It's not far."

Kallik sniffed the edge of the ice. The water smelled salty and fishy and very cold. She splashed a paw in the freezing water and drew back with a shiver. The only other times she'd been in water had been to splash through narrow channels between blocks of ice. This was really swimming, and she didn't know if she could do it. It didn't feel natural like walking on the ice—there was nothing to hold her up in the water. And she couldn't help thinking of all the bear spirits that had melted into it. Would she be swimming in spirits?

"Kallik, come on, hurry!" Nisa called again. "We have to keep moving toward the land."

Kallik knew she had to be brave. She couldn't stay on her little island until it melted. She needed to be with her mother and brother, wherever they went. She took a deep breath, closed her eyes, and leaped into the sea with a giant splash.

Sharp, salty water poured up her nose and she opened her mouth to gasp for air, but instead more water rushed in. Gagging and spitting, she swallowed what felt like half the ocean. Beating her paws against the current, she struggled to the surface and stuck her nose into the air, inhaling a quick breath before the waves swamped her again.

I can do this, she told herself. *I can swim over there because Mother is waiting for me, and Taqqiq needs to see that I am just as tough as he is.*

The force of the current was strong, trying to drag her back to her island, and she could barely see the edge of the ice in front of her as she paddled. Salty waves splashed in her eyes, and her sense of smell was overwhelmed by the sting of the sea in her nose. But she pressed on, keeping her mother's face in sight. She couldn't hear anything over the splashing of the waves, but she could see that Nisa and Taqqiq were both shouting encouragement. Finally she felt her mother's teeth sink into her neck fur and drag her onto the ice.

Gasping for breath, she shook herself as hard as she could and huddled closer to Taqqiq, who was lying flat on his belly

again. It had been freezing in the water, but it was even colder
now that she was back in the wind with wet fur.

"Swimming is horrible!" Taqqiq whispered to her.

"It's worse than being chased by giant bears," Kallik agreed.

"Unfortunately," said their mother, overhearing them, "we
will have to swim to get to land." They looked at her in horror. "It'll be short swims, wherever we run into water," Nisa
explained. "We'll rest in between as much as we can."

"Is it always like this?" Kallik asked. "Do you have to swim
so far every ice-melt?"

Nisa didn't answer for a while. Then she touched her muzzle to Kallik's. "No, it's not always like this," she admitted.
"Usually we can get much closer to land before we have to
start swimming. But we can swim, and we will. If you do as I
say and stay close to me, we will make it to land soon."

Kallik pressed her nose to her mother's muzzle, then
reared up and wrapped her paws around her mother's neck. "I
will always stay close to you," she whispered in her mother's
ear.

"And always do what I say?" Nisa teased. "Can I have that
promise on the Great Bear?" She prodded Taqqiq, nudging
him to his paws. "All right, little cubs. See that large piece of
ice over there? That's where we're going. Be brave, and move
quickly." She stood up, shaking herself off, and stepped gingerly down to the water's edge.

The chunk of ice they were on was not very large, and it
rocked unsteadily below them as Nisa moved. Kallik dug in
her claws, feeling a little seasick.

"Whee!" Taqqiq spread out his paws to balance himself. "Come on, Kallik, this is fun. It's kind of like riding on Mother's back."

"Except if you fall off her back, you're not going to drown," Kallik pointed out.

"We won't drown," Taqqiq said, padding to the edge and peering in. Nisa had slipped into the water and was starting to paddle ahead. "I'll protect you, whatever happens. We may be small, but don't forget there's two of us."

"That's true," Kallik said, feeling a little better. She followed him down to the water and dabbed at it nervously with her paws. Taqqiq scrunched himself into a ball and leaped in with a huge splash, showering Kallik with water.

"Hey!" she squealed.

"You have to get wet anyway!" he called. "I'm just helping!"

"I'll help *you*!" Kallik spluttered, jumping in after him.

She managed to splash him back, but then the current began tugging at her fur, and she had to paddle her front paws furiously to keep up with her mother. By the time they got to the next piece of ice, her legs felt as if they were going to fall off. She wondered if this was how Silaluk felt, racing around the Pathway Star forever and ever.

Kallik gripped the ice with her front paws, churning her back paws in the water as she tried to shove herself up. A firm nudge from behind boosted her up and out onto solid ice; then Kallik turned around and sank her teeth into Taqqiq's fur, helping to drag him out as well.

Nisa pulled herself out beside them, looking pleased. "See?

You're swimming like seals already!" But Kallik noticed that her mother was shaking, and she wasn't sure that it was just with cold.

At least this piece of ice was much larger than the last one. Here they could walk for a while over the snow, which was easier than swimming. But the sky was cloudy and gray, and for once Kallik wished that the sun was shining, because the freezing wind seemed to tug at each one of her wet hairs with fierce little teeth. She kept her head bent low so that snow wouldn't blow up her nose, and she pressed her flank to her mother's to shield herself from the wind as much as she could. On her other side, Taqqiq pressed close, so they could share their body warmth.

Kallik hadn't even noticed when the sun had gone away, but now there were masses of clouds above them again. She could tell from the smell of them that they weren't snow clouds; it was too warm for that, although she didn't feel warm right now. Those were rain clouds, and if they opened up, things would get even worse. The only time Kallik had seen it rain, everything got very slippery, and with the ice already melting, she knew that walking would be much harder in a storm.

The sun was beginning to set when Nisa paused at another wide channel of water. She sniffed the air and stared across to the blue-white sparkle of ice on the other side. To Kallik it looked skylengths away.

"Do we have to swim again already?" she whimpered. "Can't we keep walking along the ice?"

"We have to go in this direction," Nisa said. "The land is

that way. Can't you smell it?"

Kallik tried, but the scent of the water was too strong. "But I'm so tired," she protested.

"Me, too," Taqqiq complained. "I just want to lie here until I can feel my paws again."

"I'll take you across one by one," Nisa said. "Stay close to me, and I'll help you."

Kallik knew she had to be brave. Her mother would have to make the trip three times to take them both across, and if she could do that, Kallik wanted to show that she could be strong, too.

"You go first," Taqqiq said, flopping down on the ice and resting his head on his paws.

"Okay," Kallik said. "I can do it, I know I can."

"I'm very proud of you," Nisa whispered, her breath warm on Kallik's ear. "Everything will be all right once we get to land, I promise."

Kallik and Nisa plunged in. Kallik let out a puff of glee at the giant splash they sent up together. She tried to copy her mother's graceful pawstrokes, gliding through the sea like her, but the water kept washing up her nose, making her cough and splutter.

The ocean stretched away in every direction, dark and end-less. The waves swelled around them so Kallik couldn't see the ice they were heading for, and even her mother's head vanished a few times. Her claws tingled with fear as a new scent filled her nose—a smell that reeked of blood and rip-ping teeth and cold menace.

She spun in the water, batting frantically at the waves with her paws, trying to see what it was. There! A huge black fin was slicing through the water, bearing down on her much faster than she could swim.

Nisa roared, anger and terror mingled in her cry. "Orca!" she bellowed. "Kallik, swim! As fast as you can!"

Kallik flailed blindly, pushing with her paws as hard as she could, but there was nothing to press against here—no solid ice beneath her paws to lend her speed, no whirls of snow to urge her on her way. She was lost in the dark, cold water.

More fins appeared behind the first.

"Faster, Kallik!" Nisa roared. "Get out of here!"

"Mother!" Taqqiq screamed from the ledge of ice behind them. "Kallik! What's happening?"

Nisa swam in a circle around Kallik, clawing at the killer whales. Kallik felt the water surge around her as the orca smashed into Nisa with their massive heads. Then their tails slammed into her mother's body and spun her around.

"Mother!" Kallik cried as the world flashed white and black around her.

"Go!" Nisa butted Kallik with her head and turned to snarl at the whales again. Kallik caught a glimpse of a gaping jaw lined with yellow teeth and small, cold, black eyes.

Whimpering with fear, Kallik swam and swam and swam. She didn't know if she was still headed in the right direction or if she'd end up swimming out to sea forever.

Suddenly her nose bumped into something solid. Her eyes flew open and she gasped. Ice! She'd made it to the other side!

She dug her claws into the cold surface and thrashed her back paws in the water, trying to push herself up. But her limbs were so heavy and her waterlogged fur weighed her down.

"Help!" she shrieked, clutching the ice. "Please, help me!"

Like a spirit sent by the Great Bear, her mother appeared beside her with a whoosh of sharp-smelling water. Nisa ducked under the surface and shoved Kallik upward. With the extra boost, Kallik was able to scramble up to safety. Immediately she spun around, reaching for her mother's paws.

"Out, out, get out!" she screeched.

But Nisa's paws were already sliding back out of reach, into the water. Her mother was falling, falling away from her, and the churning water was rising to suck her down, and the fins were closing in.

"Mother!" Kallik screamed. Nisa was still fighting, her claws leaving long gashes in the sides of the killer whales, but there were too many of them. The water that sloshed over the ice was pink now, staining Kallik's paws, smelling of salt and blood and fear.

Kallik lunged forward, stretching her muzzle over the water. "Mother! Grab on to me! I'll pull you out!"

An orca tail flicked out of the water and slammed into her. Kallik was knocked back onto the ice, crashing to the ground and sliding through the snow for several bearlengths. She lay there, too stunned to move. Beneath the ice, there was a hollow knocking sound, a roar cut off, the snap of teeth.

When her ears cleared, she realized that she could no

longer hear splashing or roaring. A deep, mournful silence hung over the water. The killer whales had gone. And so had Nisa.

"Mother!" A voice sounded from far away. "Mother! Kallik! Mother!"

Taqqiq! He was calling to them across the water. Kallik lifted her head, trying to see him. But the clouds were hanging low, hiding the cubs from each other's sight. Kallik tried to climb to her paws and call back to him, but she was too winded. She couldn't catch her breath to make a sound. *I'm here, Taqqiq! I'm still alive!*

"Don't leave me alone!" Taqqiq wailed. "Mother! Come back! Kallik, where are you?"

Kallik squeezed her eyes shut, trying to force herself up. But her body would not do what she wanted, and her paws lay limp on the ice.

The wind picked up, howling and shrieking and hurling freezing sleet against Kallik's fur. Kallik heard her brother call a few more times, and then his voice started to fade. He was running along the edge of the far ice, disappearing into the snowy darkness. And there was nothing Kallik could do.

She curled into a ball, letting the storm whirl around her, and slowly slipped into white nothingness.

CHAPTER FIVE

Lusa

"*Bet you can't get up this* high," Yogi challenged, scrambling to the next branch.

"I can, too," Lusa retorted, digging in her claws and pulling herself up with her forelegs. Yogi was quite a bit bigger than her, but Lusa was determined to prove she could climb as far as he could.

The sun shone through the leaf buds on the trees, casting green shadows on the bear cubs. Along the top of the wall, the usual crowd of flat-faces was pointing and exclaiming, and the scent of strange food drifted over from them. Below her Lusa could see King and Ashia snoozing in the shade. Every once in a while King would blink, shake his head, and glare up at them, as if he expected them to fall on his head.

A shower of bark splinters rained down on Lusa's shoulders as Yogi clambered higher. "I can see into the brown bear area from here," he called down to her. "Oooh, I can see your favorite bear!"

"I don't have a favorite grizzly," Lusa said. "I don't like any grizzlies. They're too big and they're angry all the time."

"Especially Grumps," Yogi agreed, nodding his muzzle toward the old male grizzly who lived alone on the other side of the Fence. The cubs had never talked to him, so they didn't know his real name, but they called him Grumps because he was so old and grumpy. "He's rolling on his back in the dirt. It looks pretty funny."

Lusa wanted to see. She tried pressing her hooked back claws into the tree trunk and wrapping her front paws around the nearest branch. From there she could swing herself up, but it took a lot of effort.

"Hrrmph." She heard a loud grunt from the ground, but she was too focused on getting her back paws onto the branch to look down.

"HRRRRRMPH," came the grunt again. Lusa peeked over her shoulder. Her father was standing on his back legs, reaching up the tree toward her.

"It's okay, I won't fall," she called. She tried even harder, grunting with the effort, and managed to wrap all her paws around the branch.

"You'll never get to the top if you climb like that," King growled. "You're going much too slowly."

"Well, I'm still learning," Lusa replied breathlessly. She lay on her belly on the branch, letting her paws hang down while she rested for a moment.

"Don't be so timid," he said. "It's much easier if you climb the tree in quick bounds. Grab the trunk with your forepaws and push yourself up with your hind legs, like you would if it was lying on the ground."

Lusa thought it sounded more like a way to fall out of the tree, but this was her father talking. He only pawed out advice when it was something important.

"Are you sure it's safe?" she couldn't help asking.

"Safe!" King snorted. "Black bears are the best climbers in the forest. You listen to me, Lusa: Black bears don't fall out of trees. Not even puny cubs." He dropped back down to all fours and lumbered away, grumbling to himself, his ears twitching.

Lusa looked up again, up to the top of the tree where the spindliest branches waved against the cloud-dotted blue sky. Yogi had gotten bored and was climbing back down, scratching the trunk to look for insects on his way.

The best climbers in the forest, Lusa thought. *We don't fall out of trees.* Feeling bolder, she scrambled to her paws and reached up to hook her claws into the bark. Taking a deep breath, she pushed her back paws into the tree and shoved herself up in a quick leaping bound.

To her surprise, she landed almost a whole cublength up the tree. Excited, she tried the move again, and then again immediately after that, until she was racing up the tree. She didn't even stop when she got to the highest point Yogi had ever reached. She kept going, pushing herself higher and higher, until she came to a branch and realized—there were no branches above her. She had reached the very top of the tree.

The very top! Lusa sat on the branch and wrapped her paws around the trunk, panting with exertion and delight. She was up so high! Below her the other black bears were the size of caterpillars. She could see over the wall into the rest of the Bowl, to the brown bears on one side and the white bears on the other.

But she could also see beyond the Bowl itself. There was a gray path winding around several enclosures, most of them surrounded by Fences like hers. Not far away she could see some small animals that looked a bit like flat-faces, but furrier and more agile, with long swinging tails. She saw one holding on to a tree branch with only one arm, dangling in the air as if it could hold on forever.

Farther along the path she saw a large pool of water—more water than she'd ever seen in one place before. It made her wish she could leap into it and splash around. There were birds in the water, or at least she thought they must be birds, because they had wings folded by their sides, although their legs were so long and skinny that they were probably taller than she was standing on her hind legs. They were bright pink, with hooked bills, and some of them looked like they were standing on one leg. Maybe those ones only had one leg?

A roar that didn't sound bearlike drew her attention to an enclosure in the other direction, where large gray boulders formed a cliffside dotted with trees and thick bushes. She had heard the roar before, but she'd never known what kind of animal it came from. Now she could see that on one of the large flat rocks, a four-legged animal was lying in the sun, flicking its long tail. It was golden-colored, with jagged black stripes along its fur, and when it yawned she could see teeth as sharp as a bear's.

So many strange creatures! And that was only what she could see from here—she could tell that the path continued on in each direction, and that the sky reached farther than she'd ever imagined. She knew from the other bears' stories that there must be forests and mountains and other bears beyond the Bowl walls. But she hadn't realized quite how many other kinds of animals were out there . . . or how far the world reached.

Lusa sniffed the wind for a moment, inhaling the wild mixture of unfamiliar scents. Then she scrambled back down the tree and ran over to Stella, trying to hold all the images in her head.

"Stella!" she cried, clambering onto the older bear's back. Stella started awake with a grunt. Her fur was warm from the sunlight and had bits of grass in it from sleeping on the ground.

"Stella, quick!" Lusa said. "What kind of animal is sort of the color of the papaya fruit and has black stripes and big teeth and roars? And what kind of bird is tall and pink with skinny legs? And what kind of animal hangs from trees and has a squiggly tail like a worm but much longer? Are any of them like bears? Can they talk like bears? Have you ever met them?"

"Slow down, slow down," Stella grunted. She pawed at her ears and studied Lusa. "Where did you see all this? Did you climb to the top of the Bear Tree?"

"I did!" Lusa exclaimed, capering in a circle. "It was so high and so exciting and what were those animals, do you know, do you know?"

"I know their names," Stella said. "The striped cats are tigers, and the pink birds are flamingos."

"Fla-min-gos," Lusa repeated, setting the word in her mind.

"And the little climbers are called monkeys," Stella went on. "But you should ask King about them if you want to know more. He lived in the wild, after all, and he may have met some of them out there."

Lusa was intrigued. Stella loved telling stories, but for once she sounded like she thought King knew more than she did.

Lusa's father was lapping up water from the small pool near the front wall, but he swung his head up as Lusa approached and studied her warily.

"Hello, Father," Lusa said, nosing at his muzzle and scuffling her paws in the dirt. "Did you see me climb? Wasn't I good?"

"I said you would be," King said gruffly. He bent his head to the pool again. His long tongue flicked in and out as he drank.

"Will you tell me about what it's like out in the wild?" Lusa asked. "I saw all these strange animals from the top of the tree. Stella says they're called monkeys and tigers and fla-min-gos. Did you ever meet any tigers or monkeys?"

"No," King growled. "There's nothing to tell."

"But—don't you have any stories about living in the wild?"

"No, I don't." He stepped back and started padding over to the Mountains. Lusa followed along, trotting to stay at his heels.

"What about the big water?" she pressed. "Did you find any water that big out there? Did you ever go into the water like the flamingos? Could you swim?"

King raised himself up on his hind legs and clawed the air. "Black bears can swim like fish, climb like monkeys, and run like tigers. We are the kings of the forest. There is nothing that black bears can't do!" He dropped back down to his paws and stood over Lusa, staring down so fiercely that she instinctively crouched lower.

"Stop asking me questions about the wild," he growled. "You'll never live there, so why go on and on about it? Leave me in peace." He leaped up onto the nearest boulder and sat with his back to her.

Lusa backed away and slipped down the side of the Mountains to the Cave at the back. She huddled under the white stone ledge, feeling very confused. Did King hate it here? She'd never thought of the Bowl as being small before, but suddenly it felt as tiny as their watering dishes. She wanted to know what lay beyond the walls, beyond the strange animals and the long Fences and the gray paths. She wanted to see a real forest and some real mountains.

A cool black nose nudged her side, and Lusa looked around. Her mother, Ashia, pressed her muzzle to her daughter's head. "Don't be sad, little blackberry," she said. "I saw you climbing that tree earlier. You did very well. Don't mind King."

"I only wanted to know things," Lusa blurted out. "I just asked about the tigers and the monkeys, and he *growled* at me!"

"I know," Ashia said. "He doesn't really like talking. Not like you," she teased.

"He said black bears are the kings of the forest," Lusa said.

"That's true," Ashia agreed. "We're not brightly colored like tigers or flamingos, and we don't make a lot of noise like monkeys, so you might not know how important we are at first. But black bears are the best at being quiet and going unnoticed—and that's how King likes to stay. He's used to living on his own in the wild and fending for himself. He isn't so good at being friends with other bears."

"I like being friends with other bears," Lusa said, leaning against her mother's leg.

"Well, that's all right, because you're in here," Ashia said, swatting away a fly with one of her large paws. "But if you were in the wild, like he was, you would need to stay away from other bears to stay alive."

"Really?" Lusa said.

"Do you want to see what it's like in the wild?"

"Yes!" Lusa gasped. Was there a way out of the Bear Bowl? Why hadn't she heard about it before?

"Follow me, and keep quiet," Ashia instructed. She crept out of the Cave and up the Mountains into the Forest. Lusa tried to put her paws exactly where her mother had put them, although her legs were much shorter so it was difficult. She stayed low and kept quiet, watching her mother's fur shimmer brown and black in the sunlight.

"Stop," Ashia whispered, lifting her nose. "*Shh*. Here comes a big tiger."

Lusa curled her lip. "But we're still in the Bear Bowl."

"Not if you imagine we're in a deep, dark forest surrounded by wild creatures," her mother whispered back. "Now, can you smell that tiger?"

Lusa copied her mother and sniffed the air. There was definitely something coming. It wasn't a tiger, though. It was Yogi! The two of them watched from the long grass as he ambled past them and went to scratch himself on the fence. Lusa stifled a huff of laughter. Even if she pretended really hard, there was nothing fierce and scary about Yogi.

Suddenly there was a movement in the Mountains. King was standing up to stretch.

"There's another bear!" Ashia warned. "Up the tree!"

She leaped into the branches and swarmed up the trunk with Lusa right behind her. Lusa saw that her mother climbed the way King had taught her, moving swiftly and in quick leaps. It was even easier the second time, especially with her mother ahead of her. This was a good game, pretending the Bear Bowl was really a forest.

Lusa wondered if life in the wild was this exciting all the time. She perched on a branch beside her mother and looked down at the other bears in the Bowl. Maybe King was wrong. Maybe one day she would get to see the world beyond the Bowl. Maybe one day she really would live in the wild.

CHAPTER SIX

Toklo

The sky was streaked with pink and gold, and the shadows crept slowly through the forest like stalking bears. Night was falling, and under the trees Toklo rolled in the pine needles, pretending he was catching fish.

"Ha!" he growled, pouncing. "Got you!" He scrabbled in the snow and then leaped sideways, pinning down another pile of needles. "Got you, too!"

"Shh," Tobi whimpered. "My ears hurt." He was still lying in the same spot where he'd dropped after they ran up the hill from the grain spill. Toklo wished he had a brother who would play with him. He'd seen other grizzly cubs wrestling with one another. That would help him learn how to fight, and it would be fun. But Tobi was always too tired, or something hurt, or Oka wanted him to rest.

Leaves and dirt flew up as their mother dug a den for them in the snowbank. It was shallow but it helped keep them warm when they curled up together. Toklo thought his

68

mother seemed calmer now that she'd made the decision to go over the mountain. He was glad. He didn't like it when she roared at him and Tobi and tore up grass.

"We're going to sleep early tonight," she told them. "We'll need a lot of rest for our long trek tomorrow."

Tobi shuddered, pressing himself into her fur, but Toklo batted at her paws.

"Will you teach me how to catch salmon?" he pestered.

"Well, it's not the way you were playing at it today, that's for certain," she snorted. "All that jumping and yowling. They'd hear you coming the moment you set paw in the river."

"Then what *should* I do?"

"You start by wading out into the shallows," she said. "Stand with your back to the current. You'll see the salmon slithering past your paws. If you are still for a moment, they'll come right to you. And then, if you're quick"—she cuffed Toklo with one of her paws, but he could tell she wasn't trying to hurt him—"then maybe you'll catch one."

"I will!" Toklo declared. "I'll have the fastest paws in the river. I'll catch more salmon than any other bear!" *More than Tobi, that's for sure!*

"Well, that depends on the water spirits," Oka said. "They won't want to hear you bragging, especially if you don't treat them with respect."

"Are we going to meet the water spirits?" Tobi whispered with big eyes. They'd both heard this story from Oka many times—how the spirits of dead bears lived in the rivers, flowing endlessly with the salmon that had fed them in life. But they had never seen water big enough or fast enough to hold spirits in it.

"That's not how it works, little one," Oka said to Tobi. Toklo hated the way her voice got all gentle and mushy whenever she spoke to his brother. "The spirits are always there, and they may speak with you or they may not. But you don't exactly meet them."

"I remember!" Toklo said. "You have to say thank you to them so they will help you."

"Yes," Oka said. "If they are angry, they'll make choppy waves in the water so it's hard to catch any fish. But if they are friendly . . . if they like you . . . they will guide the salmon right to your paws."

"How do you—" Toklo began.

"That's enough questions for tonight," Oka said. She touched her nose to Tobi's pelt, sniffing his fur. His eyes were already closed and he was breathing shallowly. Toklo knew she wanted him to stop talking so Tobi could sleep. But even that didn't dampen his mood. Tomorrow they were going over the mountain!

Up ahead, through the shadows of the trees, Toklo could see sunlight glittering on ice. They had been traveling since dawn, climbing up through the forest toward the mountain peak. Now he could see the bare, rocky slope of the mountain where the trees thinned out and the only bits of greenery were scrubby bushes and patches of moss.

He glanced back at Oka and Tobi, shuffling through the

forest behind him. Oka stopped now and then to nose at the ground and push something edible over to Tobi. Toklo had nibbled some clover before they set out, but he was too excited to eat now. Impatiently he galloped ahead toward the sunshine and burst out into a wide, sunlit meadow. It was not far from here to the rocks—and then they'd be on the mountain!

His mother and brother caught up to him, and Oka lifted herself onto her hind legs, too, sniffing the air. "Quick, let's keep moving," she said, dropping down to all fours again.

They trotted through the meadow at a steadier pace. Even Tobi kept up, staying close to Oka's paws and only stumbling a couple of times. Soon Toklo felt hard rock below his paws instead of dirt and grass. They scrambled up a short ledge and found themselves facing a landscape of snow and boulders reaching up into the sky.

The snow was deeper than Toklo expected, and of course Tobi immediately fell into a large drift. Whimpering, he floundered around with his paws until Oka came and dragged him back onto more solid ground. Toklo didn't want the others to know, but he was having some trouble with the icy rocks, too. His claws couldn't get a good grip on the slippery frozen ground, and he found himself sliding and skidding instead of leaping gracefully from boulder to boulder as he wanted to.

But it didn't matter. He was thrilled to be climbing, to be out in the sun, to be away from the firebeasts and snakebeasts and their noise and terrible smells. Up here the wind brushed through his fur, bringing the scent of prey and snow and other bears from far in the distance. The sunbeams were warm on his back, and his muscles felt like they were moving and stretching in new ways as he learned how to climb . . . traveling like a true bear for the first time.

He spotted a stick poking out of a large patch of snow and, with a happy growl, he dove on it, clamped his jaws around it, and shook it hard.

"*Rarrgmph!*" he roared, his voice muffled by his mouthful of stick. "Mmm, I've caugmht a sagmlmon!"

"Oh, really?" his mother said, swinging her head around to look at him. "Well, you'd better hang on to it, then, because I hear that fish"—she began to stalk toward him—"can be . . . very . . . slippery!" Suddenly pouncing, she grabbed the stick from his paws and galloped away.

"Hey!" Toklo yelped. He leaped after her, landing on her back and knocking her sideways. They rolled in the snow, each of them scrabbling for the salmon stick. Toklo's joy expanded until it filled him from the top of his ears to the tips of his claws. His mother hardly ever stopped to play with him. He loved the feel of her fur tickling his nose and the strength of her paws batting him around. He knew she was holding back so she wouldn't hurt him, and that made him feel protected and safe.

"Aha!" he shouted triumphantly, wrestling the stick away from her. "It's mine! I win!"

"I don't think so," she growled, chasing after him.

"Mother!" Tobi bleated from the rock where he was

cowering. "Mother, I feel sick."

Oka skidded to a halt, kicking up snow that spattered over Toklo's back. She rushed back to Tobi and sniffed him all over. Grumpily flicking snow out of his ears, Toklo followed. He was sure Tobi was just trying to get attention. When *didn't* Tobi feel sick? Couldn't he just sit for a little while and let Toklo have some fun?

"We have to keep moving," Oka said. She sounded different now, tense and scared and angry. "We have to get over the mountain before it gets dark. Come on."

She nudged Tobi to his paws and hovered over him like a shadow as he struggled over the rocks and ice. Toklo realized that Tobi smelled strange. A sharp, rotten scent hung around his fur, and his eyes looked cloudy and confused. Toklo took one more sniff and stayed his distance.

"I can't," Tobi whimpered, collapsing onto his belly. He covered his nose with twitching forepaws.

"You can do it, Tobi," Oka murmured. Her voice was gentle now, just like it always was with Tobi. "Just a bit farther. Come on, stand up and take a pawstep. One after another, and you'll get there. A journey is nothing but a river of pawsteps. You can take one pawstep, can't you?"

"Nooooooooooooo," he moaned.

Toklo sighed. This wasn't going to get them anywhere. His ears perked up. If they were staying put for a while anyway . . . He ran over, grabbed the stick in his teeth, and ran back to his mother.

"Uh-oh!" he cried. "It's getting away from me!" He threw

his head back and flung the stick into the air. It clattered to the ground at his mother's paws.

"Not now, Toklo," Oka snapped. "We've wasted too much time already. We must get down the mountain to the river before nightfall." She grunted crossly. "We shouldn't have stopped to play."

Toklo felt his fur stand on end with frustration. Now his mother was angry at him. Yet again, Tobi had ruined his fun.

"Sweetpaws," Oka murmured to Tobi. "Little cub, be brave for me. Just climb onto my back and I'll carry you the rest of the way."

"A-all right," Tobi agreed weakly. He pushed himself up and then climbed onto Oka's back, lying there as limp as a dead leaf.

Toklo snorted. He wondered whether he'd be given a ride if he moaned all the time. He didn't think so. After all, he wasn't precious Tobi. Oka set off at a brisk pace and Toklo struggled along behind her, trying not to hear the concerned murmurs his mother kept whispering to her sickly cub.

Climbing didn't seem so much fun anymore. The wind was no longer full of warm, exciting smells; instead it was cold, and it seemed to bring darkness and whirls of snow. The sun was dropping toward the edge of the sky, and the shadows were getting longer and longer, reaching out for Toklo like creeping water spirits. His paws were aching and cold, and his claws stung from being scraped against rocks all day. Even the strong muscles of his shoulders were in pain, but still his mother pressed on, leaping over patches of ice and sharp stones that Toklo was too small to avoid.

The sun had nearly vanished all the way when Toklo stopped, exhausted.

"Mother," he called. Oka, halfway up the slope ahead of him, turned and looked back but kept moving. "Mother," he called again, "when are we going to stop?"

"We can't stop," came the reply, bouncing off the rocks all the way down to the bottom of the mountain.

Ever? Toklo thought, with a twinge of fear. They couldn't go on like this all night. His head was spinning, and he was afraid that in the dark he'd stumble and fall off the mountain . . . and that his mother wouldn't even notice. *As long as she has Tobi, she doesn't care about me,* he thought bitterly.

He took a deep breath and shoved himself up the slope, using every last bit of energy he had to get up to where his mother was. The snow was very deep and he almost had to swim through patches of it, but he pressed on, unable to feel his paws anymore because they were so cold. Finally he caught up to his mother, scrambled around in front of her, and stood in her way.

"Toklo," she growled. "I told you we don't have time to play."

"I don't want to play!" Toklo protested. "I want to rest! We've been climbing all day!"

"It's not far enough," Oka said. "We need to reach the river."

"But I don't think I can go any farther," Toklo said.

"If your brother can do it, so can you," Oka said firmly.

"If—" Toklo stammered in disbelief. "You've been carrying Tobi since sunhigh! He's not doing anything except lying there!" Toklo reared up on his back legs and held his front paws out to his mother. One of the pads behind his claws was bleeding, and there were scrapes and cuts all over them.

Oka sniffed his paws, then looked up at the sky. For the first time she seemed to notice that night was falling, and stars were twinkling up above them. She reached around and nudged Tobi with her nose.

"Cold," he whimpered, burying his face in her fur.

"All right," Oka relented. "Let's make a den for the night."

Relief washed over Toklo. He looked around and spotted a hollow under an overhanging rock.

"How about over there?" he said.

Oka grunted agreement and led the way to the sheltered spot. Tobi slid slowly off her back onto a pile of moss near the base of the rock. He curled up and immediately closed his eyes. Oka crouched beside him, licking his ears.

Toklo sat down, exhausted. His paws felt like cold rocks at the end of his legs. He glanced up at the sky, where one star shone brighter than all the others.

"I wouldn't mind being that star right now," he said to his mother. "I bet it never gets tired."

Oka looked up at it, too. "You don't want to be that star," she said. "That is the spirit of a bad bear. The other animals imprisoned it there for doing something terrible, and now they move in a circle around it, taunting it. It's trapped, not free like us."

I don't feel that free, Toklo thought, watching Tobi gasp for breath.

"What did the bear do that was so terrible?" Toklo asked.

"He disobeyed his mother," Oka said, cuffing him over the head with her paw. "Now go find us some branches."

She dug the dirt and snow around Tobi into a makeshift den while Toklo nosed around for any branches that would help protect them. He didn't find much, but he did find a few mouthfuls of dry berries. He brought them back to his mother and brother, even though his stomach was growling like an enormous adult bear. Oka took the berries without thanking him and rolled them all over to Tobi. But when they curled up together and Toklo rested his chin in the soft fur on her shoulder, she sighed and did not roll away.

Grim, pale light was glimmering through the branches and snow when Toklo awoke. He blinked his eyes several times, wondering why he felt so strange and cold. It wasn't just the uncomfortable ground below him. Something was wrong.

Toklo shifted around and discovered that his brother was curled against his back, his paws tucked into his chest. When Toklo moved, Tobi pressed his paws to his face, scraped them down his muzzle once, and then lay still. His breathing came shallow and quick and smelled funny.

Toklo nosed closer to him, smelling the same sharp scent he'd noticed on Tobi yesterday. His brother's fur was cold, colder even than Toklo had been the night before. He realized with a start that Tobi's eyes were wide open. Toklo put his face right in front of Tobi's and waited for a reaction, but there was nothing. Tobi's eyes were foggy, as if he were seeing clouds instead of his brother.

"Tobi," Toklo whispered. His brother's ears didn't even twitch. Toklo cautiously put out a paw and touched his brother's side. He could feel Tobi's breaths getting faster, and then suddenly they went very slow.

"Tobi," he tried again. "Tobi, are you going to the river? Are you going to be a water spirit?" There was no answer. Toklo was afraid but fascinated, too. How did a bear become a water spirit?

Tobi took a long, shuddering breath, then went still. Toklo quickly drew back his paw. He sat up and sniffed along the length of Tobi's body. There was still the sharp, rotten smell, but now something was missing. Tobi's eyes were closed.

He was dead.

Toklo wondered what to do. He hadn't seen his brother's spirit go anywhere. Had it gone to the river? Was it still stuck inside his fur? He tried prodding Tobi again, but nothing flew out.

There was a movement behind him, and Toklo jumped. Oka was waking up, shaking her head and getting to her paws. She looked around in bewilderment, and her eyes fell on Tobi. With a cry, she shoved Toklo aside and bent her muzzle to the dead cub. A low moan escaped her, and she rose up onto her hind legs and roared with pain and fury. The sound bounced off the rocks and rang in Toklo's ears; he crouched at his mother's paws, surprised that it didn't bring the mountain down on top of them.

Oka fell back onto all four paws and turned on Toklo, snarling. "Why didn't you wake me?" she demanded. "Why? How could you just let him die?"

"I—I didn't!" Toklo cried. "I mean, I didn't—there wasn't anything I could do."

"You could have *woken* me!" she howled. "How could you do this?" She was raging at the sky, the trees, the rocks now. "How could you take him? Why must you take all my cubs? Why must they die like this? What have they ever done to make you angry?"

She crouched in the snow beside Tobi and pushed her nose into his fur, pawing at him as if trying to get him to stand up. "I didn't even get to say good-bye to him!" she cried. "My poor cub, my poor little cub, all alone . . ."

Her voice trailed off into hushed tones that Toklo couldn't hear. He backed away and sat in the opening of the den, waiting for her to get up and keep going. They still had to get to the river, didn't they?

His fur prickled with misery. He didn't understand why she was so angry with him. He wasn't the one who was too weak to live. He was the one who would take care of her, if she would let him. The water spirits hadn't taken *all* her cubs . . . he was still here! Why didn't that matter to her? Tobi must be with the salmon in the river now. Surely that was better than when he was here, where he was cold and sad and hungry and tired all the time. It was better for Tobi, and it was better for them, too.

The light spread across the mountainside, illuminating fragments of color in the snow and turning the tip of the mountain golden-white. Oka lay next to Tobi, as still as a fallen tree. Toklo shifted his paws. Were they going to stay here all day? Weren't they going to the other side of the mountain?

A long time passed, and still Oka did not move. When the sun had risen halfway up the sky, Toklo padded a few steps toward his mother. "Mother?" he said. She didn't respond or give any sign that she'd heard him. "Mother?" he tried again. "When are we going to the river?"

Oka slowly lifted her head, turned it to look at him, and rested her chin on her paws. "Tobi will never find the river," she murmured. "He should not have died here."

Toklo waited a moment. When she didn't say anything else, he said, "But what about us?"

His mother's voice was low and raspy. "We were too slow," she growled. "It's our fault he's dead, and it's our fault the water spirits won't find him."

CHAPTER SEVEN

Kallik

As *night fell, the storm died* down, and Kallik was left in a silent, empty world. The darkness above her was filled with glittering ice spots, and the ice underneath her felt thin and hollow, as if the water was trying to push through.

Her mother was gone. She still couldn't believe it. How could Nisa be dead?

Feeling was starting to creep back into Kallik's paws and she could move her legs again, but still she lay on the ice. There was no reason to move. She had nowhere to go. She was all alone.

Up in the night sky, she could see the outline of Silaluk beside the Pathway Star. Maybe Moose Bird, Chickadee, and Robin were really orcas instead of birds, circling and trapping Silaluk and then devouring her until nothing was left but bones. A stab of fresh grief pierced Kallik's heart, and she pressed her muzzle against the ice. Was her mother's spirit down there somewhere, floating among the ice shadows?

She didn't know how long she stayed lying there. She could feel her heartbeat slowing down and her body getting colder and colder. She was dimly aware of the wind sweeping snow across the ice to pile up against her back. She thought that if she lay there long enough, eventually the snow would cover her over, leaving just a drift of white, and she would disappear forever . . . just like her mother.

Below the sound of the wind, she could hear water lapping nearby and the ice creaking beneath her. *Rrrrrraaaahhh,* it whispered softly. *Errrreeeeeeee. Oooooorrrroo.* Perhaps the ice spirits were grieving for her mother as well.

Uurrrrrrrssss, whispered the ice. *Taqqiiiqqqqq . . .*

Kallik pricked her ears.

Taaaaaaa . . . qqiiiiiiiiq . . . the ice whispered again.

Kallik lifted her head and stared into the ice. It sounded like her mother's voice. The shadows whirled and bubbled, and slowly Kallik began to see a shape below the ice. For a moment she was sure her mother's face looked back at her, and then it vanished again as the bubbles reformed, glowing in the light from the moon.

Taqqiq. Kallik remembered hearing him run away into the mist. He was still alive out there . . . and alone, just like her. Except Taqqiq was even more alone than she was, because he thought Kallik was dead. With their mother gone, he was the only thing Kallik had left in the world. She had to stay alive to find him. He needed her—and she needed him, too.

She pushed herself to her paws and shook off the layer of snow that had piled up on her fur. Her bones still ached and one of her hind legs throbbed from hitting the ice when the orca tail struck her. But her mind was clear again. She padded to the edge of the ice and looked down at the cold, dark water. Were the killer whales still lurking beneath the surface, hoping for another, even easier meal?

She lay down on her belly and waited for dawn, drifting in and out of a sleep that was haunted by nightmares full of sharp teeth and swift fins and water that turned her fur pink.

Finally the first rays of the sun peeked over the ice, bringing the snowscape to glittering life. Kallik was surprised by how much water she could see around her; the ice was melting as quickly as Nisa had said. But the shelf where they'd left her brother was still there, across the treacherous expanse of sea. If she wanted to find Taqqiq, she would have to swim back to the other side.

Kallik scanned the water carefully, searching for any orca fins. She took several deep breaths, waiting to be absolutely sure there were no whales in sight.

"Spirits of the ice," she whispered, "please help me."

The waves sloshed lightly over the edge and around her paws, and in the soft lapping of the water she thought she could hear the murmur of her mother's voice again. *For Taqqiq,* she thought, and screwed up her eyes, crouched on her haunches, and leaped into the water.

Cold water swamped over her muzzle, making her cough and splutter. She started paddling her paws furiously, trying to swim as fast as she could across the channel. At last her front paws hit ice, and she scrabbled for a clawhold. Panic shot through her when she remembered that she'd never gotten herself out of the water before. She'd always needed help from Taqqiq or Nisa. What if she didn't have the strength to climb out on her own?

She flailed her back legs in the water. Her white fur must be shining like the moon beneath the dark waves—surely killer whales could see her from far away. Perhaps they were swooping in on her right now. As she lay helpless, half in the water and half on the ice, perhaps sharp teeth were closing in to clamp down and drag her under.

"Mother!" she screamed. "Help me!"

She lunged forward and was able to get a better grip on the ice with her front paws. Straining with everything she had, she hauled herself up until she could roll her back half up and onto the ice.

She rested for a moment, panting heavily. Would it be that hard every time? How would she ever make it to land? If only she had another bear to help her . . . a bear like Taqqiq. Worry for her brother brought her to her paws, and she set out along the edge of the broken ice, heading in the direction that he'd fled.

As she walked, she wondered where Taqqiq would go and how he would take care of himself. He was always so playful and easily distracted. She wondered if he remembered any of the lessons Nisa had taught them. There was still so much they didn't know; it was too soon for them to be on their own. She made herself walk faster, desperate to find him. At least they might have more of a chance together.

The sun was only a short way up the sky when Kallik came to the edge of the drift and faced another stretch of water. Her brother must have had to swim to go any farther.

Leaping into the sea was even harder this time, since she knew the battle she would face getting out on the other side. Once in the water, the current seemed even stronger than before, but fear and determination drove her on. Kallik was exhausted by the time she crawled out onto the other side, but she shook out her fur and pressed onward on aching paws.

It was a long, terrifying day. The ice kept moving under her feet and sometimes it cracked right where she was standing, plunging her into freezing water where huge chunks of ice slammed into her sides. Often the only piece of ice she could find to climb onto was a drifting floe, barely bigger than her mother's back, and she could only stay on it a moment before she had to jump back in and swim to the next one.

If she was lucky, the floes were close enough together for her to jump from one to the next, but more often she had to paddle between them. She knew she was losing time whenever she stopped to search for orca fins before leaping into the water, but the memory of her mother's final cries still echoed in her ears. She was all Taqqiq had left. She had to stay alive to find him.

As the sun rose higher in the sky, the air grew warmer and warmer, beating down on Kallik's fur. She panted with exertion, and sometimes jumping in the water was actually a relief; at least it cooled her down.

It wasn't only concern for her brother driving her on. She

knew she had to get to land before the ice melted completely. She could not be stranded out in the bay, too far from land, when the last of the ice melted. She couldn't see any trace of land from where she was, and she knew she'd never be able to swim for long enough to reach it from here.

Fortunately she could tell which way the land was from the scents that were carried on the wind. They were strange and tangled up, but unfamiliar enough that she knew it was somewhere different from her world of ice and snow and black sea. She hoped that Taqqiq had figured out the same thing and that he was traveling in the same direction. Maybe he had even found land already . . . but what would he do when he got there? Neither of them knew anything about survival off the ice. Nisa would have taught them and kept them safe while they learned.

Kallik blinked, trying not to think about her mother. She had to focus on finding her brother, and then together they would learn how to survive.

Dusk fell, and still Kallik kept walking, as far into the night as she could before her paws were too tired to take another step. At last she stopped on the most solid piece of ice she could find and slept until another day dawned, clear and frighteningly sunny. She didn't just hate the sun now because it made her too hot; she hated it because it made the ice vanish beneath her paws.

Her belly growled with hunger, and she kept losing her footing on the ice, slipping off the edge into the water several times. Her paws were wide and usually they felt perfectly suited to the slippery smooth surface underpaw, but now they were so tired and numb that she almost felt like she was walking on stumps of ice. She could tell that she was getting closer to the land because there were fewer chunks of big ice and more stretches of fast-moving water. Her fur was constantly wet, and she spotted several large birds swimming in the water and flying over the ice. They were gray and white, the color of a snowy sky, and they made loud squalling noises that hurt her ears.

Kallik was stumbling with hunger by the end of the day. The sun was setting in a blaze of orange and red when suddenly she spotted another white bear almost a skylength away, across the ice ahead of her.

"Taqqiq?" she yelped. She began to run, galloping across the snow. "Taqqiq!"

The bear spun around, snarling, and she saw that its muzzle was red with blood and a seal carcass lay at its paws. It was much too large to be Taqqiq; this bear had seen the last burn-sky, and he was big and angry and ready to protect his food.

Skidding to a halt, Kallik spun around and ran. She didn't look back until she reached the next stretch of water. With relief, she saw that the bear hadn't chased her. But the sight of the seal had reawakened all her hunger, and she couldn't think of anything but food. She swam to the next patch of ice and padded farther onto it, sniffing the air with one scent firmly in her mind. At last she found a hole in the ice that smelled of seal. She sniffed all the way around it as she'd seen her mother do. She could remember how Nisa lay down by the hole and waited patiently for so long. At least keeping still for that long would give her a chance to rest.

Kallik stretched out on her belly, resting her head on her front paws. She kept her eyes trained on the hole, waiting for any ripple of movement, ready to pounce. Her body was exhausted, but she was too hungry to fall asleep. The suspense of waiting for a seal to emerge helped keep her awake, too, even though it seemed like the entire night was passing slowly by.

Suddenly the sleek wet head of a seal popped out of the water, its whiskers trembling as it breathed in. Kallik leaped forward, her claws outstretched and ready to sink into seal flesh, her mouth wide and ready to clamp down.

But her paws closed on empty air, and her jaws snapped shut on nothing. She was too slow. The seal had escaped.

Kallik lay down and pressed her face into the ice. Maybe she should give up. She should let the ice spirits take her, and then she could be with her mother again. But Taqqiq was on his own, too. She had to stay alive so she could find him, and then they could take care of each other.

Shoving herself to her paws, Kallik backtracked to the last stretch of water. She swam back to the large chunk of ice and padded cautiously across it, sniffing the air every other pawstep for any trace of the other bear. The night was still, and the sound of her paws crunching on the ice seemed eerily loud. But she was lucky; the other bear had moved on.

She found the seal carcass he had been eating and nosed it for any scraps he had left behind. There wasn't much, but she was willing to eat anything, even if it wasn't the most delicious parts of the fat or the skin. Her mouth watered as she chewed, and the few bits she was able to pull off helped take the edge off her hunger.

She didn't want to risk seeing the other white bear again, so she left the carcass as soon as she'd eaten every last scrap of meat. Following her nose, and steering clear of any scents that might be other bears, she hurried on toward land, only stopping to sleep for a short time when the moon was high in the sky.

The next morning, when Kallik opened her eyes, she saw something different along the edge of the sky in front of her. A smudged line of gray, like a clawstroke through the snow. She sat up and stared at it, scratching her ear. It looked a little bit like storm clouds coming, but it wasn't moving. *Land!*

She sniffed the air; the unfamiliar scents were stronger than ever. The air felt wet and soft, and the ice had a layer of melted water on the top, dripping off the edges into the sea. Kallik got to her paws and started walking toward the gray line, raising her nose so she could inhale as many of the new smells as possible. She could tell that some of them were strange animals: musky fur and fluttering feathers, scents of hunger and danger and fear, some predators and some prey. There were other scents, too, that were tangy and fresh in a way she'd never smelled before.

She swam across three stretches of water before she began to see the land in front of her more clearly. It looked gray and hard and rough, like the sharp edges of glaciers but darker.

Birds swooped overhead, more birds than she'd ever seen in her life—almost as many birds as there were ice spots in the sky. They screeched and flapped, diving for fish and preening themselves on the rocks.

Kallik shivered. What would she eat on land? There were no seals there. She was pretty sure there was no way she'd ever catch one of the birds. Without Nisa's help, how would she know what to eat? She remembered Nisa's stories about grass and berries, but she couldn't see any "green whiskers" growing out of the ground. Would she recognize them if she saw them?

She kept walking, watching the rocks get bigger as she got closer. Finally she reached a place where there was no more ice—nothing but water from here until the land. This was it . . . the place her mother had been leading them to. She had never intended for Kallik to come here alone.

Kallik dove into the water and paddled hard. The waves picked her up and drove her forward, then sucked her back. They were stronger than anything, even her mother's paws, and she couldn't control where she was going at all.

"Spirits of the white bears!" she called, gasping as water poured into her mouth and nose. "If you haven't melted into the sky yet—if any of you are left in the water—please help me before you go." Large floating pieces of ice pounded her on every side as she swam closer and closer to the rocky shore. She was nearly there when a wave seized her and smashed her into a large rock. A jolt of pain shot through her; she scrambled with her claws, trying to grip on to the rock, but the surf dragged her back into the open water again, shoving her under. Salty water surged over her muzzle, and she struggled desperately forward, scraping her claws on the rock as she wrapped all four paws around it.

I can't die now! she thought. *Taqqiq might be waiting for me on land—he might be only bearlengths away.*

It took all the strength she had to haul herself onto the top of the boulder, but finally she heaved herself free of the sea and stood, panting for breath, on the flat, hard rock. From there she could jump to the next rock, and then clamber over smaller ones until at last she stood onshore, her paws sinking into a pebbly brown surface that she guessed was the dirt her mother had told her about.

She shook the water out of her fur and breathed in deeply. She'd made it. She was finally on land.

CHAPTER EIGHT

Lusa

Snow had fallen overnight, leaving the ground soggy and cold as it squelched between Lusa's claws. Dirt clung to her fur whenever she rolled around playing with Yogi, and as they raced to get to their food, they left long streaks of churned-up mud behind them.

Lusa shook herself, trying to get some of the mud out of her fur. She trotted over to her mother, who was lying limply under the tallest tree. Ashia had been eating less and less for days, and she was starting to look thin. Lusa buried her nose in her mother's fur, which was no longer glossy and sleek but patchy.

"Mother?" Lusa whispered. "Are you all right?"

"I remember a pool of water," Ashia said, blinking. "Where is it? It was right there . . . and there were other bears . . . a cub named Ben, I think. . . ."

"What do you mean?" Lusa asked, scared. "There's no pool here. What cub? Mother, what's wrong?"

"She's thinking of the first zoo she lived in," Stella said, coming up beside Lusa.

"But why?" Lusa asked. "Doesn't she like it here anymore?"

Ashia pressed her paws to her muzzle, staring up at Lusa. "Who are you?" she asked. "You look like me. Where are the others?"

"I'm your cub. Don't you remember?" Lusa pleaded.

"She's just confused," Stella said. "Maybe she's tired. We should let her sleep."

"Don't you want to come into the den?" Lusa asked her mother. Night was falling, and Lusa knew it would be much warmer inside the stone walls. She patted her mother's paws with her own. "It's time to sleep. Let's go inside."

Ashia covered her face with her paws and mumbled something, rolling away from Lusa.

"It looks like she wants to sleep out here tonight," Stella said, heading back to the den. "Let's give her some peace."

"What's wrong with her?" Lusa asked.

"I'm sure she'll be fine," Stella said. "If she were sick, the flat-faces would take her away and make her better."

"Really?" Lusa perked up. "They can do that?"

"Unless they take her away and don't bring her back," Stella mused. "Then I'm not sure what happens."

Lusa shuffled her paws on the floor. "Has that happened to other bears?"

"Once in the time I've been here," Stella said. "But that bear was very sick, and we all thought his spirit was ready to go into the trees."

"Stop this nonsense," said a deep voice behind her. Lusa dropped to all fours and turned to face her father. King was looking at Stella sternly.

"There's nothing to make such a big fuss about," King growled.

"But what about Mother?" Lusa asked. "Will the flat-faces make her better?"

King shrugged, his fur rippling across his shoulders. "Who knows what the flat-faces will do? I don't even know why they keep us here, let alone why they fix us when we're sick. It's no use trying to figure it out. Let's wait and see." He scratched his ear and lumbered away.

Stella nudged Lusa gently with her nose. "Don't worry, Lusa. Your mother is a strong bear. Maybe she just feels like sleeping in the open tonight—the way your father does."

Lusa glanced over at King. Even he wasn't sleeping on the cold, muddy ground. He'd found a flattish boulder and was settling down on top of it, his paws hanging down on either side.

"I hope she gets better soon," Lusa said.

"Spirits of the bears," Stella murmured, gazing into the sky. "Make Ashia feel her normal self by morning." She nudged Lusa again. "Come on, let's go to sleep."

Lusa fidgeted all night, worrying about her mother and feeling the emptiness of the den without Ashia's bulk to lean against. As soon as light started to creep across the Bowl, she scrambled to her paws, shook herself, and trotted out of the den. Ashia was still lying in the same position. It looked as if she hadn't moved since the day before.

Lusa didn't know what to do. Nothing like this had happened in the Bowl in her lifetime. Why did bears get sick? How would Ashia get better? Her mother was like the boulders of the Mountains—always there, always the same. If she changed, it would be like the earth vanishing from under Lusa's paws.

Perhaps she'd feel better if she ate something. Lusa gathered some of the fruit the feeders had left for them and brought it over to her mother. "Mother?" she said, dropping the ripe berries beside her mother's muzzle.

"Lusa," Ashia whispered, pressing her paws to her belly. Relief flooded through Lusa as she saw that at least her mother recognized her. Maybe she was feeling better than last night.

"Mother, are you all right?" Lusa asked. She nosed the berries closer to Ashia. "I brought you some food."

Ashia made a groaning sound and turned her face into the dirt. Mud and snow were caked through her fur, but she made no move to shake them off. She didn't even lift her head to sniff the fruit Lusa had brought. Lusa heard a rumbling sound from her mother's belly. This wasn't better. This might even be worse.

Some of the feeders were leaning over the wall. Lusa scrambled over to them and stood on her hind legs, trying to get their attention. Couldn't they see that her mother was sick?

One of them chuckled a little and threw a piece of fruit to Lusa. Frustrated, the cub sat down again. Flat-faces never understood what you really wanted. She batted at the fruit, then abandoned it to go back and sniff her mother. Maybe if she tried harder . . . Lusa ran back to the edge of the Bowl, stood up to look at the feeders, and then ran back to her mother. She did this a few more times, clacking her teeth to show she was frightened.

The flat-faces pointed at her, and then at Ashia. They spoke in quiet, serious murmurs like the rustle of leaves in the trees. Finally a few of them came through the door in the wall and went over to Ashia, making gentle sounds and walking around her carefully.

A tall flat-face that Lusa had never seen before came into the Bear Bowl. Unlike the others, he had some bushy gray fur on his face. Two round shiny things were perched on his nose, and his removable pelt was green. He was carrying a long black-and-brown stick cradled under his arm. Lusa didn't like the way it smelled . . . like the Fence but darker and more smoky.

The other feeders brought in big poles and a roll of webbed stuff that turned into Fence when they unrolled it. They set up the poles around Ashia and put the new, smaller Fence around her. Lusa didn't realize what they were doing until they stepped away and it was too late. Now she couldn't get close to her mother. Ashia was alone inside the new Fence.

Lusa tried to claw at the Fence to join her mother, but one of the feeders came over and shooed her away. What were they doing? Why wouldn't they let her be with her mother? Lusa backed away, then scrambled up the tree, pushing herself quickly higher with her hind paws. From the branch above her mother, she could see right inside the small Fence. She saw the tall flat-face walk in and point the long metal thing at her mother.

There was a sharp popping sound, and something shot out of the black stick into her mother. Ashia grunted once, and then slowly her eyes closed.

Horrified, Lusa cried, "Mother! Mother!"

But Ashia didn't respond.

"Mother!" Lusa screamed.

She tried to climb back down, but now something loud and roaring was coming into the Bowl, and it scared her back up the tree again. It coughed smoke and swaggered so loudly that all the other bears scattered to the far corners of the Bowl, staying as far away as possible. Lusa guessed that this was one of the firebeasts she'd heard King talk about. She'd seen them from the top of the tree sometimes, charging around the paths outside the Bowl, but she'd never been close enough to smell the scent of metal and burning before.

The feeders gathered around Ashia and rolled her onto a large flat skin the color of the sky but shiny like water. Each of them picked up a corner and lifted the large, limp bear. They hoisted her onto a flat thing with round black paws, and then they hooked that to the firebeast.

With a great roar, the firebeast lurched away through the big doors at the back of the Bear Bowl. Lusa rushed down the tree as the doors were closing. "Mother!" she howled. The doors slammed in her face, and she stood up on her hind legs, clawing at the wall. "Mother! Don't go! Wait, please don't take her!"

CHAPTER NINE

Toklo

Pebbles of frozen ice caught in Toklo's claws as he dug through the snow, searching for something to eat. The sun glowed red in the sky as it crept slowly down below the trees, and an ice-cold wind raced up the mountain, slicing through his fur and making him shiver.

Oka had not moved for the rest of the day, nor had she spoken. She lay beside Tobi, unmoving, as the day passed and night crept on again. Toklo could see they would be staying here again tonight, even though his belly was howling in protest. The salmon couldn't be too far away now. Surely they were less than a day's travel from food that would finally fill him up.

What if his mother never moved again? Did Oka want him to stay here until his spirit grew so hungry it joined Tobi's in the water? He wished she would see that having one living bear cub was better than having two dead ones. It was also better than having one alive and one half dead. Now they could travel faster and take care of each other better.

His claws snagged on something soft, and he brushed away the snow to uncover a pile of moss. It was damp and soggy and crumbled in his paws, but he swallowed it down anyway. He scooped up some of it and brought it back to his mother where she lay under their rough shelter.

"I brought you some moss," he whispered, laying it close to her muzzle. Oka didn't open her eyes. The small shape of Toklo's brother lay curled between her paws, limp and still. Toklo lay down behind his mother and crept slowly nearer, dragging himself along on his belly until his fur was touching her curved back. She didn't move, so he rested his muzzle on his paws and closed his eyes, falling into an uneasy sleep.

The sudden movement of Oka's body behind him startled Toklo awake. He scrambled to his paws, noticing that the sun was starting to rise and the sky was streaked with gray clouds.

Oka stood for a moment, her head bent to sniff Tobi once more. "It's time to go," she said.

Relief spread through Toklo. He didn't have to die along with his brother after all. "To the river?" he asked.

"But first there is an earth ritual to attend to," Oka said, as if she hadn't heard him. She turned and saw the moss that Toklo had brought the night before.

"Yes," she murmured. "That is what we need." Gently she took the moss in her jaws and laid it down on Tobi's fur. Then she swung her head up and stepped out of the den, her paw-steps measured and heavy. Toklo padded after her, confused but afraid to speak in case she snapped at him.

Oka nosed through the snow, digging loose bits of earth and twigs. She clawed a pile of dead leaves together, carried them back into the den, and laid those on top of Tobi as well.

Toklo didn't know what she was doing, but he hoped that if he helped her, they could leave sooner. Copying her, he gathered dirt and branches and dragged them back to the den, where he helped her cover his brother's body until it could not be seen anymore.

Oka lifted her head and spoke, her deep growl echoing off the back of the den wall. "Spirits of the earth, I commit this innocent cub, whom we called Tobi, to your care. Take him back into the warmth of your fur and protect him. Guide his paws through the rocks and the soil to the water that lives deep within you, and let him join his fellow bear spirits in the river that flows eternally."

She paused, and Toklo wondered if he was supposed to say something. Oka scratched her claws through the dirt one way and then the other, leaving a crisscross of marks next to her cub's body. Still without speaking, she turned and walked away, out of the den onto the open slope of the mountain.

Toklo hesitated for a moment. It didn't seem right to be leaving Tobi behind. Toklo pressed his nose into the mound of dirt and leaves and branches. "Tobi," he whispered. "We're going to the river now. I know you need to get there, too, so follow me, all right? I'll take you to the river."

Toklo stepped back and shook his head, brushing off the leaves that were stuck to his fur. Then he hurried after his mother, who was setting a brisk pace down the mountain. She didn't speak to him, and he stayed silent, frightened by the tension in her shoulders and the faraway look in her eyes.

It was nearly sunhigh when Toklo noticed something at the edge of his hearing. It was a fast, rushing, happy sound, full of bubbles and life, like rain rushing across the valley. "Is that the river?" he blurted. "Are we nearly there? Are we going to catch salmon now? I can't wait! I'm going to catch so many salmon, Mother, watch and see!"

They had left the snow behind them and were coming down through thick pine trees and clearings dotted with wildflowers. In front of them he could see the river glittering in the pale sunlight—a wide, shallow rush of water with pebbly shores on either side. He galloped ahead, nearly losing his balance on the expanse of pine needles that covered the steep hill.

And suddenly Toklo saw bears.

Bears were wading in the river, staring into the water. Bears were rolling on their backs in the water, splashing with their paws. Bears were pacing along the banks and running through the shallows, their fur sodden and spiky.

Toklo had never seen so many bears in one place. They all looked so big! Most of them were larger than Oka, and they were all much, much larger than him. He slowed down at the edge of the trees and waited for his mother to catch up. Together they stepped into the sunshine, moving out of the cool shadows under the pines onto the long, pebbly riverbank. Toklo didn't like the way the other bears looked at him. They looked . . . *hungry*. One bear, an enormous adult male, stood up on his hind legs in the water to stare at Oka and Toklo as they approached the riverbank. His claws were long and sharp, and he had the largest hump on his shoulders that Toklo had ever seen. His fur was dark from the water and his muzzle was wet, as if he'd been diving for fish. He stared at Toklo with small, brown, unfriendly eyes.

As they got closer, the bear dropped to its paws and loped over, standing between them and the river and blocking their path. Oka stopped, and Toklo ducked behind her front leg, trying not to make eye contact with the large grizzly.

"Step aside," Oka said firmly.

"What's your name, pretty?" the bear growled.

"None of your business," she snapped.

"I'm Shoteka," he announced.

"We don't care," Oka snarled. "Now get out of our way. This isn't your territory—it's fair game for every bear. There's enough fish in the river for all of us."

Shoteka's eyes shifted to Toklo. "It's not the fish I'm interested in," he said. "Your cub is too old to still be traveling with you."

"No, I'm not!" Toklo squeaked indignantly. He knew most cubs stayed with their mothers for at least two fishleaps. However much he wanted to be on his own and make his own decisions, he knew he wouldn't be able to look after himself for a long time yet.

The male grizzly lifted his chin and looked challengingly at Oka. "When is he going to find his own territory?"

"We're just here for the fish," Oka said. "So step aside."

"There are no fish in this river," Shoteka rumbled.

Oka snorted. "There have always been fish in this river! You're not going to drive us off with lies like that."

She strode forward boldly and the other bear fell back, scraping his paws on the pebbles with a show of reluctance. Toklo trotted after her, staying close to her hind paws.

Just as they passed him, Shoteka lunged toward Toklo. His teeth were bared, and Toklo felt a blast of hot, rotten breath over his fur. Toklo froze.

Suddenly Oka was there, rearing up on her hind legs and roaring. She slashed at the male grizzly with her claws as Toklo ducked behind her. Shoteka stumbled back, then turned tail and ran, splashing away into the river. A few of the other bears snorted at one another. Toklo heard one of them say something about getting between a mother and her cubs, and he felt a warm swell of pride and relief. His mother was so strong! No one would mess with them now. It comforted him to know she would stick up for him, even though he wasn't Tobi.

Oka led the way upriver, moving as far away from Shoteka as possible. Toklo followed her into the shallows and gasped as the icy water tugged at his fur. It was much stronger than the streams in the valley. This water had power; he could almost believe that ancient bear spirits raced along in it. Smooth round stones shifted under his paws, and he felt the silt of the river mud drifting up like mist as he waded through it.

Toklo spun in a circle and splashed over to his mother, eager to start fishing. He could see a bear farther downriver with a large fish in its jaws, flapping and shining in the light. Other bears were closing in on it, as if wondering whether the catch was worth fighting for.

But Oka was not fishing. He could see from the looseness of her shoulders and the stillness in her paws that she was not waiting for something to swim by. Instead, she was staring into the water, talking in a soft voice. Toklo stopped splashing and listened.

"Be careful, little cub," Oka whispered. "You have a long journey ahead of you." Her head dropped lower until her nose almost touched the water. "Look after him, water spirits, I beg you. He is so little and tired, and he's not used to being on his own."

She was talking about Tobi. Of course.

Toklo sighed impatiently. He was sure the water spirits knew perfectly well that Tobi was small and weak. Why else would he have died? If he'd been bigger and stronger, he'd still be alive, like Toklo was.

Shadows danced below the ripples as Toklo gazed into the water. He searched for any sign of the bear spirits in the river, but all he could see was the vague outline of his reflection and the shapes of pebbles in the riverbed. He'd expected to see the faces of bears, or a flash of fur, or a hint of claws racing along the muddy bottom. But there was nothing here but water.

"I can't see Tobi, Mother," Toklo said. He wondered if his little brother had figured out how to follow him down the mountain. It would be awful if Tobi were stuck up in the bar-ren rocks all alone. "Do you think he's here yet? Maybe he's still finding his way."

Oka rounded on him with a snarl. "What do you know about death?" she growled. "You don't know anything."

Toklo backed away. How was he supposed to know anything if she didn't teach him? Of course he didn't know much about death. Tobi was the only bear he knew who'd ever died. And Oka had spent so much of their lives fussing over Tobi that she'd hardly told Toklo anything.

Toklo stomped over to a spot between two large rocks where the water flowed into a pool a little deeper than the rest of the river, reaching halfway up his legs. If his mother wanted to stand around talking to the river, that was fine. He'd learn to fish on his own. He looked around until he spotted a golden-furred female bear who was properly fishing. She was crouched in the water, keeping still and watching. Suddenly she leaped forward and dove into the water with her front paws. She must have missed what she was jumping for, because she pounced a few more times, chasing the fish around in a circle and sending up a spray of sparkling water drops. Finally she emerged, dripping wet, with a small salmon in her jaws. She looked nervously at the other bears and then sat down with her back to them, the water foaming around her fur, eating quickly as if she wanted to finish before they noticed her catch.

Toklo's mouth watered. Surely he could do that, too. He could be patient, and fast, and determined . . . couldn't he? He turned around in the water a few times, looking for a good place to stand. He set his back to the current and left his legs planted wide apart, so the river could flow between them.

He waited for what felt like a very long time. His vision started to get blurry from staring at the water for so long. He kept expecting to see the dark shape of a fish swim between his paws, but there was nothing but the shimmer of sunlight on the ripples.

Something dark moved just out of his reach. Toklo pounced, landing on his belly with a big splash as his paws closed around a mossy stick.

He had barely a moment to feel disappointed. As soon as he lifted his paws off the stones, the current seized him and began dragging him downriver. He let out a startled yelp as the river swept him past his mother and a few other bears, but Oka didn't look up from her conversation with the river, and the other bears just seemed curious or amused. Flailing his paws, Toklo saw the huge grizzly who had attacked him earlier waiting on a rock downstream. Shoteka had planted himself right in the path of the current and was watching as Toklo was swept closer and closer.

"Mother!" Toklo yelped. "Help me!" He tried to stretch down and dig his claws into the pebbles, but the water swamped over his muzzle. He scrambled up to the surface, choking for breath, just as he crashed into the tree-trunk legs of the male grizzly. Immediately two massive paws seized his shoulders and shoved his head below the water.

Toklo held his breath and lashed out with his paws, trying to claw at Shoteka's legs or kick his way free. His hind legs hit the bottom of the river, and he shoved himself to the surface

again, sucking in a quick breath before the grizzly forced him
under once more. Water flooded up Toklo's nose and surged
into his mouth and ears. He tried biting and scratching the
paws that held him down, but he could feel his strength starting to fade and his movements getting weaker.

The murmurs of the river seemed louder underwater,
crashing in his ears like the spirits shouting at him.

All at once the weight disappeared from his back. Toklo
bobbed up to the surface, gasping for air. His paws scraped the
stones on the bottom of the river and he was able to pull himself into the shallows, where he collapsed onto his belly. He
looked up and saw his mother driving Shoteka out of the water.
She growled and charged at the male bear, her claws reaching
for him and her mouth wide open. Shoteka roared angrily and
scampered up the bank, disappearing into the trees.

Toklo dragged himself to his paws, panting and shivering.
Oka slowly came back, her sodden fur clinging to her thin
frame. She stopped on the edge of the riverbank and stared at
him.

"I'm sorry, Mother," Toklo whimpered. "I'm so sorry I tried
to fish on my own. I won't do it again, I promise."

Oka didn't move any closer. She seemed to be looking right
through him. Toklo felt rooted to the spot, as if his legs were
growing out of the riverbed. Why didn't his mother come to
comfort him?

When she finally spoke, her voice was hoarse.

"I can't do this," she said. "I can't watch my cubs die. I
won't let it happen again."

"Mother—" Toklo began. He'd heard about her first litter of cubs, who had all died in their first few moons.

"Leave me," Oka growled. "Leave this territory. We're all going to starve here. If you must die, do it somewhere else, far away from me. Go away, and don't come back."

Hunching her shoulders, she turned and walked away, leaving Toklo standing alone in the river.

CHAPTER TEN

Kallik

Kallik felt even more alone on land than she had on the ice. It was strange not to have smooth, cold snow beneath her paws. Here she felt heavy and awkward; her paws kept sinking into the ground, and everything smelled wrong.

The piles of rocks beside the sea gave way to a long stretch of speckled dirt that ran along the water as far as she could see in each direction. Farther back, away from the water, the land rose up for several bearlengths and then flattened out again. Kallik could catch a glimpse of unfamiliar colors and shapes on top of the ridge, but it was hard to see much detail from where she was.

Maybe if she climbed up there, she'd have a better view all along the shoreline. Maybe she'd see Taqqiq!

Kallik's paws were sore and her fur was waterlogged, weighing her down, but she focused on putting one paw in front of another as she walked across the dirt, leaving the ocean behind her. Her feet left pawprints like they did in the snow, but here the dirt tangled in her fur and her claws and it was nasty to lick off, scratching her tongue instead of cooling it.

Kallik walked along the base of the cliff, looking for a way up. Soon it began to slope and part of it had fallen away around large boulders, so she could scramble from one outcropping to the next.

Huffing and gasping, she rolled onto the top of the ridge, her fur caked with dirt. From up here, she could still hear the waves battering against the rocks. The sound was even louder than the wind that howled across the ice. Kallik wished her mother were there, so she could bury her nose in Nisa's fur and block out the noise. The farther she traveled from the sea, the lonelier she felt. The comforting whispers of the spirits below the ice were a long way behind her, and Kallik felt as if her mother were getting farther and farther away as well. It was getting dark. She needed to find a place to rest where she could be safe for the night.

There were strange tall shapes ahead of her, taller even than a large white bear standing on his hind legs. Kallik crept up cautiously, wondering if they might attack, but they kept still even when she came right up to them. They didn't seem like they could move at all; their paws were buried in the dirt. Kallik sniffed the air. She recognized the sharp, fresh smell she'd noticed from the ice.

She stood up on her hind legs and rested her front paws on the solid, unmoving body. It was the same shape as one of her mother's front legs, but wider around, and reaching up into

the sky. And it was brown, like the dirt under her paws. Up
above, it split into several arms with something that looked
like feathers attached. The feathers were a color Kallik hadn't
seen on its own before, although they looked like they might
be part of the ocean's colors. She wondered if this was the
"green" her mother had described.

She dropped down to all fours again and sniffed around the
base of the strange thing. Green whiskers were pushing out of
the dirt around its paws, and with a jolt Kallik realized that
this must be grass. It wasn't how she'd pictured it from her
mother's description. She lifted her head and studied the tall
shape again. It smelled like the grass—alive but not meat, with
scents of dirt and sky and rain in it. Her mother had told her
that was how "plants" would smell. So perhaps this was a
"tree."

Kallik felt a little better once the world around her had a
few more names attached to it. Her mother had talked about
the land for a long time, so all Kallik had to do was put
together her mother's stories with what she found in front of
her eyes.

Around the other side of the tree there was a hole where
the dirt had caved in below its roots. Kallik squeezed between
two of the roots and found herself in a small shelter, surrounded by dirt walls that reminded her of the snowy dens
her mother would sometimes build. Even if an adult white
bear found her here, it wouldn't be able to fit through the
roots to get to her. She dug her claws into the dirt and spread
it around, making herself a comfortable spot to sleep in. She

didn't like the feeling of the crumbly brown earth coating her paws and getting stuck in her fur, but she guessed she'd have to put up with it until burn-sky was over.

Kallik curled up and rested her muzzle on her paws. Outside the ice spots were twinkling in the sky, and right over her head, brightest of all, she could see the Pathway Star. Despite her loneliness, she felt comforted by the sight of it. Even if she couldn't reach the ice spirits during burn-sky, at least the Pathway Star would always be there for her. She remembered the story of the place where the ice was always frozen and the bears danced. If the Pathway Star could lead bears there, could it also take her to Taqqiq?

Her eyes closed drowsily, and sleep washed over her before she could worry any more.

In the bright light of the next morning, Kallik's spirits rose as she scrambled out of her hidden den. The trees around her rustled and whispered almost like the bear spirits in the ice, and the sun sparkled brightly off all the new colors and shapes around her. Surely her mother would be proud of her for getting this far by herself. Wherever she was, she must know that Kallik was looking for her brother.

"I'll find him, Mother," Kallik murmured. "We'll be all right."

Her belly growled loudly as if it was answering her, demanding food.

"I know, bossy," she said playfully to her stomach. "Let's see what I can find." She knew there were no seals on the land, but her mother had said they could eat berries and grass and other kinds of plants, too. Kallik sniffed the grass around the tree and tried tugging up a mouthful of it.

It tasted sharp and dirty, nothing like the rich, chewy warmth of meat or seal fat. "Blech," she said, spitting it back out again. She'd only eat that if she had to.

Shaking herself, she trotted back toward the water, following the sound of the waves. She stopped every few paces and sniffed the air or nosed the ground, searching for scents of food. But before she found anything to eat, another familiar scent hit her nostrils. White bear! Could it be Taqqiq? She dashed to the edge of the ridge, where she could see out across the shore and the water.

In the distance, about half a skylength away, she spotted a large white bear lumbering along the edge of the bay. Disappointment prickled her fur when she realized it was too big to be Taqqiq. But perhaps if she followed it from far away, she might be able to eat any leftover prey it couldn't finish. She thought for a moment, shuffling her paws. It wasn't safe to get too close. Her mother had told her and Taqqiq about cubs being killed by extremely hungry white bears.

Suddenly a movement caught her eye farther along the shore. It was another white bear—heading in the same direction! The two bears were far apart and clearly not traveling together. But they were going the same way. . . .

They must be heading to the gathering place! Her mother had spoken of a place where the white bears gathered to meet the ice. All Kallik had to do was go the same way—and stay as far away from the other bears as possible.

"Please, Silaluk," she whispered, "show Taqqiq the way to go, so I can find him at the gathering place." She prayed that he remembered what Nisa had said about the place where the ice came back. She prayed that he'd made it onto the land at all. From here she could see right out into the bay. The wind whipped ripples across the open stretches of water, and birds circled overhead, shrieking.

Kallik decided to stay on top of the ridge, keeping the shore in sight as she set off around the bay. Then she could hopefully see any other bears coming from a long way off. Round gray things rolled and clacked beneath her paws, and she guessed these were "stones." Or maybe "rocks." She had never figured out what the difference was from the way her mother described them.

She traveled the whole day, staying low when she got too close to another bear ahead of her. She found no abandoned prey, no carcasses to chew on, and finally she had to stop and eat some grass, despite its bitter taste. She followed the scent of plants into a group of trees . . . a "wood," if she remembered her mother's words right. Here there were short, fat trees, and some of them had little round balls growing on them in sharp colors that made Kallik blink. Were these "berries"? Some of them were black like her nose but some were bright red like blood. She wondered if they tasted like meat. They smelled all right to eat, but she worried . . . how would she know? What if they made her sick?

The roaring in her belly made up her mind. It was this or

starve to death. She closed her teeth over the berries and tugged them free. They tasted sweet, nothing like meat but much better than grass. If she could survive on these, maybe burn-sky wouldn't be so bad.

But the problem with berries, as she discovered, was that not even all the berries in the wood could add up to a seal. They were just too small. She ate every berry she could find, and by the time she moved on she was feeling a bit more hopeful, even if she was still hungry. Her muzzle was stained with red berry juice and her claws were all sticky, but her head felt a little clearer, and she could imagine surviving long enough to find Taqqiq. She hoped he'd discovered berries and learned to eat them, too.

That night she found another makeshift den in a pile of rocks. It was colder than the den in the tree roots, and closer to the bay so she could hear the waves crashing all night long. It was hard to sleep with all the noise, and it worried her that she hadn't found Taqqiq yet. When the first rays of sunrise slipped in through the cracks in the rocks, she climbed out and started walking again. It was strange to see so many new things pushing their way out of the ground or along the arms of the trees. Sometimes it seemed like there was a light dust that smelled of plants floating through the air, which made her sneeze and her eyes water. The snow was melting away quickly and the ground was wet under her paws, squishing between her claws as she put her weight down.

Whenever she could, she stopped to find berries, and once she was lucky enough to find a carcass with some meat still on it. The animal was unfamiliar to her, and it didn't have the salty, fishy taste of seal, but she ate it anyway. As she traveled, she tried to attach more of her mother's words to what she saw.

At one point, she found herself walking through a muddy, watery, weedy territory that she thought might be a "marsh." She was watching her paws, concentrating on finding the driest spots to step on, so she didn't see the herd of animals in front of her until one of them snorted.

She looked up and jumped back in surprise. They were *enormous.* They didn't look as heavy or solid as white bears, but they were much taller than she was, perched on four long, skinny legs. Their short, shaggy fur was brown and they had long, wobbly-looking muzzles. But strangest of all, several of them had two sets of giant claws growing out of the top of their heads.

Caribou! Kallik thought. She stared at them. Most of them were grazing, nibbling at the plants and ignoring her. A couple had lifted their heads and were watching her, but they didn't look very concerned. Kallik backed up until the bushes hid her from view, and then she turned and found a different way through the marsh.

Toward sunset, as the light around her was turning orange and hazy, she came to a small pond. Trying not to slip on the mud, Kallik crouched at the edge to lap up the water. All at once the dirt beside her paw moved. Startled, she froze and stared at it. Whatever it was moved again, just twitching a little, then suddenly it jumped straight up into the air.

Kallik didn't even think about what she was doing. With a quick, instinctive pounce, she clapped her paws around the jumping thing and pinned it to the mud. Her claws sank into it and it flailed one more time, then lay there, limp and unmoving.

Had she killed it? Kallik lowered her head and sniffed it without lifting her paw. It certainly seemed dead. The creature, which was smaller than her paw, had two small legs and two long legs with webbed paws. It was slimy and lumpy, its skin like a cross between a fish and a seal. It was greenish brown, and its belly was pale white. Two bulging eyes sat on top of its head, and when she leaned on it she could see that it had a long tongue inside its mouth.

Curious, she nibbled on it and discovered that it tasted quite interesting. Its texture was a lot like a seal's, except it didn't have any fat and it wasn't quite as meaty. She devoured it in a few bites and felt a little odd afterward, but it was more of a meal than berries. She sniffed around the pond for a long time but didn't see any more animals like that. She tried digging in the mud around the water, but all that did was make her fur dirtier. She'd have to try again at the next pond.

The days grew warmer and warmer, and Kallik panted under her thick fur coat. A couple of days were so hot, she couldn't even come out of her shelter. Instead she lay in the shade below a thicket of branches, trying to conserve her energy and keep cool. It was hard to sleep, though, since the ground below her was damp and flying insects kept buzzing around her muzzle. Kallik wasn't sure which were mosquitoes and which ones were flies, but she remembered that her mother hated both of them.

Every day she thought about Taqqiq and wondered if he was all right. Had he remembered all the things their mother had told them?

One morning she found a strange den that smelled of an animal she hadn't yet met. It was large, with flat walls made of dead trees, and it was raised up on long legs above the water-logged ground. The faded scents of unfamiliar food wafted from it, but it looked deserted, as if the inhabitants had been gone for a while.

She sniffed around the outside but couldn't find a way in. Still hopeful, she moved in a circle around it, sniffing the area in search of scraps.

Aha! There was a dent in the wet ground, and half buried in it were two lightly speckled brown eggs. She had seen eggs already on this journey, but never anywhere she could reach them. But she was pretty sure she could eat them. Like the seal pups her mother had pulled from their den, these were the beginning of birds, and she knew she could eat birds.

Kallik crouched low to the ground, like her mother had taught her, dragging herself forward on her belly as slowly and quietly as she could. She imagined crunching through the shells, and her mouth watered with anticipation. She crept closer and closer, dreaming of the delicious taste of the eggs . . .

An angry screech sounded from the sky. Kallik didn't have time to roll away before a bird launched itself at her head, scratching and pecking. Kallik's heart leaped with terror and all her fur stood on end as she tried to dodge her attacker. The bird shrieked again, swooping away and then diving back down, jabbing at her with its claws. Its sharp beak hammered at her head and the claws swooped close to her eyes, scratching at her muzzle.

Terrified, Kallik fled. The bird pursued her out of the marsh, only giving up when she scrambled into a patch of trees and hid under a pile of branches. She could still hear its angry cries as it wheeled away and flew back to its nest.

Kallik curled herself into a ball, feeling wretched. She couldn't even hunt a pair of eggs that were just lying there. How was she ever going to catch real prey on her own? The land was too strange and too frightening. She belonged on the ice, with the bear spirits guiding her paws and snow whistling through her fur.

Maybe she should try to find the place of the Pathway Star, where the ocean was frozen forever and the spirits danced in the sky in many colors. No matter how far away it was, it had to be better than this nightmare of mud and heat and starvation. Maybe Taqqiq would have gone that way, too. Maybe that was the only place a white bear could ever truly be safe.

CHAPTER ELEVEN

Lusa

Lusa stared sadly at the closed doors. The walls of the Bowl didn't feel cozy and sheltering now. They felt hard and unfriendly, trapping her somewhere she didn't want to be. She wanted to know what was going on outside. She wanted to be with Ashia while she was sick, but she couldn't. There was no way for Lusa to find out what was happening to her.

What if they had taken her mother away forever?

Four sleeps passed, and on the morning of the fifth day, Lusa started pacing around the walls of the Bowl, desperation rising inside her. She wondered how things would be different in the wild if a bear got sick. At least then she could be with her mother and see what was happening to her. She wouldn't be stuck inside these stone walls with no way to escape and no choice about it.

There was a rumble at the back, near the big doors. Lusa galloped over, sniffing the air. She could smell the metal firebeast—and Ashia!

The doors opened a little way, and a cage was backed into the Bowl. One of the feeders unlatched the door, and Lusa's mother climbed out, blinking and shaking her head in the sunlight.

"Mother!" Lusa barked. She capered around her mother's legs, jumping up to touch Ashia's muzzle with her own. "You're all right! You're alive!"

"Of course I am," Ashia said. She sounded sleepy.

"Are you hungry?" Lusa asked. "I saved you some really good berries. And it was hard, because I really wanted them! But I saved them for you because Stella said you would be back, and I told the Bear Watcher I would be good and not eat the berries as long as he brought you back so you could have them, wasn't I good?"

"Very good, dear," Ashia said. She lowered herself to the ground between two of the boulders and raised her head, as if she wanted to feel the sun on her shoulders. Yogi and Stella bounded over and crowded around her.

"Where did you go?" Yogi demanded. "What was it like?"

"Did you see the forest?" Stella asked.

King strolled up, nudging the others aside. "Give her some space," he ordered. He bent his head and sniffed Ashia, pressing his nose into her fur. "You look well," he said gruffly.

"I am," Ashia said, lifting her muzzle to his.

"Mother!" Lusa butted in, bouncing on her paws. "We want to know everything! Tell us where you went and what you saw, please please please!"

"It was quite strange," Ashia said sleepily. "I woke up inside a cage, like the one that left me here just now. The cage was in a flat-face den, with straight walls on all sides, like the ones in our stone den, but even straighter and with no openings that I could see. I felt strange, as if I'd just woken up from a long sleep, and heavy. I couldn't move my paws or my head or anything."

"Were you scared?" Yogi asked with wide eyes.

"No," Ashia said. "I felt like I was dreaming. I remember staring at the ceiling a lot. And when I dozed off I had a lot of strange dreams, about the forest and the river and berries growing on bushes, thousands and thousands of berries."

"What are thousands?" Lusa asked.

"It means lots," Stella explained. "Only more than lots . . . so many lots and lots that you need a bigger word for them."

"Oh," Lusa said. "So, like the *thousands* of fleas on Yogi."

"Hey!" Yogi protested. "That's not true!" Lusa chuffed with laughter and ducked away as he swatted at her head.

"Then what happened?" Stella prompted Ashia, ignoring the cubs.

"The furry flat-face in green was there," Ashia said.

"I didn't like him," Lusa interjected.

"He was very nice," Ashia admonished her. "He spoke gently to me and fed me and took care of me until I was well again."

"Then why did he shoot you?" Lusa challenged.

"I don't know what that was," Ashia said. "But it only stung for a minute, and then I fell asleep, so it can't have been anything too bad."

"Hmmm," Lusa said skeptically.

"And then when I stopped hurting inside, and wanted to eat again, they brought me back here."

"Did you see the tigers?" Lusa asked. "And the fla-min-gos?"

"I did!" Ashia said, looking a bit more awake. "There are so many different animals out there, very close to us. Most of them are behind Fences like ours. I saw one with long, long, skinny legs and a neck so long and tall, it could reach up to the top of the tallest tree in our forest."

"No!" Lusa cried. "How did it get like that?"

"Maybe it just kept reaching and reaching for berries until its neck stretched," Yogi suggested. "Maybe that'll happen to you if you keep dancing for the fruit the flat-faces throw you."

"I also saw an animal that was big and gray with a long dangly nose," Ashia interrupted, warding off another argument. "Its ears were the size of our biggest water dishes, and it had two long fangs, like curved claws, sticking out of its mouth on either side of its nose."

Lusa tried to picture this, but her imagination failed her. How could a nose be long and dangly? She touched her forepaw to her own shiny black nose and blinked in confusion.

"And there was a tall Fence running all the way around the whole place," Ashia went on. "Inside, with the animals, there are mostly trees and grass and gray paths in between. But on the other side the paths are wider and full of firebeasts roaring and running around. Next to the paths are flat-face dens—like our stone den but much bigger."

"Why do flat-faces need bigger dens than us?" Lusa asked. "They're much smaller than we are."

"I don't know," Ashia answered. "Perhaps they keep their trees and boulders inside their dens instead of using the ones outside."

Yogi scratched his ear with his back paw. "Or perhaps the firebeasts live in their dens, too. They're pretty big!"

King *harrumph*ed and waggled his head. "I've stuck my nose in a few flat-face dens," he growled. "They hoard things, like squirrels and magpies do. Their dens are full of food, if you can figure out how to get to it, and they collect shiny treasures that aren't any good for eating."

"Why?" Lusa wanted to know.

"Don't ask me," King grunted. "Flat-faces make no sense."

Ashia lay down and looked up at the puffy white clouds floating in the sky above them. Her eyes kept closing, and her voice dropped to a murmur. "And in the distance," she whispered, "beyond the paths, beyond the dens, beyond the firebeasts . . . I could see a mountain. A huge mountain, one that makes our boulders look like specks of sand. This mountain has snow on the top and dark forests all along the sides . . . forests that could swallow our small trees whole." She sighed. "It was beautiful."

King reared up on his hind legs and made an angry huffing sound. "Don't talk about that sort of nonsense," he ordered. "The mountains and the trees that we have here in the Bear Bowl are big enough, and there's no use dreaming about what we cannot have."

"Is that the mountain you came from, Father?" Lusa asked. "Have you been up to where the snow is?"

"Look what you've done," King snarled at Ashia. "That's enough talk of the outside. Do not speak of it again—that goes for all of you." He dropped to all fours and lumbered off, his rage radiating through his fur.

Lusa watched him curiously. Why did stories of the world outside the Bear Bowl make her father so angry? She waited until he'd settled himself in the far corner, out of earshot, and then she whispered to her mother, "I want to know more about the mountain. Please tell me more!"

But Ashia was already snoozing, a light sleepy hum coming from her nostrils. Lusa nudged one of her mother's paws, and Ashia twitched but didn't wake up.

Lusa sat down to wait. This wasn't the end of it, whatever her father said. She wanted to know more about the wild, and she would find out . . . one way or another.

CHAPTER TWELVE

Toklo

Sadness and confusion swept over Toklo, like the river washing over his paws. He looked around at the other bears gathered by the river. Most of them were still fishing, but a few had glanced up to watch his mother walk away from him. Oka climbed onto a large rock and sat with her back to Toklo, hunching her shoulders and acting like he wasn't even there.

He didn't understand what was happening. Why had she rescued him if she was just going to ignore him? He couldn't figure out why she was so angry. It wasn't his fault the giant bear had tried to kill him.

The river gurgled and splashed around his paws, scattering chilly droplets in his fur. Clouds had blown in on the wind, dimming the sunlight so the day felt grayer and colder. Toklo gazed up at the snowy mountains towering over the forest and felt suddenly small and very lonely. He didn't want to lose his brother and his mother both at the same time.

"Mother!" he called. "I said I was sorry!"

Oka didn't turn around. She shook her head and then lowered it to the rock, letting the fur settle on her shoulders.

Fine then, Toklo thought crossly. *I don't need you, either.* He turned away and stepped purposefully through the water to the other side of the river. He found a rock opposite his mother and sat down on it, watching her.

After a long time, Oka got up and stepped off the rock. Toklo sat up, wondering if she would come over and say she was sorry. But she didn't even look at him. She began pacing along the riverbank, back and forth, back and forth. She seemed to be talking to herself. Another bear wandered near her, dabbing its paws in the water as it searched for fish. Oka spun around and snarled at it. Startled, the other bear reared back and galloped farther downstream.

Toklo felt his fur prickle along his back. Why was his mother acting so strange? Oka turned in a circle, following her stumpy tail around and around, and then sat down in the water. Even though there were no other bears near her—all the bears along the river were giving her a wide berth now— she snarled at the air as if she were being attacked.

Finally she lay down, half in and half out of the water, and sank her head onto her paws. Toklo could see the fur rising and falling on her back as she breathed. He curled up on his rock with his back to her. He wasn't going to watch her anymore. If she didn't care about him, he didn't have to care about her, either. He would just stay right here until she came over to apologize and take care of him again.

The sun sank slowly behind the mountains as Toklo lay

there, waiting. A deep purple dusk settled over the valley, and
he was starting to fall asleep when he heard the shuffle of
large paws on the pebbles nearby. He scrambled up, his head
spinning from the sudden movement. Hope leaped into his
chest as he saw a large female bear approaching him . . . and
then died again when he realized it was not his mother. He
glanced sideways and saw that Oka was still lying in the same
position.

The large female came closer and sniffed him curiously.
"Why are you by yourself, little cub?" she asked. "Where is
your mother?"

Toklo didn't want to admit that his mother was right there
but pretending he didn't exist. He shrugged his shoulders.
"I'm waiting for the salmon," he said. "Like every other bear
here."

The she-bear shook her head, her brown eyes sad. "They're
not coming anymore," she growled. "The bear spirits must be
angry with us."

The bear spirits, Toklo thought. *Like Tobi.* Was Tobi angry with
him? Did he blame Toklo for his death, too, like Oka did?

"Why would the bear spirits be angry?" he asked nervously.

"Or maybe it's the flat-faces," the bear said. "They're building a dam upriver that stops the salmon from getting
through."

Toklo knew what a dam was. He'd seen beavers building a
dam in a stream on the other side of the mountain. That had
been a good day—Tobi had been feeling stronger than usual,
and they had played a little bit in the water while Oka caught

them a hare to eat. A pang of grief stabbed at Toklo's heart.

The she-bear tilted her head and looked at him kindly, as if she could sense his sorrow. "Tell me where your mother is, little cub," she said.

Toklo slid off his rock and padded over to the river's edge. He pointed with his nose to the dark shape of his mother, lying partly in the water on the other side.

"You should go back to her," the female bear said. "Or she'll start to worry about you."

I wish, Toklo thought. The she-bear stepped into the river as if she were going to walk him across.

"It's all right," Toklo said quickly. He didn't want her to see how strange his mother was acting. "I can go by myself."

"Very well," said the she-bear. "Good luck to you both." She touched her nose to Toklo's muzzle, then turned and lumbered away into the dark. Toklo watched her go with an ache in his heart. Why didn't his mother care about him as much as this strange bear did? Why wasn't Oka the one checking up on him and nuzzling him and making sure he wasn't alone?

He splashed through the cold river, picking his way carefully across the rough current as his claws slipped on the smooth pebbles underwater. Oka didn't move as he got closer, and he was afraid to speak to her in case she snarled at him like she'd snarled at the other bear earlier. He climbed a short way up the bank and lay down, as close to her as he dared to get.

Snowflakes drifted past his nose, and the air was sharp and cold. Toklo wished he could cuddle into his mother's fur. He almost couldn't remember what that felt like; she hadn't let him snuggle into her since Tobi had died. He rested his chin on his paws and watched her. She was growling in her sleep, muttering to herself. He saw her front paws twitch and flex, as if she was dreaming about pinning something down with her claws.

Toklo didn't like the feeling it gave him to see his mother like this—it was as if the trees in the forest had shaken the dirt off their roots and started walking around, or the river had switched direction and started flowing up the mountain. She was supposed to be his protector; she was supposed to be strong and to teach him the ways of being a bear. She certainly wasn't supposed to drive him away.

His mind teeming with dark, lonely thoughts, Toklo finally drifted into an uneasy sleep.

In his dream, Toklo found himself safely tucked under the ground. He looked around, blinking, and saw that he was back in his BirthDen. The earth walls curved around him, keeping him and his brother warm. Tobi was curled up beside him, opening and closing his mouth as if testing out how it worked.

Toklo could smell the richly packed earth. The scent of leaves and moss filled his nostrils. His nose twitched, and he sneezed, which startled him awake. He opened his eyes and saw his mother standing over him. There was a strange, heavy feeling in his fur, and he realized it was full of dirt and leaves. Oka had her eyes half closed and she was murmuring something. . . .

"Guide his paws through the rocks and the soil until his soul reaches the water that lives deep within you—" she said softly. She was saying the words of the death ritual!

Toklo scrambled to his paws, shaking his fur. "Mother!" he yelped. "Stop! I'm still alive, see? I'm not dead!"

Oka's eyes were vague, as if she was looking into the distance instead of at her cub. She seemed shocked that he'd gotten to his paws.

"Mother?" he said again. "Look, it's all right. I'm not dead."

Her eyes narrowed and she bared her teeth. "You *should* be dead," she snarled.

Toklo took a step back and noticed a sign in the earth beside him. It was the same crossing-claws mark that Oka had made next to Tobi's body. What if the earth spirits came to get his spirit, thinking he was dead? Or what if he died somewhere else and they never found him, because the mark was here?

"Get out!" Oka roared. "There is nothing here for you."

"But—but you're my mother," Toklo whimpered.

"I have no cubs," Oka growled. "Go away!" She lunged at him, her claws outstretched.

Toklo turned tail and ran for the trees as fast as he could.

He glanced back when he reached the trees and saw Oka standing on her hind legs, roaring. Her eyes were wild and she looked like a stranger—not like his mother at all. Toklo had lost more than his brother when Tobi died. Perhaps his mother's spirit had followed her cub too far into the dark river.

He ran into the woods, determined to put as much distance between himself and Oka as he could. *Every cub leaves his mother someday,* he told himself. That was true—but usually they had several more moons of learning to hunt and fish with her first.

"I can teach myself," he said out loud. "I will learn to hunt and forage on my own." *She wasn't teaching me very much anyway. Perhaps I'll be better off by myself. Now I can go where I please and make my own choices. I can stay in the mountains, far away from the stinky trails of the firebeasts.*

The light grew brighter in the clear blue sky as he wove through the whispering, sun-speckled trees, following the bubbling sound of the river, and he felt the warm breeze ruffling his fur. It carried with it the promise that earthsleep was ending and fishleap was on its way—the smell of things growing and changing.

If he had to live this way, so be it. If there was any cub who could survive on his own, it was Toklo. He'd find a way to live.

He had to.

CHAPTER THIRTEEN

Kallik

Hunger gnawed at Kallik's belly and her paws trembled with exhaustion. The long shadows of the night were slipping away across the wet grass as the sun peeked over the edge of the sky. Above her, there were streaks of clouds like long claw scratches.

She reached a scrawny tree, one of the few she could see in either direction, and sat down to rest for a moment. Kallik looked up at the Pathway Star, shining as brightly as it had all night. She'd been trying to follow it while staying close to the shore; even up on the ridge, or when she had to travel inland to get around boggy swamps, she made sure she could smell the bay not too far away.

The small spot of ice gleamed in the sky above her, reminding her of Nisa and Taqqiq. Maybe her brother was looking at the same star right now. She felt the strong pull of the star, almost as if she could smell the place of never-ending ice already. She knew she had to find it, because Taqqiq would be looking for it, too. She got up to walk again, drawn by the fading light of the star. Her paws made a squishing sound as she stepped onto an expanse of marshy grasses that stretched far in front of her. She felt mud squelching up between her claws and she shuddered, wishing all over again that she could be back on the clean ice and snow over the frozen sea.

As she slipped and stumbled through the marsh, she stopped to try and eat some of the grass, but it did almost nothing to ease her hunger. She nearly walked straight past the small lump of brown fur, half hidden by the long grasses. But the breeze whisked by at just the right moment, parting the stems so she could spot it.

Kallik pounced, realizing as her claws hit the flesh that it was a rabbit, and it was already dead. She couldn't tell how it had died, but she was too hungry to care. "Thank you, ice spirits," she whispered, ripping off the skin with her claws. "Wherever you are, thank you."

She devoured the rabbit in a few bites, feeling strength return to her legs. When she was finished, she padded toward the shore, following the sound of shrieking. There were birds everywhere now—birds sailing through the air, birds floating in the water, birds darting along the sand, leaving tiny three-clawed tracks behind them. Kallik had never seen so many living things in one place. She knew some of them were ducks and some were plover; from her mother's stories, she guessed the long-necked ones were geese.

Shortly before sunhigh, she emerged from the marsh onto pebbly sand. The sea was going out and she spotted five plovers fighting over a small fish. The silver scrap of food was lying on the sand, with birds diving at it and squawking at one another. One of them was standing over it, attacking any others that came near, but another was able to dive in and grab it before a third seized the tail and tried to yank it away.

Kallik dropped into a crouch, then lunged forward. With a yelp of satisfaction, she pounced on one of the plovers, pinning it to the ground.

She couldn't believe it! Live prey, and she'd caught it herself! Kallik bit down quickly before the bird could flap its way free of her paws. With her claws she sliced away the feathers and then chewed her way through the meat of the plover, its tiny bones crunching in her teeth.

Even the bright heat of sunhigh didn't bother her as much when there was food in her stomach. Feeling triumphant, she padded through the sand, watching the masses of birds whirl and flap and dive for fish in the bay. Hints of green were starting to appear on the bushes along the shore and Kallik could see more trees again, farther inland.

She stopped and sniffed the air. The smell was almost overpowering, like all the rain in the world. She started trotting toward it, drinking in the scents it carried of mud, reeds, and tree roots. She threaded her way through some bushes and skidded to a halt. Ahead of her was a tongue of brown water flowing into the bay. She stared across to the other side.

The brown water was half a skylength wide!

More swimming? The water looked deep, with a fast current. She started shivering, remembering her mother crying out and the whales attacking.

There had to be a way around it.

She turned her back on the bay and trotted along the brown water's pebbly shore.

The brown water twisted and turned through scrubby trees and long grasses. Every time she rounded a bend, hoping to reach its end, she saw it stretching away even farther. She felt she might travel forever and never get to the end.

When her feet started to hurt she made her decision to try and swim across. Although the brown water was deep, she was thankful that it was moving more slowly now.

She climbed down its muddy side and stepped tentatively into the water. It was cold and refreshing. In a few more steps she was up to her nose. *Silaluk, please help me to the other side,* she whispered and fell forward into the current. She pulled with her front paws and let her back legs hang behind, steering her.

Kallik swam farther into the brown water. It felt wonderful, the cold water tugging her fur and soothing her muscles. Soon she was far from shore. She was wondering if she was over halfway when something bumped against her legs.

She pushed her head beneath the surface and, although it was too murky to see anything, she could hear strange sounds. The water was making clicking, whistling and clanging noises. She lifted up her face to see smooth gray bodies swimming all around her. There were so many of them! It was like the pebbles on the bed of the brown water had come to life. Panic shot through her. She remembered the black fins and sharp teeth of the orca that had taken away her mother. *Save me, spir-*

its of the ice! she thought.

A spout of water shot into the air, dousing her head with salty spray. The next moment, a head popped out of the water, and Kallik saw that the swimmers weren't killer whales at all. These were small gray whales. The one looking at her had a chubby white head and short flapping fins. It squeaked cheerfully, and another small whale broke off to join it. They both clicked and whistled at Kallik, and she wondered what they were saying.

One of them ducked under, came back up, and spat water at Kallik. The other swam around her, flapping its fins and spinning slowly. For such peculiar-looking animals, they moved with an odd grace in the water. Kallik felt clumsy and awkward beside them.

They splashed around her as she swam toward the shore, and a light giddiness welled inside her. She'd been too terrified to notice before, but the icy water was a relief after so much mud and dust and rocky ground under her paws. Kallik rolled in the water, ducking her head under and sending splashes into the air that made the whales whistle. She felt cooler and lighter, the dirt and grime of many days' travel washing out of her fur. The water tasted of ice: freezing and sharp and full of promises. But there was no ice to be seen—the waves stretched on and on, all the way to the edge of the sky.

Kallik felt sand under her paws and she dug in, pushing herself out of the water up onto the shore. A loud whistle sounded from a larger whale swimming by, and the two little whales flipped over and dove away, swimming rapidly to catch up to the others. Kallik watched them go with a deep pang of lone-liness. They had one another to play with, and lots of other whales to keep them company. She never got to play anymore, not without Taqqiq, and she had no one to look after her.

Kallik was too tired and wet to go any farther today. A short way along the shore she found a hollowed-out rock sticking out of the sand. She crawled underneath it, digging through the sand until she'd created a space big enough for her to curl up in. From here she could see and smell the sea. It made her think of the spirits in the ice, and she drifted off to sleep wondering how long they stayed around when the ice melted. Was her mother's spirit out in the water somewhere? Or had she already splashed up into the sky, to become a star looking down on Kallik?

The shore of the bay started to change the next day as Kallik kept walking. There were more stones underpaw here, the sand giving way to pebbles and larger round rocks. Soon after the sun came up she saw a large cliff cutting across the beach far ahead of her, blocking her view of the shore beyond.

As she got closer to the rocky wall, a dank, heavy smell hit her nose almost at the same time as she heard grumbling and snorting from up ahead. She slowed down, wondering what it was and whether it was safe to go any closer. It sounded a bit like thunder, or many bears bellowing in pain.

Kallik crept up to the edge of the cliff that cut in close to the sea. She peered around it to the strip of land beyond, where the shore curved into a miniature bay enclosed by rocks.

All along the sandy beach, huge, fat animals were lying on their stomachs. Walruses, so many and so packed together that Kallik couldn't see the ground underneath them. They were the ugliest creatures Kallik had ever seen. Two long yellow teeth jutted straight down from their top lips. Tiny eyes peered out of the folds around their faces, and their muzzles were squashed and bushy.

Kallik padded out from behind the wall and trotted along the curve of the small bay. As she got closer, a few of the walruses swung their heads around to look at her.

Suddenly the closest one charged at her, barking, its brown flesh wobbling. Its teeth sliced through the air only whiskers away from Kallik's nose. With a yelp of fear, Kallik fled back the way she came, terror giving extra speed to her paws. She skidded around the end of the rocky cliff and raced inland. She would go as far as she could while keeping the smell of the sea in her nose.

She trotted faster, fear spurring her paws along. Visions flashed through her mind of those long, sharp tusks stabbing into her fur. Had her brother run into walruses on his journey? She looked up at the sky, knowing the Pathway Star was out there, even if she couldn't see it in the daylight. *Please, spirits of the ice, if you can hear me,* she whispered, *please protect Taqqiq. Help him to follow the Pathway Star. Tell him I'm coming for him. Tell him to stay alive until I find him. Please.*

CHAPTER FOURTEEN

Lusa

Lusa's nose twitched. There was something new in the air—something that made her paws itch and her fur prickle. She could smell things growing and changing around her, although the Bear Bowl still looked the same. Every day more and more birds flew overhead. Sometimes she would sit and watch them and wish she could go wherever they were going.

"It's the seasons changing, little blackberry," Stella explained. "Cold-earth is ending, and this is your first leaf-time. This is the time when we would be searching for new kinds of food in the wild. But we don't have to do that here, because we haven't gone short of food during cold-earth. We're safe, and nothing's going to change. You'll get used to it. Now, go and play with Yogi. He's probably feeling just as restless as you are."

Lusa didn't think so. Yogi couldn't even be bothered to climb to the top of the Bear Tree to see what was outside the Bowl. But she didn't want to be lonely as well as bored, so she went to find him.

They were playing on the Mountains, jumping off and scampering around to climb back on again, when Lusa heard a whirring noise and doors rattling on the far side of the Fence, in the grizzly enclosure. She leaped off the rocks and galloped over to the Fence, pressing her nose against the cold web.

"Lusa!" Yogi cried. "Where are you going? What about our *game*?"

"Yogi, come see!" Lusa called. "Grumps is getting a friend!"

The burning smell of the firebeast filled her nose as it prowled into the center of the brown bear enclosure. It was pulling a cage, like the one Ashia had been taken away in. Inside, Lusa could see a large pile of shaggy brown fur.

She had never seen a new bear arrive in the Bowl before. She stood up on her hind legs and hooked her front claws in the Fence, stretching to get a better view. Two of the feeders came around to the back of the trailer, wearing extra pelts on their paws and faces. They unhooked the mesh door and reached in to pull out the shiny skin the new bear was resting on. They dragged it and the bear onto the ground, then slid the skin out from under her.

The new grizzly was sound asleep, her back rising and falling in an even rhythm. She was very thin, with patchy fur and scratches along her muzzle. Lusa wondered what had happened to make her look so battered. Had she been in a fight? If so, she'd lost, by the look of it.

Grumps ambled over from his corner. He sniffed the

newcomer with a grim look on his face, and then lumbered back to his corner, where he sat down with his back to her, grumbling.

"I don't think Grumps wants to share," Lusa said to Yogi.

"Maybe he's worried she'll want to eat all his food," Yogi said. "She's so thin—she must be starving!"

"Where do you think she comes from?" Lusa wondered. "Do you think she's a wild bear? Did she come from the forest and the mountain? Has she been out there her whole life? Do you think she's met tigers and elephants and flamingos?"

"How should I know?" Yogi said. "She's just a brown bear. It's not that interesting." He turned and wandered over to the food bowl, searching for leftovers.

Lusa ran to the Bear Tree and clambered up. She pulled herself onto a long branch that stretched out close to the Fence, from where she had a clear view into the brown bear enclosure.

The she-bear kept sleeping. She seemed to sleep for a very long time. Lusa lay down on the branch and waited, watching her. She had so many questions! Especially if this was a wild bear. A real wild bear!

Ages later, the bear stirred. Lusa sat up on her branch. Was she awake? The grizzly rolled onto her side and twitched her paws. It looked like her eyes were still closed, but her mouth was moving as if she was talking to herself. Lusa scrambled down from the tree and ran back to the Fence. She strained her ears, keeping very still so she could hear.

It sounded like the grizzly was murmuring the word *Tobi*

over and over again. Sometimes her voice was soft and sometimes fierce. Then the grizzly grunted in an unhappy way and whispered, "Toklo."

Lusa didn't understand either of those words. Was the grizzly speaking another language—not bear language? It didn't sound like the flat-face language, either. Then she caught the word *mountain*. The she-bear's paws jerked and batted at the air, as if she was dreaming about running.

"River," she whispered. "To the river. Careful. Toklo . . . Tobi." Her murmurs trailed away and her paws went limp again. She'd fallen back into a deeper sleep.

Lusa was confused but also excited. If the bear was talking about mountains and rivers, surely that meant she'd come from the wild. Maybe when she woke up, Lusa would be able to find out more.

Most of the day passed before the strange bear awoke. Lusa had given up watching her and was practicing climbing the tree again, digging her claws into the bark and experimenting to see if she could climb down headfirst, which didn't seem to work very well. Yogi was perched on a boulder, calling out unhelpful suggestions.

"Let go and jump!" he shouted. "Maybe you'll find out you can fly!"

Lusa ignored him. He wasn't as interested in climbing as she was, which meant she was already much better at it, even though he was moons older than her.

Suddenly an angry roar split the air. Startled, Lusa nearly lost her grip on the branch, but she dug her claws in before she could tumble out of the tree. She clung to the trunk, panting. She'd never heard a roar with so much fury and outrage and pain in it before. King's roars were stern and commanding. Grumps sometimes roared in a grouchy, irritated way. But this roar was different. It had to be the new she-bear.

Lusa crept along the branch and peered down into the brown bear enclosure. The new grizzly was running around and around the Bowl, charging at the Fences. She reared up on her hind legs and scraped her front claws against the back wall, roaring furiously.

Grumps looked bewildered. He was up on his hind paws, looking from the she-bear to the wall where several flat-faces were watching.

Yogi came running over and scrambled up the tree beside Lusa. His eyes were enormous and he was shaking like the trees in a storm. "That bear is crazy!" he declared.

"I think she's sad," Lusa said. The she-bear had *sounded* sad when she'd been whispering those odd words. "Maybe she's lonely."

"Lonely?" Yogi snorted. "She's got a brain full of bees."

"She needs a friend," Lusa decided.

"She doesn't want to make friends!"

"How do you know?" Lusa challenged. "Maybe I'll be her friend."

"Ha!" Yogi flicked his ears. "She won't talk to you. You'll just make her madder if you try."

"We'll see," Lusa said, lying down on the branch to watch the raging grizzly.

Finally the she-bear wore herself out. She stopped running and collapsed near the fence, breathing heavily with exhaustion.

"Here I go," Lusa said, sitting up.

"You're going to get your nose clawed off," Yogi growled.

Lusa climbed down the tree and padded over to the Fence near the new bear. She crept up carefully, trying not to make any sudden noises. The grizzly swung her head around and saw the black bear cub approaching. She lowered her head and barked, but Lusa couldn't tell if it was an unfriendly noise or not.

"Hello," Lusa said, scratching the dirt nervously with her paws. "I'm Lusa. What's your name?"

The grizzly sighed and closed her eyes. Lusa waited for a moment, and then, disappointed, she turned to go back to the tree.

"It's Oka," the brown bear growled. Lusa jumped. At least the bear wasn't speaking that strange language anymore.

Lusa pressed closer to the Fence. "Welcome to the Bear Bowl, Oka," she said. Feeling bolder, she lifted herself onto her hind legs and sniffed the air, trying to figure out what she could smell in Oka's scent. "Where did you come from?" she asked. "Were you in the wild? Did you live on the mountain? Have you seen a forest?"

But Oka turned her massive head away and buried it between her paws.

"I *told* you she wouldn't want to make friends!" Yogi called from the tree.

"Maybe later?" Lusa said to Oka, backing away. "Whenever

you're feeling better, I'll be right here." Of course, she had nowhere else to go.

Oka slept for the rest of the day, staying outside when night fell instead of going into the grizzly Caves with Grumps. Lusa came out the next morning to find Oka stomping around on the other side of the Fence, growling and muttering. Sometimes she would attack the tree that grew at the back of the grizzly enclosure, shredding its bark and snapping savagely at its branches. This worried Lusa a lot, because if there were bear spirits living in that tree, they wouldn't be very pleased. She hoped they were all right.

She stayed away from the Fence, playing with Yogi and rolling around to make the flat-faces laugh. It was the first really hot day of leaftime, and lots of flat-face cubs were visiting, chattering and pointing at her. Lusa was able to get three different feeders to throw her extra fruit, which made her feel very clever.

"It's going to rain tonight," Stella announced as they ate their evening meal. "I can feel the air getting thicker and wetter."

Lusa sniffed. She could see what Stella meant—clouds were rolling in and the sky seemed all crackly around the edges.

"Oka will sleep in the Caves if it's raining, won't she?" Lusa said.

"Who's Oka?" Stella asked.

"The new grizzly," Lusa said, pointing toward the Fence with her muzzle. "She slept outside last night, but if there's a storm—"

"You shouldn't be worrying yourself about grizzlies, little blackberry," Stella interrupted. "It's not your problem if she sleeps outside in the rain."

But Lusa *was* worried about Oka. A heavy rain started shortly after dark, and as Lusa crept back under the shelter, she could see Oka's blurry hulking shape crouched in the corner near the Fence, away from the trees or anything that could shield her from the storm.

The rain pounded on the roof all night as Lusa dreamed about the sad, lonely bear outside. She woke up near dawn when the rain finally stopped. Yogi was sprawled across the den with one of his paws flopped over her head. Lusa climbed free carefully so she wouldn't wake him and went outside.

Birds were twittering in the trees, and the air had a fresh, newly washed feeling to it, like the best fruit the feeders brought before Yogi trampled on it. There were still piles of gray clouds in the sky, but light pink rays of sunlight were starting to peek through as the sun came up.

Oka was lying in the corner where she'd first met Lusa. Her wet fur was steaming in the cool early-morning air.

Hesitantly Lusa approached, but although Oka was watching her, the grizzly made no move to run away. Lusa sat down by the Fence and tilted her head, studying the brown bear. "Did you stay out here all night in the rain?" she asked. "Don't you mind getting wet?"

Oka closed her eyes and didn't respond.

"Maybe you're used to it," Lusa guessed. "You must get rained on all the time in the wild. Right?"

Oka still didn't answer.

"I wish I could go into the wild," Lusa went on. "I'd like to see a forest and catch my own prey."

Oka snorted, making Lusa jump. "There is no prey," the brown bear snarled. Her eyes were open now, black and fierce. "There's nothing to eat."

"But you must have eaten something. I thought the wild was full of food."

"It used to be," Oka growled. "Fishing . . . finding fish in the rivers was what we used to do. Back . . . back then."

"What's a river?" Lusa asked.

"It's a long tongue of water that rolls through the hills and mountains and forests, carrying fish."

"I don't think I've ever eaten a fish," Lusa admitted. "But I know they bring them for Grumps sometimes. And the white bears eat them, too, so I know what they smell like." She wrinkled her nose.

"Fish is a brown bear's favorite food," Oka said. She still had her eyes half closed. "Toklo would have liked fish. He would have been good at catching fish. Maybe he is now . . . but I'll never know." She stopped abruptly.

"Who's Toklo?" Lusa prompted.

"Tobi," Oka murmured, curling onto her side and resting her muzzle on the ground. "Why did you leave us? I'm sorry I couldn't feed you enough, but didn't I try? Couldn't you have held on?"

"Who are Tobi and Toklo?" Lusa begged, pulling herself up on her hind legs by hooking her claws in the fence. "Oka, please tell me who they are."

"You don't know what I've had to do, Tobi," Oka whispered without looking up. "What I had to do to poor Toklo. What I was forced to do, just to stay alive. Scavenging from flat-face dens, eating scraps out of metal containers, running for my life from the firebeasts." A violent shudder wracked her body. "Toklo," she cried again. "I'm sorry, Toklo."

She closed her eyes. Lusa stared at Oka in dismay. She hadn't meant to upset her. Quietly she dropped to all fours and backed away. Whatever had happened before Oka came to the Bear Bowl, it must have been truly terrible.

Lusa left Oka alone for a few days, worried that she'd upset the brown bear again if she tried to talk to her. But Oka stayed huddled by the Fence most of the time, and finally Lusa decided to try again. Maybe Oka needed a real bear to talk to instead of her sad memories. Perhaps telling Lusa about them would make her feel better.

The sun was high in the sky, and Yogi and Stella were lying in the Mountains being boring instead of playing. Lusa climbed out of her perch in the tree and padded close to the Fence. She passed by Oka's spot, waiting to see if the grizzly would respond. Nothing happened, so she turned around and walked past again.

Oka grunted. Lusa stopped immediately. It wasn't quite a "hello," but it didn't sound like "go away," either. She sidled closer.

"Hi, Oka," she said. "How are you feeling today?"

Oka blinked and grunted again.

"The Bear Bowl isn't so bad, is it?" Lusa tried. "I know Grumps is kind of . . . grumpy . . . but the bears on this side of the Fence are nice, I promise. That biggest one over there, drinking from the water dish, is my father, King. My mother, Ashia, is inside the Caves, napping. And that lazy lump of fur on the closest rock is my friend Yogi. You might like him—he's funny when he's not annoying."

Oka's ears twitched. Lusa hoped that meant she was listening. She sat down and ran her claws through the dirt.

"King came from the wild, too, like you," she went on. "He wouldn't tell me about the mountain, though. Mother said there's one you can see from outside the Bear Bowl. Is that where you came from?"

"There are many mountains," Oka murmured. Lusa perked up her ears. "I came through many, many mountains. . . . They caught me on one shaped like a bear's snout, with snow at the top . . . cold snow, freezing my paws . . . Poor Toklo."

"What else did you see?" Lusa prompted.

"There was a river," the brown bear said, gazing up at the sky. "A long journey . . . I followed it until I found a dry riverbed to walk along. Journey . . . journey . . . three lakes at the edge of a dead forest."

"A dead forest?" Lusa echoed with a shiver. "Why was it dead? Who killed it?"

"The fire from the sky," Oka whispered, as if talking to herself. "The fire that roars like a bear when it rains."

"I know that fire!" Lusa cried. "I've seen it in the clouds! It's so loud, my ears hurt for days afterward. I didn't know it could come down from the sky!"

"It can," Oka said, "and when it touches a tree, it can spread fire through a whole forest."

Lusa stared at her in alarm. "But what about the spirits in the trees? The dead bears?"

"Dead bears?" Oka roared. "What do you know about dead bears? Why are you asking me all these questions? Leave me alone!" She jumped to her paws and galloped away to the far side of the clearing.

Lusa leaped back. "I'm sorry!" she called after Oka. "I didn't mean to bother you!"

"*Shhh*, little cub," Ashia said, coming up behind her. "It's not your fault. That bear has problems you can't help with."

That didn't make Lusa feel any better. She felt sorry for Oka, and she wanted to find a way to help her, if she could.

That night she had strange dreams of racing through an ice-cold river, watching silver fish leap and splash in the water around her. Above her head birds screeched in the sky and fire flashed in the clouds. The wind rushed through her fur and the trees around her called out to be climbed, using the voices of black bears from long ago.

She woke while it was still dark, feeling restless and hot. The den seemed more cramped than usual, the walls pressing in around her. Even when she was outside, Lusa wished for more space to run, so she could really stretch her paws. She wanted new trees to climb, with different bark and unfamiliar branches that would challenge her. She wanted to eat something new and catch her own prey.

She climbed onto one of the boulders and sat down, looking up at the fading night sky. It didn't feel right to call this rock a Mountain anymore, not after the stories she'd heard about real mountains. She searched the sky until she found the Bear Watcher. It shone brightly and steadily, and she wondered if it watched her as closely as it watched wild bears.

"I know what you're thinking," a deep voice said from behind her. Lusa scrambled around, slipping on the rock, until she faced her father. King was sitting on his haunches, looking up at the Bear Watcher, too.

"You do?" Lusa said. "You mean you feel it, too?"

King growled. "A little restlessness is natural when leaftime starts," he said. "But I see the way you pace and sniff the air. That brown bear is filling your head with strange ideas."

"No, she isn't," Lusa insisted. "She's just telling me about the wild."

"You don't need to know about that," King said. He stood up and turned to walk away, but he paused and looked back for a moment. "I want you to leave that bear alone," he rumbled.

"But—" Lusa started.

"Don't argue with me, Lusa," he growled.

He padded over to one of the trees and began to scratch his back against the bark. Lusa watched mutinously, her fur prickling. It wasn't fair! Why couldn't she listen to Oka's stories?

The dark bulk of her mother emerged from the den behind them. Lusa could tell from the look on Ashia's face that she had heard their conversation.

"He's right, little cub," Ashia said, pressing her muzzle into Lusa's side. She licked Lusa's nose and nuzzled her. "You should stay away from that bear."

"Why?" Lusa asked, climbing onto her mother's lap and burying her face in her fur.

"Because she's not well," Ashia said. "When a mother loses her cubs, sometimes her heart gets sick and she doesn't know what she's saying."

Her cubs! Lusa thought with a jolt. *That must be who Tobi and Toklo are!* But Oka had spoken as if Toklo were still alive. Lusa wondered how she had lost him.

"You see how dangerous it is in the wild," Ashia went on. "There's no future for bears out there. We are much better off in here, where we are safe and well fed. There's nothing to attack us or hurt us, and food comes every day, no matter what. The flat-faces take care of us." She nudged Lusa's muzzle with her own. "I'm glad I didn't have to try and feed you on my own out in the wild, like that poor grizzly did." Ashia shook herself, fluffing out her fur and tumbling Lusa onto the ground.

"Do as your father says, little cub," she said affectionately. "You'll be happier if you stop listening to these stories and stop thinking so much about the wild."

She turned and went back into the den. Lusa watched her go, then looked up at the Bear Watcher again. How could she stop thinking about the wild? Especially when the air was so full of the smell of wild things growing? She padded over to the tallest tree and launched herself up the trunk, scrambling up as high as she dared to go. Then she stretched out her muzzle toward the Bear Watcher star.

"I know you can hear me," she whispered. "I know you understand, even if Mother and Father don't. If there's any way . . . anything you can do . . . just so I can see what the wild is like and decide for myself. Please, I have to know." She blinked, and the star seemed to blink back at her.

CHAPTER FIFTEEN

Toklo

Toklo's stomach was growling. He hadn't eaten in days, except for a few scraps of moss he'd been able to claw off tree roots. He'd tried to hunt for salmon in the river several times, but usually he saw no signs of fish at all—and the ones he did see moved too fast for him to catch.

Melting snow was mixing with the dirt, creating an icy mud that clung to his paws and made traveling slow and wet. The river rushed by, bubbling over large black rocks with a constant roaring, gurgling noise that was beginning to sound, to Toklo, not that different from the BlackPath.

He caught the scent of prey and lifted his nose in the air, taking a deep breath. It was coming from the trees above the river, at the top of a steep embankment.

He scrambled up the icy rocks, digging his claws into the stone and slipping on the slick surface. Sharp edges pressed into the pads of his paws and snagged on his fur as he dragged himself over the last ledge and climbed to his paws under the trees. Pine needles lay thickly underpaw, giving off a strong evergreen scent that mingled with the smell of the prey. He put his nose to the ground, sniffing, and tracked it to a spot where four trees grew close together, their trunks almost touching and their branches overlapping. The earth below them was still covered in hard, densely packed snow where the trees blocked the sunshine from reaching it.

Toklo crouched and crept closer. The scent didn't move; whatever it was didn't know he was coming. When he could smell it right below his nose, he pounced, striking hard and fast at the snow. He dove into it with his forepaws, digging ferociously, throwing back snow and loose earth with his claws. When his paws reached something that was neither earth nor snow, his mouth began to water. Toklo brushed away the snow to reveal two squirrels, a stoat, and a couple of animals he had never seen before. They looked like they had been killed only recently, and the delicious smell of fresh meat wafted up to him.

Toklo turned over the stoat with his paw and saw claw-marks on its underbelly. He sniffed deeper and realized that under the smell of the prey there was the muskier scent of another bear. That bear must have buried this prey here, saving it for later. Toklo's fur burned with jealousy. It wasn't fair that this other bear had so much that he could bury meals like this.

His mother must have taught him how to hunt properly, Toklo thought.

He glanced around, pricking his ears and sniffing the air.

There was no sign of the other bear. Whoever had buried this would be furious if some of the catch went missing. . . . Toklo remembered his mother telling him never to steal prey.

Why should I care what she thinks anymore? She doesn't care about me! And she's not here to tell me what to do.

He crouched and sank his teeth into the soft flesh of a squirrel. He could feel his strength returning with every mouthful, and his thoughts of Oka melted away like the snow.

After he had eaten as much as he could, Toklo covered the rest of the kill pile with earth and snow. He tried to pat it down so it looked undisturbed, although he was worried that his scent would still be on it. Quickly he searched through the tangled undergrowth until he found some strong-smelling leaves and spread them over the hiding place. Perhaps that would help to hide his scent, at least long enough for him to get out of the other bear's territory.

Feeling better after his meal, Toklo bounded into the woods. One day he would have a territory of his own, too. He just had to keep moving, find enough food to stay alive, and stay alert for other bears until he was old enough and big enough to fight for his own range somewhere.

He kept his ears pricked for the sounds of another bear as he climbed up through the trees, heading farther up the mountain. He deliberately avoided the wet patches of dirt so he wouldn't leave a trail of pawprints. There was enough frozen, packed snow still on the ground for him to walk on, and he found more and more of it as he went farther up through the trees.

The wind seemed to get colder as he traveled, buffeting his fur and making his eyes water. Toklo was scrambling up a slope littered with large rocks among the trees when he saw a large dark shape moving through the woods several bear-lengths away. He froze in the shadow of one of the rocks.

It was an adult bear—and from the scent drifting on the wind toward him, it was the one he'd stolen the prey from. The strange bear's shoulders were broad and his fur was matted with mud. Toklo kept very still, knowing that any sudden movement might catch the bear's eye, and even the crackle of a twig beneath his paws could attract its attention. He was glad that the wind was blowing in his face instead of carrying his scent toward the bear.

Toklo crouched lower, hoping the rock would keep him hidden. The breeze dropped for a moment, and in the stillness a bird squawked loudly, as if it could see Toklo and was shouting, "He's over here! Come get him!"

Toklo's heart started to pound. He saw the other bear stand up on its hind legs and sniff the air. *Please don't smell me. Please keep going.* Toklo buried his face in his paws and waited for a heavy paw to clamp down on his shoulders.

After a long moment, he opened his eyes again. The bear was shambling down the mountain toward the river. Toklo hoped he wasn't heading for the hidden newkill, but just in case, he picked up the pace and began running through the trees.

Ahead of him he could see the shimmer of sunlight, and with a burst of speed, he shot out of the trees into a wide open meadow. Suddenly he was surrounded by bright yellow warmth, and for a moment he had the confused feeling that he'd run right into the sun. He blinked until his eyes adjusted to the light. He was standing in a field of yellow flowers, the color both startling and comforting, like a pool of melted sunlight. In the distance, beyond the meadow, a mountain rose into the sky. Toklo stared at it. It looked like the head of a bear, its nose raised to the clouds, its mouth half open as if calling out to the sun, which was slowly setting behind it.

He lowered his muzzle to sniff one of the yellow flowers. The stem had no leaves on it, and the yellow flower was drooping off the top. Its smell was fresh and sharp, stronger and tastier than the dandelions his mother had made him eat by the BlackPath. An even more mouthwatering smell was coming from below the ground.

Toklo dug his front claws into the dirt and scraped away the earth around the base of the flower. The stem ran down under the ground to a round white bulb. Toklo scooped out the bulb with his paw and bent his head to eat it. It crunched satisfyingly between his teeth, and after a moment he felt a curious tingling sensation of heat in his mouth and throat. He dug up the flower next to it and ate that bulb, too.

Warm and full, he moved to the bank of snow on the edge of the tree line. Night was creeping across the meadow, dimming the brightness of the flowers, and stars were beginning to appear in the dark sky. Toklo dug a shallow den for himself in the snow, making a hollow he could curl up in with some protection from the wind on all sides. He crept inside and lay down, looking up at the stars as they twinkled to life one by one.

The brightest star was up there, almost directly above him, and as the night got darker, it seemed to grow brighter, shining right down on him. He remembered his mother telling him about how it was the spirit of a bad bear, driven out by the other animals. As he watched the star, he knew how it felt. The star was alone—the loneliest star in the sky—just like he was. It didn't need any other stars to survive. It lived on its own in the endless sky, the same way he was wandering by himself across the endless mountains.

His eyes drifted shut, and in his muddled dreams he thought he could hear the star calling to him. "Toklo! Be strong like me," it whispered. And then he dreamed that he was walking through dark purple clouds right into the sky, and when he looked down, his fur was shimmering silver, and he realized that he'd become the star. It was cold in the sky, and he could hear the voices of other animals whispering from far away, but he lifted his muzzle proudly toward the moon. Whatever he'd done to get here, he was alone and proud of it, and that was how he would stay.

CHAPTER SIXTEEN

Kallik

Kallik was walking at the foot of a low cliff, watching the tide creeping up the beach. She knew she needed to turn inland before long. She reached a place where the cliffs had crumbled down onto the shore, and scrambled up. Blasts of foul-smelling wind flattened her fur and stung her eyes.

From here she could see down to a flat gray path with straight edges that stretched in either direction to the edge of the sky. Beyond it was a cluster of dens like the one she had seen several days ago, propped on squat legs with flat walls and pointed roofs.

As she lay there, a roar came from the distance, and in a moment a loud, smelly creature came galloping along the path. It shot past her with a blaring noise and a blast of smoky air. Kallik coughed and coughed, trying to breathe although her nose was filled with the horrible scent. Her mother had told her that the only creatures bigger than white bears were something called "firebeasts." Nisa had said that they didn't eat bears . . . but Kallik shivered, wondering if that was true.

On a patch of grass in front of one of the dens, three creatures were playing. They walked on two legs and had rainbow furs in many colors, like birds. Kallik thought they looked too small to be dangerous, although they were too big to be prey. She wondered if they were more like bears or birds, and she wished she was brave enough to go over and sniff them more closely. They were wrestling and chasing something, and once again she felt a pang of missing her family.

Underneath the horrid smoky smell, Kallik picked up faint traces of other scents that smelled fatty and salty, like food. They were coming from the other side of the stone path. She pushed herself to her paws and trotted down the slope to the path, her ears twitching and her nose held high. It was hard to tell which scents were old and which were new; the smell of the path overwhelmed them all.

Kallik took a deep breath and bounded onto the path. It felt strange beneath her paws, pebbly and smooth at the same time. She raced for the other side as fast as she could, but she was still a few bearlengths away when a terrifying rumble shook the ground. She glanced to the left and saw one of the firebeasts bearing down on her much faster than she could run.

With a howl of terror, Kallik picked up speed and threw herself to the grass on the far side of the path. She hit the ground and tumbled head over claws into a thorny bush as the firebeast shot past behind her. Still terrified, Kallik sprang to her paws again and kept running, blundering through bushes and thickets until she crashed into a new kind of barrier, short and white and made of wood, like a series of tiny identical leafless trees growing next to one another. In her panic, she knocked over a whole section of these wooden trees and floundered into an enclosed space of peculiarly short, even grass.

A high-pitched scream sounded from inside the nearest den. Kallik ran back through the hole she had made, following the smell of trees. She blundered into an overgrown patch of woods behind the dens and found a large bush with branches hanging low to the ground. Kallik crawled underneath and lay there, panting, until she was sure that nothing was chasing her.

She rested her muzzle on her paws. She was shaking all over and her fur felt as if it had been dragged through an ice storm. It took her a long time to fall asleep, and when she did, strange creatures chased her through her nightmares, yowling and roaring. Through the chaos of noise and color, Kallik spotted her mother, pale as snow, on the far side of the stone path. Nisa looked into Kallik's eyes, then turned and walked away. As she walked, the ground beneath her turned to ice, and the cool blue stillness spread out from her paws, rippling to the edge of the sky. Unable to move, Kallik watched helplessly as her mother walked farther and farther away across the ice.

The path seemed quieter when she woke in the early morning. Kallik sniffed the air, braced herself, and sprinted across at full speed. This time she was lucky: No firebeasts sprang out of hiding to attack her. She made it across and kept running uphill past lone scattered trees until she reached the top of the cliff that looked out over the water.

Her paws were sore and bleeding from the harsh surface of the stone path, and her coat was gray with the dirt that seemed to hang in the air around it, filling her nostrils with its scent. Her throat hurt from the scratchy air, and the bright sun beat down on her fur, scorching her nose and overheating her body.

At the top of the cliff was a stretch of dry ground covered in scraggly grass and tiny, leafless bushes. Kallik tried to eat some of the grass, but the spiky leaves hurt her tongue and throat. She sniffed the air for any scent of fresh water and was relieved to find a trace that seemed close by. Kallik padded across the bare earth to a gully, where she found a stream running along the bottom. She scrambled down the side of the gully and raced to the edge of the stream. There she stopped short in dismay.

Only a few bearlengths away, sprawled in the water, was another white bear.

He was older than her, but still young, probably only one or two burn-skies old. He was not as large as some of the bears Kallik had seen, but he was a lot bigger than her, although he looked thin and starving like she was. He was lying on his belly, letting the flowing water cool him off. Kallik took a step back, hoping he hadn't seen her yet. There was a snap beneath her paws as she stepped on a twig, and she froze.

The other bear raised his head and stared at her with small dark eyes. She took another step back, and he stood up, shaking himself so drops flew in all directions. Kallik was wondering if it would be wise to run when he spoke.

"It's all right," he said gruffly. "You can have a drink. I won't eat you."

"Oh," Kallik said. Her voice sounded strange because she hadn't spoken in so long. "Thank you." She padded to the edge of the stream, keeping her eyes on the other bear. When he didn't move, she ducked her head and drank quickly.

The bear was still standing there when she stepped back. Kallik didn't know if it was really safe to talk to him, but he hadn't attacked her yet, and maybe if he was friendly, he'd help her find her brother.

"Hello," she said cautiously. "My name's Kallik."

"Hmm," grunted the other bear. She waited. After a long pause, he said, "I'm Purnaq."

"Are you all alone?" Kallik asked. It was such a relief to be talking to another white bear that she couldn't stop the words tumbling out, quicker than water. "I am. My mother was killed by orcas and I lost my brother—I don't know where he is, but I'm looking for him—he ran off into the snow and I've been trying to find him." Purnaq cocked his head, listening. "It was so horrible," Kallik went on. "I was in the water with my mother when the whales attacked, and she pushed me onto the ice but they pulled her under. And my brother is out there somewhere, all alone, and I have to find him. . . ."

"It's a sad story," Purnaq agreed with a shrug. "But things are tough all over right now. Most bears have stories like that to tell."

"Most bears?" Kallik echoed. "Have you seen a lot of other bears, then?"

Purnaq looked surprised. "Don't you know where you are? Just look up there." He nodded to the far side of the gully. Kallik splashed through the water and pulled herself up the dusty slope to the top.

The sparse, dry ground stretching in front of her was covered with white bears! More bears than she had ever seen in her life, more than all the claws on her paws. They were standing well away from one another, but most of them were close to the sea, which she could see glittering ahead of her. All of them looked thin and wretched.

She had done it. . . . She had reached the gathering place. "Taqqiq!" she cried.

CHAPTER SEVENTEEN

Lusa

It was a warm morning in leaftime, almost a moon after Oka's arrival. There were a lot of flat-faces clustered at the top of the wall, watching the bears in the Bowl. Lusa was in the Bear Tree, listening to them chatter. She lay on a branch, stretching her paws and feeling the sun warm her fur. The flat-faces sounded noisier than usual.

The doors in the wall on the other side of the Fence started to clank open. Lusa turned her head to look down into the grizzly enclosure. Oka had been clawing at her tree all day, roaring now and then with rage. She'd frightened Grumps off to the far corner, where Lusa could hear him grumbling about the damage to his poor tree. She wasn't sure if there was anything making Oka angrier than usual, but the she-bear seemed very upset.

One of the feeders stepped through the door, carrying a bucket of fish. Lusa recognized the flat-face; he often brought her food and when she was very little he had sometimes play-wrestled with her.

Oka spun around when she heard the door clang shut. Her ears twitched and her eyes narrowed. She looked like she had just spotted a juicy piece of prey. Lusa sat up, sensing something was wrong. She barked, trying to warn the feeder, but he had his back to Oka and was setting the bucket down on the ground.

All of a sudden, Oka charged. In less than a heartbeat she had raced across the clearing and slammed into the flat-face. He fell over with a shout, and the grizzly pinned him to the ground with her paws. He reached up with his hands, trying to push her away, but her huge jaws yawned over his face and her claws ripped at his chest.

Lusa scrambled back to the tree trunk, wrapped her forepaws around it, and pressed her face into the bark. She could hear the flat-face visitors screaming and shouting from the wall. Even louder than them, she could hear the feeder howling in pain. The terrible sound seemed to go on and on and on.

Finally she heard the door clanking again, and she turned to see another feeder come running through, pointing a metal stick at Oka, which let out a loud *pop*. Oka reared up from the first feeder and turned to the new one, roaring and lashing out with her claws. For a moment Lusa was afraid that the other flat-face would be hurt as well, but then Oka stopped, swaying. She blinked, shaking her head, and then her eyes closed and she toppled to the ground with a crash that sent up a cloud of sand.

The second feeder ran to the flat-face on the ground, and more came running in behind him. They pressed what looked like white pelts over his wounds, but blood came welling up under their paws. All of them were shouting, and Lusa could see the flat-faces at the wall being herded away.

Lusa stayed in the crook of the trunk, trembling. She'd never seen a bear treat a flat-face like prey before. She didn't understand how any bear could be so savage and violent. Ashia and King must be right—there was something wrong with Oka.

The flat-faces moved the hurt feeder onto a tightly stretched white pelt and carried him out of the enclosure. Two of the feeders stayed behind, looking down at Oka's sleeping form, murmuring in their language and shaking their heads.

Lusa scrambled down the tree and ran over to Ashia and Stella, who were sitting on the Mountains looking shocked. "Why did she do that?" Lusa blurted out. She buried her face in Ashia's fur, and her mother patted her head with her paws.

"It's all right," Ashia soothed. "It's over now."

"I knew that bear was crazy," Stella said, shaking her head sadly.

"Can the flat-faces make her better?" Lusa asked. "Like they fixed you, Mother?"

Stella and Ashia were quiet for a moment, exchanging a long look.

"I remember a white bear," Stella said finally. "A long time ago, when I first came here. He clawed a feeder very badly."

"What happened to him?" Lusa whispered.

"The flat-faces took him away," Stella said. "And he never came back."

Lusa whimpered.

"We don't know for sure that this will happen to Oka, though," Ashia said quickly.

"Maybe they'll take her back to the wild," Lusa said hopefully.

"I doubt it," Stella said, her voice gentle. "You can see how unhappy and dangerous she is. She wouldn't be any better off out there, and they're probably worried that she would attack other flat-faces if they let her go."

Lusa crept over to the back corner of the Fence and waited there for the rest of the day, watching Oka sleep. As the last of the daylight was fading, Oka grunted and woke up, staggering clumsily to her paws. She looked around the enclosure, and then her eyes turned to the Fence, where she saw Lusa waiting.

The grizzly dragged herself over and lay down with her muzzle on her paws. She sighed heavily. Lusa didn't know what to say.

After a long pause, Oka squinted up at Lusa and said, "It's all right. I know what I did."

"You do?" Lusa said.

The brown bear flexed her claws, looking down at the dark, dry splashes of blood on her fur. "I was so angry—with myself for losing Toklo, with the flat-faces for keeping me here—just with everything. I don't even know why." She stopped and looked at Lusa again. "They're going to send me into the longsleep, aren't they?"

"I—I don't know," Lusa whispered.

"It's all right," Oka said again. She took a deep breath and closed her eyes. "There is nothing for me here anymore. At least now I can be with my Tobi."

Lusa lay down on her side of the Fence. She wished she could reach through the web and press her nose into Oka's fur. "I'll stay with you," she promised. "Until they come."

"Thank you," Oka said.

They lay for a while in silence. Lusa could hear King grumbling to Ashia, but she knew her mother would understand. She would let Lusa stay with the brown bear tonight.

As the sky darkened, Lusa lifted her head and searched for the Bear Watcher. There it was, shining fiercely in the dim orange-lit sky. "The Bear Watcher is looking down on us," she said.

Oka followed her gaze to the bright star and snorted. "That is the saddest star in the sky."

"Why?" Lusa asked.

"It is the spirit of a very bad bear—a bear who did terrible things. As a punishment, it was imprisoned in the coldest and most lonely place the spirits could find. It's all alone up there . . . like me."

"The star isn't alone," Lusa said, trying to sound reassuring. "There are other animals in the sky to keep it company. I know you can't see them very well from here, because of all the lights, but Stella says they're there. Like me—I'm here with you, so you're not alone, either."

Oka's voice softened. "I am glad you're here."

"Do you think you'll be put up in the sky, too?" Lusa asked. "I thought the spirits of bears became trees. Maybe you'll become a tree. Maybe you'll grow on this side of the Fence and I can climb you and we can still be friends."

"That's not what happens to brown bears," Oka said. "My spirit will find its way to the Great Salmon River and be washed out to sea. Don't worry about me, little cub." She sounded gentler than Lusa had ever heard her be. "I welcome the longsleep," Oka murmured. "It will bring me peace at last."

She fell silent again.

"What is salmon?" Lusa said, wanting to make Oka talk some more. Her silence made Lusa feel scared. "You said Great Salmon River—is it a place?"

"Salmon is a kind of fish," Oka explained. "They're silver and slippery and they are the best food in the world."

"Better than blueberries?"

Oka grunted with amusement. "Much better than blueberries." She stared into the distance. "Toklo loved blueberries, too. But he would have loved salmon even more. If only I had been strong enough to stay with him." She clawed at her muzzle with a sad whining sound.

"Tell me about Toklo," Lusa prompted. This was her last chance to find out what had happened to Oka's missing cub.

"I abandoned him," Oka said in a low, raspy voice. "I don't even know if he's still alive. He's so brave, and so strong . . .

such a good cub. He'll be a great bear one day, if he survives.
But he's so young . . . and he's all alone, and it's all my fault."

Her voice rose to a keening cry and she clawed at her face
again, this time leaving deep scratches in her muzzle. "My
cub!" she cried. "My poor cub. How could I leave you? How
could I drive you away like that?"

Lusa didn't know what to say. Oka was crazed with sadness,
and Lusa was afraid she might hurt herself badly. But what
could she do? There was no way to help her.

"I'm sure Toklo will be fine," Lusa said. "He sounds like he
can take care of himself—he'll find food, I'm sure he will."

"No, he won't," Oka snarled. "He's too little—he's even
younger than you are, and you could never survive in the forest."

"Yes, I could!" Lusa cried.

Oka huffed and lay down. "You're better off here," she said,
"where it's safe, where there's enough food, and you have a
mother to look after you—one who will never abandon you.
You'll never know what it's like to live in the wild."

"But I do know," Lusa protested. Her mind filled with
images from her dreams—endless dark trees, glimpses of sun
through the branches, rain pattering on thick leaves. It was
where she belonged, wasn't it?

"You'll never know, because you're shut in this place. While
Toklo wanders alone, starving and helpless. I tried to find
him, I really did. But what's the use? His spirit probably
joined the Salmon River long ago. He'll never know that I'm
sorry, that I loved him just as much as Tobi."

Lusa couldn't bear the despair in Oka's voice. It wasn't fair she should go to the longsleep without being able to help her last surviving cub. And Toklo didn't even know she loved him. "Oka!" she cried, jumping up and pressing her muzzle to the Fence. "Oka, listen. I'll go to the wild. I'll find Toklo for you and make sure he's all right, and I'll tell him that you loved him. You can go to the Salmon River and find Tobi. I'll look after Toklo."

The large brown bear met Lusa's eyes. For a moment they stared at each other. No words needed to be spoken. Lusa just nodded.

I will find Toklo for you. I promise.

CHAPTER EIGHTEEN

Toklo

A long sharp claw was prodding Toklo awake. He blinked and rubbed his eyes. At first he thought it must be his mother waking him, but then he remembered she'd left him by the river. He looked up and a bolt of terror shot through him.

It was the full-grown bear from the day before—the one whose prey he'd stolen. He had a deep scar across his muzzle and an unfriendly look in his eyes.

"What are you doing here, cub?" the bear growled.

"I—I'm—" Toklo stammered.

"Where did you come from?" The bear nodded his head toward the woods, where the pile of prey had been buried. "Did you go through there?"

"No!" Toklo lied. "I came down off that mountain over there. I haven't gone into those woods."

"Well, you'd better not," the bear snarled. "This is *my* territory." He reared up onto his hind legs. "See the marks on this tree?" He indicated a set of deep scratches in the bark. "That means this place is mine."

"Fine," Toklo said. "I didn't know. I won't go in."

"Go back to where you came from," the bear growled, dropping to all fours again. "There is nothing for you—or any other bear—here."

Snarling, he lumbered off into the trees, and Toklo backed away into the meadow, watching the grizzly until he couldn't see him anymore.

The sun rose higher in the sky, heating the earth beneath his paws. He could tell that the season of fishleap was truly beginning. Toklo kept journeying up the mountain, following the line of melting snow, digging up flower bulbs to eat all along the way. Their taste didn't compare to squirrels or hare, but it helped his legs stay fast and strong . . . which they needed to be in case he encountered other hungry bears with strong feelings about sharing their prey with cubs.

He could smell the scent of prey in the air around him— small animals roused, like him, by the new-growing grasses and flowers. Toward the end of the day, he found a burrow that smelled promising. He paused at the entrance and listened. Not far inside, he could hear muffled shuffling sounds, and the scent of juicy prey made his stomach growl. There was a rabbit inside! Panting with eagerness, he sank his claws into the earth and scrabbled down into the hole, but the rabbit fled out of reach, its feet drumming on the earth. Toklo's stomach rumbled loud as thunder as he drifted off to sleep that night, and he dreamed of sinking his teeth into rabbit flesh.

Three sunrises later, Toklo had made his way near the peak of the mountain. He stayed closer to the open meadows above the tree line to avoid the thick forests in the valley, which all seemed to be claimed by grizzlies already. He had his nose to the ground, sniffing for fresh water, when another rabbit leaped out of the bushes almost directly in front of him. Toklo raced after the rabbit as it fled up a small ridge. His paws pounded on the ground and the wind swept through his fur, making it ripple like grass. As he reached the crest, the rabbit vanished into a hole, and Toklo skidded to a stop. He was at the edge of a path like a huge claw scratch down the side of the mountain. On either side were trees and rocks, covered in snow, but the scratch itself was bristling with bright green shoots, standing out sharply against the bare trees on either side. At the bottom was a heap of snow-covered boulders and snapped tree trunks, as if a bear had kicked them off the top of the mountain and sent them crashing down the steep slope.

Toklo realized that this must be one of the mountain slides his mother had told him about. He looked around nervously, wondering if any other parts of the mountain were about to fall off.

"Listen to the birds," Oka had said. "They will warn you. If you prick up your ears and hear no birds, run away as fast as you can."

Toklo twitched his ears. Birds were chattering all around him, singing and whistling at one another. That must mean there was no danger from the mountain here. He sighed with

relief. The claw scratch was alive with the smells of wildflowers, and he scrambled onto it, rooting around for food.

Toklo padded up the scratch, nosing through the mountain
grasses and digging up roots. About halfway up, he came
around the side of a gray boulder twice his height and nearly
crashed into a full-grown grizzly.

"HEY!" the bear roared, standing on its hind legs. "Get out,
get out!" He dropped to all fours and leaped at Toklo.

Toklo jumped back with a startled yelp. "I'm not bothering
you!" he protested. "There are enough bulbs and roots here
for lots of bears."

"Is that what you think?" the bear snarled. "That just shows
what an ignorant cub you are. Get out of here, before I rip
your fur."

"Why can't I stay?" Toklo whined. He was sick of being
driven away. How could every pawstep on this mountain be
part of some other bear's territory?

"The uplands are not for cubs," the adult bear said bossily.
"Go back down to the valley. Only the strongest bears can
hunt up here." He lunged with his claws outstretched, swiping
at Toklo's side. Toklo felt a sting of pain as the claws grazed
him, and with a howl, he turned and ran back down the
mountain. He could feel the other bear's eyes on him as he
stumbled over the rutted earth, his angry gaze pricking the
back of Toklo's ears.

Toklo tumbled to a stop at the bottom of the scratch and
leaned against a rock, panting. It wasn't fair! His mother
should be here to fight for him, to make sure he got enough

food. He could still hear the other bear roaring, so he forced himself to keep going, on down the mountain and into the trees, even though his belly felt pinched and empty.

After a while he heard the sound of firebeasts ahead of him, so he knew there must be a BlackPath close by, like the one in the valley where he'd lived with Oka and Tobi. This valley had many of the same smells—flat-faces, burning and metal, rotfood—but the shape of the mountains around it was different, and there was a river flowing through it that had split off from the one he'd been following earlier. Following the sound of the firebeasts, he clambered down through dark trees until he reached the edge of the BlackPath.

Something was lying on the grass that smelled like rotfood, but it wasn't an animal, as far as Toklo could tell. It looked like moldy bits of lots of different things, wrapped in a thin black skin with no fur. The skin ripped easily when he sliced his claws into it, and what was inside came spilling out along with many confusing scents. Toklo stepped back, wrinkling his nose, trying to sort out the different smells. It definitely seemed like there was *something* in there he could eat.

He found a few bones with chewed meat still sticking to them, and he gnawed all the rest of the meat off and crunched the bones with his teeth. Then he found a hollowed-out shape with something sweet inside, and he stuck his tongue in to lick it all up. This wasn't so bad. While he was stretching his tongue to get the last trace of sweet, sticky stuff, a blast of noise came from a firebeast racing past, and Toklo jumped. His muzzle scraped against a sharp metal edge and he felt his skin tear. The new stabbing pain in his mouth joined the throbbing in his side where the bear had clawed him.

Toklo backed away from the rotfood and padded back into the forest, climbing up the slope through the trees. Blood was dripping from his muzzle, warm and salty, and as soon as he found a snowbank, he stuck his nose in it. When his nose felt numb, he pulled it out and dug himself a shallow hole in the ground. He curled up and pressed his nose into the earth, breathing in the warmth and the clean growing scents of the dirt until sleep finally overtook him.

The next day, the firebeasts were quieter on the BlackPath, and Toklo was able to hear the splash of the river in the woods behind him. He followed the noise until he reached the bank and carefully stepped into the water. This river was smaller, shallower, and faster than the one where he'd tried fishing for salmon with his mother. The banks were made of soft earth that crumbled, instead of pebbles that sloped straight into the water. Toklo stood with his back to the current, watching the reflections dance and sparkle on the surface. He tried to listen for the bear spirits, but all he could hear was the rushing and splashing around his paws.

All at once, something silver slithered between his paws. Toklo was so surprised, he reacted instinctively and leaped for it. He landed on his belly in the water, soaking his fur, and the fish twisted away just out of reach, vanishing downriver.

But I was close! Toklo thought. He scrambled onto his feet and waited for another one to come by. Before long, he spotted the flash of movement again and dove at it. Once again, he ended up flat on his belly with a noseful of river water. He stood up, shaking his head. Every time he dove, water splashed in his eyes so he couldn't see anything. But he couldn't think of another way to do it.

Toklo tried to catch fish for the rest of the day. There was no shortage of fish—almost every time he stood up, another one darted between his paws. But that just made it even more frustrating when he couldn't catch any. At last he stomped up the bank and sat on a rock, glaring at the river. He could see the dark shapes of fish flitting past, casting shadows on the riverbed. They seemed happy and unafraid, as if they knew they had nothing to fear from him.

"Thanks a lot, river spirits," Toklo muttered. "Fat lot of good you are. Can't you do anything useful, like send a fish to my paws? Stupid bunch of weasel-brains. You're as useless as a black bear. Longsleeping, squirrel-faced, hollow-headed salmon-brains!"

The river kept burbling past, ignoring him. Toklo got up and began following it, pacing along the bank. The water seemed to be in a hurry, swirling by in a flurry of choppy waves and frothing splashes. He wondered where it was going at such a fast pace, and if all the bear spirits were going there, too. His mother had said that the bear spirits floated down-river until they reached the end, a place of forgetfulness where they faded from every bear's memory.

Well, if that's where Tobi's trying to go, he hasn't gotten there yet, Toklo thought. He certainly hadn't forgotten about his brother, although he wanted to. Every time he remembered the sad scrap of fur lying in the half-built den, alone, Toklo had to remind himself that he didn't *want* Tobi here, whining and dragging his paws and feeling ill all the time. He wished Tobi would hurry up and get to the end of the river so Toklo could stop thinking about him.

A noise ahead snapped him out of his thoughts. Toklo crept up the slope until he was hidden from the river by a thick line of bushes. He edged along to a place where he could peer through at the water below. Not three bearlengths from him, a brown she-bear was standing in the shallows with two cubs. The cubs were wrestling, splashing in the river and dunking each other underwater.

"Little ones," their mother scolded gently, "this is not the time for playing. Pay attention to me."

The bigger, darker cub obediently sat down, but the smaller one, with a patch of light blond fur across her shoulders, couldn't resist swatting one last splash of water at him.

"Hey!" the bigger cub protested.

"SIT," their mother ordered. They both snapped to attention, watching her.

"Now watch me," the mother bear said. She paced through the water until she found a spot where boulders channeled the current directly between her paws. She stood and waited, her head lowered to stare at the water, but it wasn't very long before she pounced. When she lifted her head, she held a fat, flapping salmon between her teeth. She shook it hard until it stopped flapping about. Then the mother bear brought it over to her cubs.

"The trick is to look before you jump," she explained, dropping the fish on the pebbles beside them. "Don't pounce on where you see the fish—pounce on the spot where it's going, because by the time you land, that's where it will be. Take a moment to plan it out, because as soon as you move, the water will splash in your eyes and you'll have to rely on your paws to find it and hold it down."

Toklo pricked up his ears. He hadn't thought of that. . . . He had just leaped as soon as he saw anything move. He curled his lip. How could he know what to do, anyway? Oka should have taught him.

The cubs were splashing through the shallows, chasing after their mother and trying to imitate her. The smaller cub kept batting hopefully at the water with her paws. Toklo could see that she didn't have enough patience for this task yet. Like him, she would jump before thinking, sending cascades of water over herself and her brother.

But the bigger cub stood calmly, staring at the river. Toklo's paws prickled with tension as he waited, feeling every whisker on his body quiver. When the cub finally leaped and emerged from the water with a fish in his mouth, Toklo wanted to shout with triumph. The cub had done it! He'd caught a fish!

"Good job, Fochik!" his mother praised him. "That was terrific!"

"Wow," said his little sister, circling her brother. "Maybe you're not such a slippery-paws after all."

"Thanks, Aylen," the cub said.

Toklo watched Fochik drag the fish to the edge of the river, using his claws to keep it from being dragged away in the current. The cub nudged the salmon's body with his muzzle until it lodged on some stones, just out of reach of the water. Toklo narrowed his eyes, thinking. He could steal that fish. The cubs were smaller than him, so he wasn't afraid of fighting them if they tried to stop him. The mother bear was a different matter, but she was back in the stream, watching the current— Toklo could slip in and out before she even noticed. It wasn't as if the bears would go hungry if he took this fish. The she-bear would just catch more for them. He needed that fish more than they did because he didn't have a mother.

He snuck through the shadows of the bushes until he was less than a bearlength from the riverbank. Aylen was scampering around her brother at the edge of the water, begging for a bite. "Come on!" Toklo heard her cry. "Just a little! Let me try it!"

"Go catch your own!" her brother answered good-naturedly. He was standing over his fish, watching its tail lift when the water lapped against it. "It's not that hard. Don't you think you can do it?"

"Of course I can! I just need something to keep up my strength, that's all. One bite!"

Fochik turned his head to shove his sister away. At once Toklo darted out of the bushes, plunged down the bank, and snatched up the fish in his jaws.

"HEY!" Aylen yelped. "Stop! That's ours!"

"Mother!" Fochik yowled.

Toklo scrambled up the bank. He glanced back and saw

Aylen chasing after him. "You thieving badger-face!" she howled. "Are you a wolverine or a bear? Come back, scavenger!"

Her words pricked at Toklo's pride but the taste of the salmon was already flooding his mouth, so he kept running. Then he heard the crash and crackle of the mother bear charging through the bushes after him, and his heart began to pound with terror. How far would she chase him? He knew she must be faster than he was. He dodged under a low-hanging branch and slipped on a pile of leaves, wasting precious moments as he scrabbled back to his paws.

He risked another look back as he burst out of the bushes and raced under some spiny trees. The mother bear was pushing her way out behind him, her mouth hanging open and her pink tongue lolling. She let out another bellow when she saw Toklo. "We fish the river here!"

Toklo's legs were so tired, he didn't think he could run anymore. If he stopped, would the mother bear take the fish back and leave him alone? Or would she attack him, ripping into his fur like the bear on the mountainside, leaving him bleeding and dying on the leaves? His breath came in ragged gasps and all he could hear was the blood pounding in his ears. His footsteps slowed and, without looking around, he braced himself for massive paws to slam down on his shoulders.

Nothing happened. Toklo slowed even more until he staggered to a stop, the salmon still gripped in his teeth. He turned around. The mother bear was standing behind him, several bearlengths back, under a prickly tree with small curly leaves. "This is my territory!" she roared. "Stay away from us!"

Toklo didn't answer. His legs were trembling too much to carry him another step. He just stood still, waiting for the she-bear to catch up to him. But she didn't. Instead, she turned away with an angry huff and trotted back toward the river. Toklo sank onto the dry leaves, panting and dizzy. She had chased him out of her territory—that was all she had wanted. He was safe. And he had food.

That night he slept with a full stomach in a den under some tree roots. For once, he did not dream of Tobi dying or of Oka driving him away. He didn't even feel guilty about stealing the salmon. His sleep was dreamless and peaceful.

CHAPTER NINETEEN

Kallik

Kallik stared at the sea of white bears. Maybe Taqqiq was there, so close to her she might be able to smell him. She wondered if it was safe to go down and walk among them. They didn't look as if they were talking to one another like a big group of friends—in fact, they seemed to be ignoring one another, as if they were here on their own. Perhaps they would ignore her, too.

One large male with patchy gray fur and scrapes along his muzzle was pacing along the edge of the sea, staring out over the waves. "Why have you abandoned us?" he howled. "Spirits of the ice, where are you? We need you! You are failing us!"

It made Kallik feel nervous. She couldn't help thinking that yelling at the ice spirits was only going to make them angrier.

Behind her, Purnaq scrambled up the slope. He stopped next to her at the top, scraping the mud off his claws.

"What's going on?" Kallik asked. "Why are all these bears here?"

"This is where we come every burn-sky," he said. "We're waiting for the sea to freeze."

Relief washed over Kallik. "So we all wait together?" Maybe now she could learn everything she hadn't had time to learn from her mother.

"It's not exactly like that," Purnaq said. "But we don't fight one another here—it's hard enough just to survive."

Kallik could hear a note of warning in his voice, like he was telling her not to expect too much, but she felt better anyway. The other bears would give her a better chance of learning where to find food, and she might even be able to share a left-over carcass. With other bears, she would also be safer from walruses and the other animals she'd seen.

Purnaq started toward the beach, trotting down the slope of the hill. Kallik bounded after him and caught up to trot alongside. Purnaq stopped and turned on her, his lip curling.

"Stay away from me," he snarled. "I have trouble finding enough food for myself. I don't need a stupid cub tagging along behind me."

Kallik stared at him in astonishment. "I—I wasn't tagging along," she stammered. "I was just going the same way."

"Good," he growled. He whirled around and stalked off without looking back.

Kallik stayed where she was, waiting for him to get far enough away so it didn't look like she was following him. Gray-and-white birds hopped along the edge of the sea, shrieking and flapping their wings at one another. They seemed unafraid of the gathered bears and walked right up to them to pick up bits of seaweed and other tidbits.

Kallik walked among the bears, feeling the sand trickle between her claws. She looked at each of them closely, trying not to seem like she was staring. Many of them were lying very still, ignoring the insects buzzing around their ears. Others were tugging up the spiky blue-green grass to chew it. The air felt hazy and warm, blurring the sun's rays into a heavy pelt of heat that pressed them into the ground. By a cluster of boulders, she saw a pair of young male bears play-fighting. Her heart started to thump, and she edged closer to get a better view, but after a moment she could tell that they were both too big to be Taqqiq.

Other bears clearly didn't have enough energy to wrestle. They looked as if they had been lying in the same place for days, leaving a permanent bear-shaped imprint on the sand. Kallik guessed they were saving their energy, not sure when they would be able to eat again.

A yelp of laughter startled her, and she spun around. Nearby, two cubs were leaping and rolling on the pebbles. One of them snatched up a clump of seaweed and galloped off with his brother in close pursuit. A large female bear roared at them, and they both swerved to run back to her side. She cuffed them gently with her paw and then lay down so they could scramble over her. Memories of Taqqiq and her mother made Kallik's eyes blur, but she blinked hard and forced herself to move on.

On the far side of a group of sleeping bears, another cub was dabbing his paws in the water, flicking his ears at the squelching sound they made when he lifted them out. Kallik could imagine Taqqiq being fascinated like that. He'd have been happy to play with all the new things she'd found. Maybe this cub *was* Taqqiq. . . .

She padded over, her muzzle lifted, trying to catch his scent. It didn't smell like Taqqiq—this cub smelled more like trees and dirt than fish and snow, but that would happen to any white bear once it had been on land for a while.

"Taqqiq?" she called. The cub lifted his head. "Taqqiq!" she called again, speeding up.

A wall of white fur slammed down in front of her, and Kallik skidded to a stop. A she-bear reared up over her, snarling. "Leave my cub alone," she growled.

Kallik crouched down, ducking her head, too scared to speak. Dropping to all fours, the female turned and herded her cub back up the beach. Now Kallik could see a tilt to the cub's ears that Taqqiq didn't have. She wanted to find him so badly, she tried to see him in every cub. But Taqqiq wasn't here. She kept walking through the bears, feeling more and more hopeless as she saw that each cub the right shape and size had a mother to travel with. There were no other lone white bear cubs here.

A strange grumbling noise drifted toward her, from behind a shallow ridge of ground. Kallik stopped and perked up her ears. She stared in alarm as an enormous creature crawled over the ridge, growling deep in its throat as it headed straight for the bears. Kallik looked around, but none of the other bears had even raised their muzzles to sniff for the creature's scent. She turned back, determined to be brave like them.

The creature was a bit like the firebeasts Kallik had seen on the stone path, with the same round black paws and bitter, burning scent, but it was larger and shaped like a huge white block of ice. Suddenly she realized there were holes in the side of the creature, and *inside* were the two-legged animals she'd seen before. Had the firebeast eaten them? How were they still alive? She could clearly see them moving and pointing their paws at the bears. They didn't seem afraid of being trapped inside the firebeast at all.

Kallik glanced over her shoulder again. Maybe one of the other bears would know what this was. She could see Purnaq beyond a cluster of bears around a patch of brittle grass, but she didn't want to get snarled at again. Closer to her there was a female bear lying on her side who looked only a few seasons older than Kallik. Her eyes were half closed, and she looked comfortable and peaceful. Kallik hoped she wouldn't be too unfriendly.

"Excuse me?" she said, padding up to the bear. "I'm—I'm sorry to bother you, but could I ask you a question?"

The bear opened her eyes and grunted without sitting up. Kallik took that as a yes.

"Can you tell me what that is?" she asked, pointing with her muzzle to the white creature with round black paws. "Is it a firebeast? Are those live animals inside it? Do you know what they are?"

The bear sighed. "This is why I don't want cubs," she muttered. "Always asking stupid questions. We call them white firebeasts," she said grudgingly. "You don't need to be scared of it. It just comes out here to stare at us. Firebeasts carry around the no-claws—those are the two-legged animals you can see inside."

"Oh," Kallik said. "If they have no claws, that means they can't hurt us, right?"

"Ha," said the older bear. "You *are* an ignorant cub, aren't you? Don't you know about the no-claws' firesticks?"

Kallik shook her head.

"If you ever see a no-claw pointing a long stick at you, run as fast as you can," the bear advised. "They make a noise like cracking ice, and they're even more dangerous than the tusk of a walrus, because they can hurt you or kill you no matter how far away the no-claw is."

Kallik shivered. How could a stick hurt you without touching you? She looked at the white firebeast and the no-claws peering out through the holes in its side. None of them seemed to be carrying sticks, but a lot of them were pointing at her with their paws. It made her nervous.

"Thank you for your help," she said to the female bear, who grunted and lay down again. Kallik began to walk toward the sea, but it seemed like the white firebeast was following her. When she stopped, it stopped. When she moved again, it started crawling to keep up. She wondered what would happen if she ran away.

Suddenly a furious roar came from down on the shore. The bear who had been ranting at the ice spirits reared up on his hind legs, clawing the air with his front paws. Then he dropped to all fours and charged up the shore, over the pebbles and spiky grass, right up to the firebeast. Lowering his head, he smashed into its side with a hollow, ringing sound. The white firebeast lurched but didn't fall over. The male white bear reared up and slammed his front paws into its side, raking his claws down it with a squealing sound that made Kallik wince. She could see that he only had some of his claws left, and there were red spots on his fur where the others must have been torn out. She could smell his blood on the air.

The firebeast didn't fight back. Instead it crawled away quickly, leaving long tracks in the dirt behind it. The bear slumped to the ground, whimpering.

Some of the bears were on their paws now, walking along the edge of the shore in the same direction as the white firebeast. None of them even looked at the wounded old bear. Kallik wondered where they were going. She looked around until she spotted Purnaq, who had stopped to drink at a stream.

"Hello," Kallik said. He whipped his head up and glared at her. "I'm not following you," she said quickly. "I just want to know where those other bears are going."

Purnaq nodded in the direction the white firebeast had gone. "If you keep going that way, you'll come to a territory of no-claw dens." He hesitated, then added, "You can get food there, if you're lucky, but you have to be careful of the no-claws."

"Are you going there?" she asked.

He hunched his shoulders and looked down at his paws. "I haven't decided yet."

Kallik got the feeling he was only saying that so she wouldn't tag along with him. "All right," she said. "Well, thank you."

"*Hrm,*" he muttered, turning back to the stream.

Kallik padded away in the opposite direction, aiming for the shore. She walked casually, without looking back, but when she reached a group of boulders, she slipped behind one of them and peeked out at Purnaq. He had crossed the stream and was heading purposefully up the shore, aiming inland, the same direction as the white firebeast had gone.

She snuck out and followed him, staying at a safe distance. He was her best chance of reaching the no-claw dens and possible food. What's more, if Taqqiq had heard that there was food to be found in this place, he might have gone there as well.

CHAPTER TWENTY

Lusa

Lusa watched through the Fence as the feeders took Oka away. They had made the grizzly sleepy first with the same popping stick that had been used on Ashia. Lusa guessed she would never see her again. She just hoped Oka would find Tobi where she was going.

Her fur prickled as she thought about the promise she'd made. She had no idea how she'd get out of the Bear Bowl, or how she'd survive on her own until she found Toklo. But she had to: Somewhere out there, Toklo was alone, convinced his mother didn't love him, and he needed her to tell him the truth.

"Crazy old furlump," Yogi said, coming up behind her. "I'm glad she's gone."

"Well, I'm not," Lusa said. "Oka wasn't crazy. She just had a lot of bad things happen to her."

"*Pffft,*" Yogi grunted. "Maybe now you'll forget all this stupid talk about the wild and come play with me instead."

"Yogi, some things are more important than playing," Lusa said, trying to sound grown-up.

"Like what?" Yogi looked at her as if he thought she might be as crazy as Oka. "Sticking your nose in the clouds and dreaming of places you'll never go?"

"But I *will* go there!" Lusa blurted. "I promised Oka. I'm going to leave the Bear Bowl and go into the wild to find her lost cub, Toklo."

Yogi snorted. "That's very funny, Lusa! I'd like to see that— baby Lusa in the wild on her own!"

"Why not?" Lusa cried. "I could take care of myself! And I'm going to find Toklo and help take care of him, too! You'll see!"

Yogi stared at her. "You're serious," he said. "Wow, I didn't know that bear's craziness was catching. Hey, Stella!"

The she-bear got up from her basking place by the tree and ambled over. "Sorry about your friend, Lusa," she said, nudging the cub with her muzzle.

Yogi interrupted before Lusa could speak. "Lusa's going to escape the Bear Bowl! Ha! Can't you see it? Lusa wandering the forest by herself. Lusa climbing wild trees. Lusa chasing berries! Ha!" He rolled on his back, making loud grunts of laughter.

"Shut up!" Lusa growled at him. "It's not funny!"

"What's going on?" Ashia asked, coming out of the den.

"Lusa's going into the wild!" Yogi cried. "She thinks she can survive on her own. You can't dance for your food in the wild, Lusa!"

"Your father was right, dear," Ashia said softly. "This is what comes of listening to crazy stories. That wild bear has filled your head with cloudfluff."

"It's not cloudfluff!" Lusa insisted. She turned her back on the other bears and ran over to the Bear Tree. She scrambled up it quickly, digging in with her claws, until she was at the very top. Perhaps from here she'd be able to see a way out of the Bowl. At least up here she could forget about the others, telling her she'd never go to the wild, never find Toklo, never keep her promise to Oka.

Lusa stayed up in the tree all day. She stared at the paths that wound around the Bowl and the other cages nearby. She wished she could see farther, to the high Fence that ran around everything, so she could figure out how to reach it. Nothing she saw from the tree gave her any ideas about how to escape—she knew she couldn't climb out of the Bowl, and the Fences and walls were all too strong and solid to knock down. Finally, as dusk was falling, she heard her mother calling from the bottom of the tree.

"Lusa! Time to eat!"

Her stomach was growling. She hadn't eaten anything since yesterday morning. As much as she didn't want to face the other black bears, she was too hungry to stay in the tree any longer.

Lusa clambered back down to the ground. Ashia was waiting for her with a pawful of blueberries and a sympathetic look in her eyes.

"Thanks," Lusa muttered, lapping up the blueberries with her tongue. The burst of sweetness in her mouth made her feel a little better.

"I understand that you're upset," Ashia said. "It's never easy to lose a friend, and what happened yesterday was very shocking. I'm sure that right now it seems like the outside world would be a better place to live, but believe me, it isn't."

"That's not the point," Lusa said. "I promised Oka I'd find her lost cub."

Ashia shook her head. "You don't know how big the world is," she said. "It would be impossible for two cubs to find each other. And besides, there's no way out of here." She stretched out her muzzle and pointed with her nose at the Fences on all sides of them.

"I know," Lusa said, "but black bears are the best climbers in the forest. There *must* be a way out."

Ashia sighed. "Please don't say anything to your father about this berry-brained idea, Lusa. It would only make him angry."

After eating, Lusa went looking for King. If he was the only one who didn't know about her plans to escape, perhaps she could get some information out of him. The bulky black bear was sitting by one of the boulders, tearing an apple apart with his claws. Lusa padded up to him and sat down. She had to think of a way to ask him questions without giving away her plan. She scratched her ear until an idea occurred to her.

"I don't see how it can be that hard to live in the wild," she began. "I mean, doesn't food grow on trees and bushes out there? It's just everywhere, isn't it?"

King grunted. "It's harder than you can possibly imagine. Even if you do find food, you have to be careful about where you take it from—and who might be angry if you do."

"What do you mean?"

Her father jerked his head toward the Bear Tree. "Have you ever looked carefully at the bark on that tree?"

Lusa shook her head. King stood up and lumbered over to it. "See here," he said, rising onto his hind legs and patting the trunk with his front paws. "These scratches right here."

Sure enough, there were deep gouges in the bark of the tree, right where her father's paws reached. Lusa was surprised she hadn't noticed them before. She must have been too busy climbing.

"If you saw scratches like this in the wild," King said, "you'd have to be very careful, because it would mean you'd entered the territory of an adult black bear. A bear that won't take kindly to a cub stealing his food."

"Oh," Lusa said.

"And of course there are grizzlies. A brown bear would snap you up in a heartbeat, as if you were just a hare or a caterpillar. I'm telling you, there's danger around every bush in the wild. It's no place for a soft cub like you."

"How do wild black bear cubs survive?" Lusa asked, hoping he wouldn't get cross and storm off again.

King rumbled deep in his throat. "There is one thing you can do that a brown bear can't: Climb trees. Look at your claws."

Lusa lifted one of her front paws and examined it.

"See how your claws are curved? A brown bear's claws are straight. They're made for digging, not climbing. Cubs in the wild stay near trees and use them to escape from danger. But that doesn't mean it's safe for them. They spend half their time racing up trees at the smallest noise. No bear wants to live like that."

Stella, resting on her back on the other side of the tree, chimed in. "Trees can give you food, too," she said. "The best food of all is honey, and it comes from a Buzzy Tree."

"What would you know about it?" King scoffed.

"I've heard stories!" Stella protested. "The tree buzzes and buzzes and stings you to keep you away, but if you keep trying, you can dig out the most delicious, sweet stuff, even better than blueberries."

King snorted and turned to walk away.

"Wait," Lusa said. "I want to know more."

"What's the point?" King snarled. "You'll never see a Buzzy Tree, or taste honey, or have to escape from a grizzly. And you should be glad of it!"

He stomped off to his corner again. Lusa sighed. Now he'd be too grumpy to talk about the wild for ages. But at least she'd learned a few things.

For the next couple of days, Lusa lurked around the door in the wall of the Bowl. It was the only way she knew that led out of the enclosure, and if she could slip through when it opened, she might be able to make a run for it.

"What are you *doing*?" Yogi whined, poking her with his nose. "Come play with me."

"No," Lusa said, keeping her eyes on the door.

"You're not still planning to escape, are you? Are you going to fly over the wall like a bird?"

Lusa ignored him. Yogi circled her, looking worried. "You're really going to try, aren't you?" he said. "How? What are you going to do?"

"Like I would tell you!" Lusa snapped.

"Maybe I can help," he offered.

"Ha," she said. "I don't need your help."

He skulked away, pawing at pebbles in the dirt.

Suddenly Lusa heard the familiar clang of the door. She braced herself, rocking back on her paws. The door slowly swung open, and she could see one of the feeders coming through. A little bit farther . . . a little bit farther . . . now!

Lusa sprang. She dug her paws into the ground and raced forward, aiming for the space that was opening up.

All at once a sharp pain jolted through her bones. Shocked, Lusa leaped back and saw that the feeder was holding a long stick. He poked it at her again, but this time she scrambled back before it could sting her. She retreated to a safe distance and watched the feeder come in and close the door behind him.

She sat down, scraping her claws in the earth. She was disappointed and puzzled. The stick hadn't shot something into her, like the one the feeders had used on Ashia and Oka, and she didn't feel sleepy, but it had *hurt*. Frustrated, she dug her claws through the dirt. If the only way out of this enclosure was that door, then she would have to find a different way of getting through it.

The next morning, Lusa lay down under the tree and didn't get up for the whole day. When Ashia tried to bring her food, Lusa pushed it away and pawed at her stomach with a whine. She remembered exactly how her mother had acted when she was sick. Whimpering, she pressed her paws to her muzzle and closed her eyes.

Ashia and Stella hovered around her all day, trying to take care of her. Lusa felt bad about lying to them, but she remembered her promise to Oka. Ashia and Stella had each other, but if Toklo was still alive, he had no one.

That night she slept out in the open, even though the cold wind made her shiver and there were lots of strange noises from outside the walls. The sky was cloudy so she couldn't see the Bear Watcher, which made her anxious. Was he still watching her? Would he take care of her if she made it to the wild?

When she still hadn't eaten anything by the end of the next day, the other bears started to get worried. Yogi came over and nudged her.

"Get up, Lusa," he said. "I'm sorry I teased you. Come play on the Mountains with me."

"I don't feel well," Lusa mumbled. It was starting to be true; she was so hungry, she felt like her stomach was going to cave in and eat itself.

At long last, the door in the wall creaked open and a pair of flat-faces came through. They looked at Lusa carefully, probing her fur and shining a light in her ears. The feeder in green with the furry face came in behind them, and Lusa tensed. What if the stick put her to sleep and she never woke up again? She had to force herself not to jump up and run back to the Caves. She closed her eyes as the feeder got closer and closer. She thought about Oka and Toklo, and how much he needed her. She had to be brave.

There was a soft *pop*, and Lusa felt a sharp tickle in her side. She opened her eyes and saw her mother watching from the Mountains. Lusa lifted her paw in farewell, and then let it drop as a strange heaviness filled her body. Her eyes drifted shut again, and she tumbled into darkness.

Lusa dreamed she was floating down the Great Salmon River. Sparkling water flowed around her and through her fur, but she didn't feel wet. In the bubbles she caught glimpses of large silver blueberries flashing past, but when she tried to catch them, they slipped out of her paws. Although the river glittered with light, when she looked up she could see the night sky, full of more stars than she'd ever seen before.

In among the stars there were strange animals. Some of them Lusa recognized: a monkey, a flamingo, a tiger. Then there were ones she had never seen before—the long-necked skinny creature and the big one with the long dangly nose that her mother had described. They bobbed their heads at her and danced from side to side.

Lusa tried to move her paws, but they were too heavy. She started to panic. Lifting her muzzle to the stars, she called out for help . . . and then she saw the Bear Watcher. It was shining brightly right above her. The star beamed down at her, and Lusa gazed back. It seemed like it was getting bigger, as if it were coming closer and closer to her. Maybe she was dead, and it was coming to turn her into a tree.

Gradually Lusa realized that her eyes were open and she wasn't dreaming anymore. She was staring up at a warm yellow fire-globe dangling from the roof of a flat-face den. The floor under her was cold and hard, and she was inside a cage of metal bars. She pushed herself to her paws. She felt groggy and slow—her fur heavier than usual, her muscles floppy. She was alone, in a large den full of silvery, shiny things. She couldn't smell any flat-faces nearby. She couldn't see the sky, but something inside her told her that it was nighttime outside, which meant she had slept the entire day.

Lusa sniffed around the edges of the cage until she found the door, where there was a short piece of metal sticking out. Did this make the door open? She prodded at it with her paws, hooking her claws around it and waggling it. Then she tried sticking her nose through the bars and closing her teeth around the bit that stuck out. The cold metal smelled bad and it made her teeth hurt, but she felt something sliding loose. She poked it again with her paws.

There was a small *clang* and the door swung open. Lusa stared in astonishment. She was free!

She took a tentative step outside the cage. The shiny white

floor was smooth like water below her paws. Her paws dragged on the slippery floor and her legs felt heavy as stones, but she managed to stagger over to the tall door in the nearest wall. She had no idea how to get through it. She didn't want to wait for a flat-face to come along and open it. . . . She could try to run for it again, but the pain from the shocking stick was fresh in her mind.

Lusa looked around the room for something that might help her open the door. A fresh breeze drifted past her nostrils, carrying the scent of wild animals and burnt flat-face food. She stood on her hind legs, searching for the source of the smell, and spotted an opening high in the wall at the far end of the room. She slithered across the floor and heaved herself up on a shiny ledge the color of the buckets the feeders brought their food in. Her claws lost their grip on the slippery surface, and her back end slid off the ledge. She hung for a moment, scrabbling with her forepaws, and then, with a grunt, she dragged herself back on top once more.

As she cleared the edge, one of her back paws hit a stack of objects. They toppled to the floor with a crash that sounded like an entire forest falling over. More desperate now, Lusa shoved her head through the opening. It was a tight squeeze, but she managed to pull her shoulders and paws, and finally her rear end, through the small space. She felt herself falling through the air and wondered for a terrified moment what was below her. Then her paws hit the springy branches of a leafy bush, and she bounced off it and tumbled to the ground unharmed.

She scrambled to her paws and raced into the nearest patch

of shadows. She remembered her mother talking about the high Fence that surrounded all the animals' Fences. She also remembered Ashia telling her about how quietly black bears could move. Lusa dropped into the stealthy crouch her mother had shown her and crept through the shadows, watching where she placed her paws.

Excitement and fear tingled through her fur and her muzzle quivered. There were so many new smells out here! Not only that; now she could hear the grunts and snores of other animals coming from behind their Fences. She could also hear the distant noises of the flat-face world and smell a faraway scent of flowers. Her ears and her nose were more useful than her eyes in the dark, so she let her vision blur and concentrated on what she could hear and smell instead.

Two flat-faces were coming along the path. They were moving fairly quietly, for flat-faces, but Lusa's ears picked up the low murmur of their voices and the rhythmic beat of their pawsteps. She ducked behind a large metal den that smelled of rotten food. Some of the scents were tempting. . . . Her stomach was roaring with hunger. But this wasn't the time to go foraging.

The flat-faces walked by without seeing her. When they were out of sight, Lusa ran along the side of the gray path, keeping to the grass so her claws didn't tap on the hard stone, until she spotted the high Fence. Beyond it she could see the outline of flat-face dens, lit up by their fire-globes. A wide path stretched along the other side of the Fence, and more paths branched off from it, leading between the dens.

Glancing around, Lusa sniffed the air. With so many flat-face smells here, it took her a moment to be sure that none were close by or heading her way. She paced over to the fence, hooked her claws in the metal web, and began to climb.

As she pushed herself up, she thought of the bears she had left in the Bowl. She would probably never see them again—never roll around the Mountains with Yogi or pretend to stalk through the wild with Ashia or listen to one of Stella's stories. She wouldn't even hear Grumps roll around growling on his side of the Fence. Her heart thudded and her legs began to tremble, so that she had to tighten her grip on the Fence to keep herself from falling off. She was leaving her family, her best friends, everything she knew, for the sake of a promise made to a bear she had only just met.

Then she thought about Toklo, somewhere beyond the mountain and the three lakes and the dead forest that Oka had described. She imagined him wandering alone, convinced that his mother hated him. She thought of Oka's dying words, and she knew she would do everything she could to keep her promise.

She reached the top of the Fence just as the clouds parted, and when she looked up at the sky, there was the comforting shimmer of the Bear Watcher. Her family would never have a grand adventure like this—they would be surrounded by the same walls, the same trees, the same "mountains" for the rest of their lives. But she was going to see something amazing. She was going to discover the world.

Although she was afraid, the Bear Watcher was looking down on her. She was not alone.

CHAPTER TWENTY-ONE

Toklo

Toklo stopped to rest his paws, exhausted and panting. All the snow near the river had melted, and the sun beat down through his fur. Sometimes it was so strong, he had to find shelter under shady, low-hanging trees during the hottest part of the day.

Stepping into the river also helped cool him down, letting the water wash over his paws as he walked. Some days the river wound slowly through stands of tall trees, and then he would find it rushing wildly through a gorge with steep slopes of rock and sand rising up on either side. He had decided to follow the river to the far end of the valley, circling the mountain where he'd been chased off by the last bear. Toklo couldn't shake the feeling that Tobi's spirit was in the river, traveling alongside him. Tobi might be lonely if he took a different route. That would be just like his little brother, too feeble to enjoy his own company. Besides, rivers were shared territories—Toklo figured he couldn't get in too much trouble with other bears as long as he stayed near this one.

The river led into another valley, enclosed by steep snowy mountains. In the distance, Toklo could still see the bear snout mountain, higher than the other peaks, stretching up to sniff the clouds. The smell of roots and berries was stronger in this valley, and there were more bushes and wide stretches of grass instead of forest trees. Somewhere ahead of him there were unfamiliar smells and the sound of chattering—like birds, but lower pitched. Toklo climbed up to a bank of rocks and saw a BlackPath ahead of him, crossing over the river.

Down by the water, almost underneath the BlackPath, was a gathering of strange animals that Toklo had never seen before. They looked a bit like bears, standing on skinny hind legs and waving their paws around, but they were much smaller. Their pelts were not shaggy and black or brown, but smooth and multicolored—some of them were even the color of berries or flowers or leaves. Their muzzles were pale and smooth and strangely flat, and patches of fur grew on top of their heads.

Some of them were seated on things that looked like four-legged tree stumps, in front of flat wooden surfaces, also raised up on wooden legs. Many of the interesting smells were coming from the surfaces, where the creatures had spread out stacks of what must be food, because they were lifting it to their mouths with their paws and eating it. Toklo's mouth watered. He wondered if he could get some of the food away from them. He studied the creatures more closely. They looked small and soft, which meant they should be easy to fight—but so did skunks! He knew not to pick a fight with the little black-and-white animals because once he had, and the terrible scent had clung to his pelt for ages, making his eyes water and hiding the taste of anything he'd tried to eat.

Besides, these new creatures were very loud and there were a lot of them. He couldn't be sure what sort of hidden claws or fangs they might have. Even worse, they were being protected by a large firebeast. It was hunkered down on a patch of gravel by the BlackPath, staring at the creatures with its shiny round eyes. Its sides gleamed like the sky in the evening. Unusually, it wasn't growling or giving out belches of sour smoke. Toklo froze, hoping it hadn't caught his scent. It didn't move and after a long, long moment, Toklo figured that it was just sitting there.

That didn't mean he wanted to attract its attention. He climbed farther up the valley, staying away from the BlackPath. There weren't many firebeasts traveling along it, although he saw more of the smooth-pelted creatures playing along its edge, always with a firebeast crouched beside them.

That night, Toklo found a tree with large roots and dug a den under them, taking the time to make it sturdy and densely packed. This was made easier by the soft, moist earth in the valley, which he could sink his claws into as if it were water. He drifted off to sleep, wondering if he could make this place his territory. There was plenty of food, he hadn't seen any other bears, and the breeze was warm and gentle, stroking his fur like the feel of his mother's tongue.

Bang! Bang! Bang!

Toklo scrambled to his paws, his ears ringing. Outside his

den, the thin gray light of dawn was seeping through the trees along with a light mist.

Then the noises started again—sharp popping sounds so loud they echoed around the valley. When he sniffed the air, all Toklo smelled was the bitter, heavy scent of smoke and metal. Smooth-pelts were shouting from a distance, like their chatter yesterday but harsher and louder. Toklo crouched at the back of his den, pressing himself into the earth and squeezing his eyes shut. The popping noises went on and on, and once he heard dogs barking in the distance. He'd seen a few dogs running through the forest when he was a cub, but his mother had always hurried him and Tobi in the other direction, so he didn't know much about them, just that they were like wolves with snappier voices.

Around sunhigh, Toklo crawled to the mouth of his den and clawed some of the blackberries from the bush outside. But he couldn't bring himself to eat them. There was a tension in the air that made his belly clench, and he felt as if he was in danger without knowing exactly why.

Night came, and the noises stopped. It took Toklo until moonhigh to fall asleep. He dreamed that he was the lonely star in the sky again, but this time he was being chased by the other animals, who made loud popping sounds and breathed smoke out of their mouths.

When he woke up the next morning, his heart was still pounding. He couldn't take another day of those noises, and clearly there was something dangerous about this place that kept other brown bears away. He should have known it was too good to be true. He scrambled out of his den, tasting the early morning air. The hills were silent and the breeze was chilly and damp. He was too scared to search for food; he wanted to get out of here as quickly as he could.

The sight of the bear snout mountain in the distance made him pause at the edge of the trees. Maybe he should try going that way, climb the mountain, and explore the valley on the other side. He padded down toward the river. The sun was peeking over the horizon, sending glittering shafts of light across the snowy peaks, but Toklo wasn't comforted by the warmth on his fur. He kept his head down, miserably listening to the growling of his empty stomach.

A scream shattered the quiet, and Toklo's head jerked up. "Help! No!"

There were raised smooth-pelts voices as well, harsh and angry-sounding. Toklo crouched lower to the ground. Maybe he could hide until they went away. He crept quietly over the leaves until he found a fat bush with a hollow in the center, which he climbed into.

But the voices were coming closer, and a moment later Toklo saw a brown bear cub racing toward him. Behind him were four smooth-pelts, some of them red like berries, others in a glowing orange brighter than any flower Toklo had seen. The cub skidded to a stop beside Toklo's bush and spun around, trapped. Two of the smooth-pelts came closer and jabbed at it with long black sticks.

"Stop it!" the cub howled.

One of the smooth-pelts picked up a stone and flung it at

the cub. It flew past him and into the bush, smacking Toklo in the shoulder. Toklo let out a yelp of pain.

Instantly all of the smooth-pelts pointed their sticks at the bush, barking gruffly at one another. Now that they knew he was there, he had no choice but to run. Toklo sprang out of the bush, almost knocking the other cub off his paws.

"Come on! Run!" he yelled, racing up the slope deeper into the woods. The cub followed. There was a huge *bang* and the cub squealed. Toklo glanced back and saw smoke bloom from one of the sticks.

Bang! Bang! The sound of the metal stick rattled the branches around them. Something really bad was happening. Toklo's paws pounded on rocks and twigs as they swerved around bushes and leaped over fallen logs. Dogs began barking behind them, and Toklo could hear the smooth-pelts shouting as they crashed through the trees.

There was another *pop-bang* sound, and the cub beside him let out a howl of pain and tumbled to the ground. Blood spurted from his shoulder.

"Get up!" Toklo cried. He shoved the cub back onto his paws and they ran on, as fast as the wounded cub could manage. Toklo watched his blood splattering the leaves on the ground and listened to the sound of the smooth-pelts not far behind them.

He tried to think. The trail of blood would lead the dogs right to them, if their own scent wasn't enough to do that already.

"Over here!" he bellowed, veering to the right. There was a

stream this way, branching off the main river and heading for
the base of the mountains where the meadows gave way to
pebbly ravines. Toklo perked up his ears, hearing the rush of
water ahead of him. Suddenly the trees fell away on either
side and they were at the top of a rocky slope, with the stream
sparkling at the bottom. They raced down, scrambling over
the boulders; Toklo winced as one of his claws was wrenched
back by a sharp stone. There was no time to lick the pain away.
They had to get across the stream to hide their scent.

Toklo saw the cub hesitate, so he ran over and shoved him
into the shallow water. "Come *on!*" he growled.

They headed up the stream through the water. The pebbles
rolled under Toklo's paws, making it hard to run, and the current tugged at his fur, slowing down both him and the cub.
Toklo hoped staying in the water would be enough to throw
the dogs off the scent trail; if they guessed which direction the
bears had gone, it wouldn't take long for them to catch up.

He heard the dogs behind them, baying angrily, but the
sound was fading. Good, they must have lost the scent. Toklo
kept running until the sound faded away, and then scrambled
out of the stream, shaking the water from his pelt. They were
at the bottom of a ravine with steep rocky sides. The
wounded cub was breathing heavily, his head hanging low, and
his shoulder was bleeding even more. Toklo knew he couldn't
run another pawstep.

He looked around until he spotted a dark hole halfway up
one side of the ravine. A faint trail of smaller stones led up to
it. Toklo nudged the cub onto the path, and kept pushing him

with his nose until the cub had stumbled and clawed his way up to a ledge outside the small cave. The hole was just big enough for two bears to lie down comfortably, with a flat, sandy floor.

The cub staggered inside and dropped to the floor, his sides heaving. Toklo stayed at the entrance, listening. There was no sound of the smooth-pelts or their metal sticks or the dogs. They were safe, for now. Although he wouldn't have been in danger to start with, if the cub hadn't run into his bush. Toklo rounded on the wounded bear.

"What were you thinking?" he demanded. "Don't you know to stay away from smooth-pelts? Couldn't you smell them coming?"

The cub buried his nose under his paws and didn't answer.

"What's the matter?" Toklo asked. "Did they hit your tongue with their metal sticks, too?"

The cub curled up on his side, his eyes tightly shut.

"Fine," Toklo muttered, stomping out of the cave. "Yes, I know I nearly lost my fur rescuing you. No problem. You're welcome."

He scrambled up to the top of the cliff, where prickly bushes and yellow dandelions grew between the boulders. Toklo sniffed around for roots, his belly roaring hungrily. The sun still hadn't reached the middle of the sky yet; if he ate something to keep up his strength, he might be able to make it to the bear snout mountain by nightfall.

A whiff of rabbit scent drifted past his nose. Toklo paused, tracking it, and then crept across to a tangle of dead branches that might once have been a leafy bush. Just as he got within paw's reach, a flash of brown fur darted out from underneath, and Toklo pounced.

Yes! His claws sank into flesh, and he bit down hard, shaking the rabbit until he was sure it was dead. He tore off a mouthful of meat and gulped it down.

A vision of the skinny cub came to his mind, curled up and bleeding on the cave floor.

"I don't owe him anything," Toklo told himself. "He nearly got me killed."

But there was something about him that reminded Toklo of Tobi, weak and exhausted and starving . . . and this time Toklo had real food he could share.

With a sigh, he picked up the rabbit with his teeth and stamped back to the edge of the cliff. The warm prey bounced against his paws as he eased himself down the rocky path to the cave.

"I found some prey," he announced, dropping the rabbit next to the cub.

The bear rolled over, turning his back to Toklo, and said nothing.

"Well, fine," Toklo growled. "I'll eat it all myself then." What was *wrong* with this cub? At least Tobi could talk.

Toklo took a large bite out of the rabbit, determined to eat the whole thing. But then he looked up at the shape of the cub's ribs, sticking through his thin fur, and with a growl, Toklo shoved the rest of the rabbit toward him. "I'll just leave it there," he muttered.

He was too exhausted to go any farther that day. His paws hurt from running across the rocks, and he still felt cold and wet from wading in the stream. He didn't want to go searching for another shelter, either. This cave was not very large, but it was out of the wind, and it didn't smell of other bears. Hoping the cub wouldn't wake up and claw out his eyes, Toklo curled up with his back pressed to the cub's bony spine. The touch of his fur reminded him of his brother, and a wave of sadness washed over him again as he lay there. *Stupid Tobi,* Toklo sighed, pushing the thought away. After a long while, he fell asleep.

It was dark outside when Toklo drifted awake. The heavy bulk of the other cub was no longer pressed against his back. Toklo opened his eyes and rolled over to see where he had gone.

Crouched on the floor of the cave, staring at Toklo with round dark eyes, was a young smooth-pelt. The brown bear cub was nowhere to be seen.

Toklo leaped to his paws. "Where is he?" he roared furiously. "What did you do with the cub?"

The smooth-pelt flinched away, clutching his left shoulder. His light brown skin was stained with blood from a small round wound. The smooth-pelt held out his paw—a tiny, hairless thing with no claws.

"Peace," the smooth-pelt said in bear language. "I am your friend."

CHAPTER TWENTY-TWO

Kallik

Purnaq followed the tracks of the white firebeast for a whole day, barely stopping to eat or drink. Kallik's paws ached but she was determined to keep up, staying far enough back that he didn't notice her. The full moon was floating high in a cloudless sky by the time Purnaq found a dip in the ground and curled up to sleep. Kallik dragged herself over to a leafless bush and dropped to the dirt. She hoped Purnaq wouldn't double back and catch her following him. She was too exhausted to run away if he did.

She awoke at dawn, as silvery pink clouds trailed across the sky. When she scrambled out from behind the bush, she realized with a stab of despair that she couldn't see Purnaq anymore. The hollow where he'd gone to sleep was empty. Kallik wondered if he had scented her and deliberately moved on early so he could lose her.

There were no other bears in sight, either, and panic gripped her as she spun around, searching the empty horizon. How would she find the place with food—the place where Taqqiq might be going—if she couldn't follow another bear? She padded over to the hollow where Purnaq had been sleeping and sniffed around, searching for his scent. She caught a hint of it heading up the hill, away from the sea. The hollow felt warm, as if he hadn't been gone for long. Maybe she could still catch up.

She raced up the hill, bracken crackling beneath her paws. At the top she stopped short with a gasp. Stretching out before her was a gathering of no-claw dens like the ones she'd seen before, but many, many more of them. They glowed with eerie yellow lights like tiny suns, and there were puffs of smoke drifting into the air from some of the roofs. It was quiet, but she could see gleaming firebeasts crouched outside several of the dens.

It was terrifying to think how close she was to the no-claws and their sticks that could hurt from a long way away, but she was transfixed by the smell of food coming from the dens. Hot food, *meat* . . . Kallik couldn't remember the last time she'd eaten anything but grass. Her head was swimming, and she could barely stay upright on her paws. Even the faintest scent of real food made her belly feel as if it were caving in like a loose snowbank.

She padded forward, keeping watch for any other bears. As she reached the edge of the no-claw place and stepped onto one of the stone paths, she heard a clatter of loud popping noises. Death sticks!

Kallik froze, squeezing her eyes shut. Her heart pounded as she waited for the biting pain. "Mother," she whispered.

"Spirits of the ice, please save me." A moment passed, and then another, and she realized that she was still alive and unhurt. To be certain, she sniffed herself all over, but there was no trace of any blood.

She looked around but couldn't see any no-claws. Curious, she backed up a few steps, and the noises went off again, making her jump. But nothing happened to hurt her; as far as she could tell, it was nothing but noise. She wondered why the no-claws would want bangs going off every time they came close to their dens. Perhaps they liked loud noise—maybe that was why they traveled with the roaring firebeasts. Or perhaps they were trying to scare away other animals.

Well, it's not going to work on me! she thought. She was too hungry to go back, no matter how loud the noise was.

She padded along one of the stone paths, the unfamiliar surface scraping her paws. A clatter came from one of the dens, making her jump, and she scrambled over to the side of the path to hide under a bush. She watched as a no-claw emerged from the den and climbed inside the firebeast crouched beside it. With a growl, the firebeast woke up, backed away from the den, turned, and sped off along the stone path.

Kallik realized that other firebeasts were waking up nearby. She could smell no-claws moving about outside their dens. She could also smell the same wolflike animals she'd seen with the no-claws before, and some of them were barking and howling as if they could smell her, too.

Kallik crept along in the shadow of the bushes beside the path until she found a smaller stone path that went off to the left. She followed this to a stone clearing behind a flat-face den. A few firebeasts were squatting here, but they all seemed to be asleep. Next to the large den were three enormous containers, each twice her height, overflowing with rotting food and bits of discarded flat-face things. Kallik squeezed between them and the wall of the den. There was just enough space for her, and it was dark and well hidden from sight. The smells from the containers were driving her mad with hunger, but her terror won out, and she crouched lower, hoping the smell would help to hide her scent from the firebeasts.

She crouched there all day, dozing uneasily but snapping awake every time there was a noise outside. Twice she heard no-claws come out of the den and throw things into the containers, making clanging sounds that hurt her ears. Firebeasts growled in and out of the clearing, squatting there while their no-claws went into the den and came out carrying strange-smelling things.

Kallik dreamed of plump seals crunching between her teeth, chewy fat sliding down her throat. She reached for another mouthful, but the seal was sliding away across the ice, and when she reached out for it, her nose hit cold metal and she woke up. The air was full of the smell of food—hot sizzling fat from somewhere close by. Kallik's head swam and her belly growled. She had to find that smell.

She squeezed out from behind the containers and tracked the scent, using her nose the way her mother had taught her. She followed it along the walls of the dens, staying in the shadows. It was difficult because there were bright sun-globes everywhere, many of them growing on the top of tall, leafless trees that lined the stone paths.

When Kallik reached the den where the scent was coming from, she smelled something else: another bear. She hid behind a container like the others until she could see the approaching bear. It was a female, starving and thin with a mud-splattered pelt. Kallik watched her nose through the entrance of a den and wander inside. She must have been tracking the same scent. Quickly Kallik followed. This was *her* prey!

She poked her nose inside the open door and discovered a narrow space that smelled overpoweringly of food. The she-bear was at the other end of the room, standing on her hind legs and roaring at a no-claw. The no-claw screamed and threw something at the bear that clattered on the floor. Other no-claws came rushing in, all of them shouting.

Kallik glanced around, her stomach roaring so loud it filled her ears. On a ledge just above her head, there was a large hunk of blood-red meat. *Yes!* She stood up on her back paws and fastened her teeth in it, dragging it down to the floor. She tore into it, ripping strips off and gulping them down. Nothing mattered but the meat, precious food, rich and warm and filling her belly. . . .

A bang split the air and the other bear slumped to the ground. Kallik saw blood spilling across the floor and trickling between her claws. It felt warm and sticky, and she suddenly remembered pink water washing over the ice, staining her fur. She looked up and saw a no-claw standing a bearlength away.

He was pointing a death stick right at her.

CHAPTER TWENTY-THREE

Lusa

Lusa dropped to the ground below the fence, feeling the hard surface of the flat-face path below her paws. She sniffed the air for a moment, wondering which way to go.

A low rumbling trembled through the ground and she twitched her ears, trying to identify the noise. It got louder and louder, and suddenly a pair of enormous bright eyes blasted out of the darkness and roared past her, belching smoke and fumes. Lusa leaped backward and rolled into the fence, covering her muzzle with her paws. She lay there, quivering, wondering if the terrible beast was going to come back and eat her. As her heartbeat slowly returned to normal, she realized that it must have been a firebeast—a larger, louder version of the ones the feeders rode around in to visit the animals.

Were the firebeasts everywhere in the wild? She didn't want to make any of them angry. She didn't want to see what they would do to her in a fight.

She ran across the path to a patch of grass outside one of the flat-face dens. The soft green tickle under her paws made her feel a little better, so she took a moment to stop and study her surroundings. Bright fire-globes stood all along the flat-face path, casting wide circles of light that drove the shadows into the corners. If she stayed on the path, she'd surely be spotted by a flat-face. She wasn't afraid of them—she knew that flat-faces liked her and might give her food if she danced for them. But she worried that if the feeders found her, they would shoot her with the stick that made her sleep, and then they'd take her back to the Bear Bowl. It would be very diffi-cult to escape the same way again. The feeders would be watching her too closely. She had to make it work this time.

There was a side path that looked darker than the main one, so Lusa padded down it, staying close to the fences and keeping her paws on grass as much as possible. She made it past several dens when she heard flat-face voices coming toward her. Lusa spun around. Next to her was a wooden fence about twice her height. She scrambled over it and dropped onto grass on the other side. The fence made a square, like the walls of the den in the Bear Bowl. Lusa raced across the grass and swung herself over the fence on the other side.

She was in another enclosure! Lusa began to despair. Was there nothing out here but fences and enclosures, like one Bear Bowl after another?

A wild screech came from behind her, making her jump. She turned and saw a small animal crouched beside the door of the flat-face den. The animal's back was arched, its long tail was standing up straight, and its orange fur was sticking out all over. It hissed at her and screeched again, showing a row of tiny sharp teeth.

Lusa was puzzled but amused. The creature was barely a quarter of her size. She could easily knock it over, if she wanted to. But she admired its bravery. Lusa backed away and climbed over the next fence.

She found herself in yet another enclosure. There was another animal here, but different, with a loud, fearsome bark. This one was much closer to Lusa's size. It charged at her with its slavering jaws wide open; Lusa stood rooted to the spot, transfixed by the gleaming teeth and lolling pink tongue. But when it got to a bearlength from her, it jerked to a sudden stop, falling back with a yelp.

A long chain stretched tautly behind it, holding the creature back. It strained at the end of the chain, flailing its paws toward her and barking furiously.

Lusa rose onto her hind legs and huffed. "Don't mess with me!" she snarled, although she knew it couldn't understand what she was saying.

To her surprise, the animal fell quiet and dropped to the ground, laying its ears flat. Lusa stalked past him . . . but made sure she stayed out of the chain's reach.

The next fence led to a tiny lake in the middle of a grassy enclosure. Lusa padded up to it. Could this be one of the lakes Oka had mentioned? It was smaller than Lusa had imagined. As she got closer, she saw that the floor of the lake was not

dirt; it was hard white stone like the floor of her den in the
Bear Bowl.

Lusa ducked her head to the water and sniffed, wondering
if it was safe to drink. It had a sharp smell, but she reached out
her tongue and lapped it cautiously.

Yuck! Lusa spat and wiped her tongue with her paws. This
didn't taste like real water at all. It couldn't be the lake Oka
had talked about. Besides, there weren't two others next to it.
She climbed over the next fence and at last found herself back
in a dark open space, with a path running along in front of
her. She paused, taking a deep breath, and looked up to search
for the Bear Watcher again.

There, outlined against the orange sky, was a mountain! It
looked like a bear's snout, just as Oka had described. And it
was huge! It had to be at least ten or twelve times the size of
the boulders in the Bear Bowl! Surely she'd be able to get to it
very quickly—it was so large, it must be close by. The Bear
Watcher star was gleaming right over the mountain, as if it
was waiting for her.

Lusa ran all night long, darting into the shadows whenever
flat-faces or firebeasts went by. But as the sun started to come
up, she didn't seem to be any closer to the mountain than she
had been when she started. She was too tired to keep walking,
and flat-faces could see her more easily now that it was daylight. She needed to find a place to sleep. She padded along the
path until she found a fence with more greenery growing over
the top of it than the others had. Where there were bushes
and trees, there might be a place to hide. Shoving herself up

with her back claws, she scrambled over the fence and dropped down into an enclosure that was full of bushes and vines in a tangle of branches and leaves.

Keeping her ears pricked for flat-face noises, Lusa padded through the web of vines to the end of the enclosure farthest from the flat-face den. Here she found a place where three thick bushes grew close together, concealing a hollow space underneath. She crouched low on her belly and crept into the space, curling her paws around to fit and digging away some of the dirt to make it more comfortable.

Once she was safely hidden, exhaustion finally hit her. Lusa rested her muzzle on her paws and, within moments, she was fast asleep.

The sound of her stomach growling woke her up shortly after dark. She had never been this hungry before; it was as if someone had scooped out her insides with a giant paw. Lusa scrambled up and poked her nose outside, sniffing for danger. As far as she could tell, there were no flat-faces or strange animals around. But she did smell something else . . . something very tempting.

She followed her nose through the tangled vines to the side of the flat-face den. The scent was coming from two large cans next to the wall, a bit like the ones the feeders brought her food in. Lusa crept up to them on silent paws.

She rested her forepaws on the edge of one of the cans, poking her muzzle inside. A wave of delicious, peculiar, startling scents hit her nose. Lusa nosed through crinkly things, sharp things, and fluffy things until she found a mouthful of meat. It tasted a little sour, but it was better than nothing. She also found some rotten bits of banana and scraps of bread farther down, where she had to lean in to dig them out.

As she dug her paws into the can it tipped over with a crash, scattering its contents everywhere. Lusa looked up and saw a light come on outside the den. A flat-face roar sounded from inside. It didn't sound like a friendly roar, from an animal that would appreciate her taking food from its cans.

Lusa raced to the fence, hauled herself over, and ran down the road. She didn't stop running until the overgrown place was far, far behind her.

When she finally slowed down, she noticed that nearly every flat-face den along the paths had the same big silver cans stacked outside. She padded past them, sniffing, until she found a den with no firebeasts crouched beside it. Cautiously she snuck up to the cans and stood up on her hind legs, sticking her nose inside. A thin white skin surrounded the contents, but she was able to slice through it with her claws, spilling more crinkly, shiny, crumpled things out into the can. She leaned in, resting her weight on the edge of the can, and it toppled over, clattering deafeningly on the path.

Lusa sprang back in dismay. Beside her was a small tree, and although it wasn't as tall as the Bear Bowl trees, it was still a place to hide. She scrambled up and clung to a top branch, waiting.

Nothing happened. No flat-faces came out to yell at her. After waiting a long time, Lusa snuck back down and started pawing through the mess that had fallen out of the tipped-over can. Some of the things she thought were food were horrible. She bit down on one black lump and spat it out again immediately, wiping her tongue with disgust. But another smell caught her attention, and she dug farther until she found some short sticks of potato that were covered in salt and tasted like fat. She gobbled them up and licked her paws clean afterward. She thought they might be the most delicious thing she'd ever eaten.

The next morning she hid in a small wooded area where leafy bushes concealed her from the flat-face cubs that raced around playing during the day. When she continued walking the next night, she kept the bear snout mountain in sight and headed toward it as much as she could, although she often had to veer around large flat-face dens to avoid bright lights or the sound of the barking and screeching animals. If this was living in the wild, she couldn't understand why King had been so worried or grumpy about talking about it. It was easy! She had food and places to shelter, and she knew which way to go.

On the third night, when she awoke, clouds were hanging low over everything, shrouding the world in fog. She couldn't see the stars or the mountain anymore—she could barely see her paws in front of her. The air hung heavily around her, clinging to her fur and leaving damp droplets on her muzzle. Lusa was too nervous to go on without the sight of the Bear Watcher or the mountain in front of her, so she dug herself deeper into the hollow under the tree roots and waited, restless and hungry, for the sky to clear.

The fog continued all night, in the morning shifting to rain that left Lusa dripping, cold, and unhappy. But finally it cleared, and she stuck her nose out into a damp mist shortly before sunset. Ahead of her, the bulk of the mountain loomed against the darknening sky. She padded toward it until she came to the edge of a large flat-face path, wider than any of the ones she had crossed before. It smelled strongly of the firebeasts, and even as she was standing there, one of them roared past.

Lusa shivered. This path was clearly their territory. She paced back and forth, sniffing the air and scratching at the dirt below her paws. She needed to keep going toward the mountain, but in order to do that she'd have to cross the fire-beasts' path. Finally she decided to travel along the path and hope she found a safe place to cross farther up.

She padded along in the shadows, ducking into the bushes whenever a firebeast went by. There were a lot of them at first, but as the night wore on, she saw fewer and fewer.

It was close to moonhigh and the low clouds were starting to break up like shredded spiderwebs when Lusa smelled something that might be food. She hadn't eaten yet that night because the flat-face dens along this stretch of path were too brightly lit and full of noise, and she was afraid to approach them. But this smell was coming from somewhere close by. She stood on her hind legs and took a long sniff.

It was coming from the path! She dropped to all fours and walked a little farther, until she spotted something on the ground in the center of the path. From the scent, she guessed that it was the salty potato sticks she'd tasted before.

Did she dare step onto the path? She hadn't seen a fire-beast in a long time. Perhaps they had all gone somewhere to sleep.

Lusa stepped tentatively onto the path. She waited, her whole body tensed, but she couldn't feel the rumbling of an approaching firebeast. The air was silent, with the faintest breeze drifting through the light fog. She took another paw-step, and then another, and soon she was racing across the path to the discarded food. To her delight, it was a crumpled carton of the potato sticks with several left at the bottom. She pinned it down with her paw and stuck her muzzle into the carton as far as it would go, licking up the salt with her long tongue.

BWAAAAAAAAAAAAAAAAAAAAAAAAAAAMP!

A large firebeast was hurtling toward her, its eyes blazing with fury.

Lusa bolted to the other side of the path just as the fire-beast hurtled by. As she leaped onto the grass at the edge, she felt a sharp pain stab into her paw. Whimpering, she crept under some bushes and sat down, lifting up her forepaws to see what was hurting her. One of her paws had something sharp and glittery sticking out of it, and blood was trickling from the wound. Lusa blinked, feeling ill and anxious. It wasn't a thorn, but it felt sharp like that. It looked like the clear, shiny stuff she had seen in the flat-face dens. And it *hurt*.

She crouched there for a moment, staring at her paw and wondering what to do. What would King do? Or Oka?

They would be brave. They would fix themselves and keep going.

She put her teeth around the sharp object and tugged it free from her paw. As it came loose, a gush of blood followed it, and Lusa felt dizzy. She shook her head, gritting her teeth, and began to lick her paw. To her relief, the flow of blood slowed and then stopped, and her paw felt a little better. But when she tried to stand on it, the pain sliced through her again. She would have to find somewhere safe to hide until it had a chance to heal.

The mist clung to her fur as she limped out of the bush, heading for an open grassy space not far from the firebeast path. It wasn't as sheltered as some of the enclosures she had been in, but the grass was very tall—almost as tall as her—and there were three trees growing close together at the far end, near a fence. Lusa curled up in the roots of one of the trees and went back to licking her paw.

She stayed there for three days, until she could walk again. During the day she could hear the firebeasts roaring and racing past. She wondered if she had made them angry by stealing food from their territory. She hoped they wouldn't come off the path to look for her.

Luckily there didn't seem to be many flat-faces in the area. She did see several of the furry screeching animals stalking through the grass, but they could smell her there, and they stayed well clear of her hiding place. She felt weak from hunger and pain. *Everything is going wrong!* How would she ever make it to the bear snout mountain, let alone find Toklo once she got there? At least she could still see the Bear Watcher from her hiding spot. It was comforting to know the star was still watching her.

On the night Lusa was ready to resume traveling, the sky was covered in clouds and she couldn't see any stars at all. She sat up, pointing her nose at the spot where she was sure the Bear Watcher should be. She couldn't see it—but somehow she knew she was looking in the right place. It was like a tug in her fur, nudging her that way. Just then, the clouds drifted apart and for a heartbeat, the Bear Watcher beamed down from the dark blue sky. It vanished again almost at once, but that was enough for Lusa. As long as she knew where the star should be, she wouldn't get lost!

She climbed to her paws, gingerly testing her sore paw. It still ached when she leaned on it, but she took a few steps and decided that she could walk, at least a little way. Now that she had her sense of where the Bear Watcher was, she wanted to keep going. She climbed over the fence and headed toward the mountain and the star again. She'd been walking for a short while when a light rain started to fall, filling the air with a clean, fresh scent.

There were fewer flat-face dens in this direction. The ones she saw were surrounded by wide expanses of grass, and there were short stretches of woodland in between them. The growling murmur of the firebeasts faded the farther she walked. She liked the quiet, but it also made her a little nervous. She wasn't sure how she was going to find food once she left the flat-face dens behind.

The rain lifted close to dawn, and Lusa sneezed, shaking her soaked fur. Everything around her smelled green and alive, and for once there were lots of places where she could hide. But first she wanted to find something to eat. The last meal she'd had was the potato sticks in the firebeasts' territory three days earlier, and she was beginning to stumble with weariness and hunger.

She trotted warily over to the nearest flat-face den. In the pink and gray early-morning light, it looked quiet and closed up. Not a sound came from inside, and she couldn't see any lights shining through the windows. A high wooden fence ran along the back and sides of the grassy enclosure, with tall trees just beyond it.

Lusa sniffed around to the back of the den, where she found one of the silver cans. This one had a lid tightly stuck on it. She dug her claws under the rim and shoved at it with her front paws. The can tipped over easily, knocking off the lid. The clatter was fairly loud, but still nothing seemed to move inside the den. Maybe the flat-faces were out hunting for prey. She stuck her muzzle inside the can and scrabbled out a small skin stuffed with things. She ripped open the skin and spread the contents out around her, sniffing each one.

Something rattled behind her, and Lusa spun around. Standing on the back steps of the den was a male flat-face cub. He looked like the flat-face cubs who had often visited her at the Bear Bowl. Perhaps if she danced for him, he would throw her fruit, like her feeders used to. Her mouth watered at the thought of blueberries. Feeling hopeful, Lusa stood up onto her hind legs and batted at the air with her forepaws.

The flat-face cub screamed.

Startled, Lusa fell over backward. Her ears were still ringing as she scrambled back to her feet. The door of the den
slammed open and a large male flat-face stormed out, shouting and waving his paws. In one of them he held a long metal
stick. As he swung it around to point it at her, Lusa realized
that it looked like the ones the furry feeder had used to send
her and her mother to sleep.

She turned and raced for the nearest fence. She didn't want
to be sent to sleep! With a huge leap, she sank her claws into
the wood and scrambled up to the top. Just as she was hauling
herself over, a bang went off behind her, and the edge of the
fence near her exploded into splinters.

Lusa lost her balance and tumbled onto the other side,
knocking the wind out of herself as she landed. Painfully, she
climbed upright again and limped into the woods. She wasn't
sure what had just happened—but she suspected that if the
metal stick had hit her instead of the fence, *she* might have
been the one exploding into bits.

She found a hollow between two trees and crawled into it,
shivering. Part of her wanted to stay in there forever. This
wasn't how her journey was meant to be! Maybe King was
right, and she should have stayed in the Bear Bowl. The other
part of her knew she should keep moving as soon as it was
dark again. She needed to get to the forest and the mountain.
Once she was truly in the wild, away from the flat-faces, she
knew there would still be dangers . . . but she couldn't believe

they would be as scary as what she'd faced so far.

Lusa slept all day, and when night fell, she had to force her-self to leave the hollow. Another flat-face den was only a few bearlengths away through the trees, but she didn't want to risk another attack from a spitting stick. She would get to the forest, and then she would start looking for food again.

She wove through the trees until she came to a path, where she stopped and looked up at the night sky. Her breath caught in her throat. There were so many stars! She'd never known there were so many up there—the orange glow of lights around the Bear Bowl and among the flat-face dens must have hidden them. But out here, where there was much more darkness, she could see all the tiny stars glittering clearly in the pure black sky.

"*Thousands* of stars," she breathed.

Now she could see the stars from Stella's stories. She could see the little black bear that had the Bear Watcher in her tail, and the big brown bear that chased her around the sky. That little bear had to be brave, and so did she.

Lusa padded along, keeping her eyes on the dark shape of the mountain ahead of her. She ran across patches of short grass, through stands of trees, behind quiet flat-face dens. She walked all night. And then, at last, just as the sun was sending trickles of pale gold sneaking over the horizon, Lusa crossed one final stone path and looked up to see the slope of the mountain rising above her.

Ahead of her stretched a forest for as far as she could see, touching the ends of the sky and climbing up the mountain.

The trees were vast, gigantic—so much bigger than the spindly trees in the Bear Bowl. Lusa could believe that this was where bear spirits came when they died. Already she thought she could hear their whispers in the soft breeze that rustled the leaves.

She stood at the edge of the forest and looked up into the branches.

"It's me, Lusa," she whispered to the tree spirits. "I'm here."

CHAPTER TWENTY-FOUR

Toklo

Toklo stared at the smooth-pelt cub. It could speak his language!

"Please help me," the young smooth-pelt said. "I won't hurt you." The cave echoed with his growls, which sounded very strange coming from a smooth-pelt muzzle.

"What do you want?" Toklo growled. "Where is the cub?"

"I am the cub," the stranger said, pressing his paw to the wound in his shoulder. "I—I changed during the night. Please, I need you to get me an herb for this." Toklo saw that the smooth-pelt's paws were trembling and his face was very pale. His breathing was ragged and his voice kept faltering, as if he was using all his energy to talk.

"An herb?" Toklo echoed. "Why do you want an herb?" He didn't believe this butterfly-brained story about the cub turning into a smooth-pelt. But they did have the same wound, which was odd.

"The juice of the leaves will make my shoulder better. It's a tall plant with bright yellow flowers," the smooth-pelt grunted. "The leaves are long and dark and—and pointed at the ends. Please." A ripple of pain crossed his face. "If you don't get them, I'll die."

Toklo backed out of the cave. He hadn't decided yet whether to come back with the herb, but he didn't like the sickly smell coming from the smooth-pelt. It reminded him of Tobi, and he didn't want to watch another creature die, even if it was only a smooth-pelt cub. Perhaps he would bring the herb and then get as far away as he could.

As he padded up the ravine, he kept an eye out for the grizzly cub. It must have snuck out of the cave while he was asleep. He was surprised not to find any pawprints or traces of the smaller cub's scent. How had it gotten away?

In the meadow at the top, Toklo hesitated behind a pile of boulders, sniffing the air, before emerging into the field. There was no trace of the smooth-pelts or their popping sticks in the air. Only the buzzing of flying insects and the far-away hum of firebeasts reached his ears as he stepped into the long grass. He followed his nose to the main river; not far from it there was a clump of the plants that the smooth-pelt had described. Toklo bit a couple of them off at the stem, resisting the urge to stay and dig up some roots to eat. *Maybe if the flat-face keeps annoying me, I'll eat him,* Toklo thought. Did grizzlies eat smooth-pelts? He didn't think so—his mother had never mentioned them, and she would have if they were food.

He dragged the plants back to the ravine and held them carefully in his mouth as he climbed down to the cave. They tasted bitter, and he tried not to swallow any of the juice. Inside, the smooth-pelt was curled up, his ribs lifting with quick, shallow breaths, his eyes closed. Maybe he was right about dying.

Toklo dropped the plants beside him. "Is this what you want?"

The smooth-pelt opened his eyes and nodded. He picked up one of the plants in his tiny, clawless paws and started ripping apart the leaves. Toklo realized that the smooth-pelt's paws split into five bits at the ends, each of which the cub could move separately from the others. Toklo looked down at his heavy, flat paw, tipped with long straight claws. He thought it was more useful to be able to dig up roots and slice open the skin of your prey than it was to pick up small things.

"What's your name?" the smooth-pelt asked, pressing the leaves together.

"Toklo."

"I'm Ujurak," the smooth-pelt said. He put the crushed leaves in his mouth and chewed them into a green paste, which he spat out and spread over his wound. Toklo wrinkled his nose.

Ujurak held out his paw, with some of the paste still in it. "Your muzzle is hurt," he said. "Put this on it."

"No!" Toklo said. "I don't need your help."

"Trust me, it'll heal faster," the smooth-pelt said. He leaned forward so quickly, Toklo didn't have time to move. Before he knew it, Ujurak was spreading green paste over the cut on his nose.

He felt a cool tingling under his skin, and the pain faded away. Toklo stopped squirming and sat still, letting Ujurak apply the rest of the paste. After he was finished, Ujurak lay back against the wall. He closed his eyes, and his breathing slowed until Toklo realized that he was asleep.

Time to go. Ujurak wasn't dying anymore. Toklo could go on his way without worrying about this smooth-pelt cub or even thinking about him again. Quietly, so as not to wake him, he backed out of the cave and padded up the side of the ravine again. He set off across the meadow, working his way back to the river. He could feed himself now and get rid of the taste of that herb.

Standing in the river with the silvery shadows flickering between his paws, Toklo watched and waited. There! A flash of movement slithered through his paws. Toklo remembered not to leap too quickly. He saw the path the fish was taking— he aimed for the spot where it *would* be, not where it was—and then he sprang, trusting his paws to guide him.

His claws sank into flesh. He ducked his head below the water and fastened his teeth around a gleaming, flailing bundle of scales. Triumphantly he lifted his muzzle out and shook the fish as hard as he could, stunning it into stillness.

He'd caught a salmon!

Toklo splashed over to the riverbank and dropped the fish on the pebbly shore. He pinned it down with one paw and ripped off a chunk with his teeth. The taste was startlingly delicious. It tasted even better than the salmon he'd stolen a few days earlier.

Suddenly he pricked his ears. Something was coming through the bushes. Toklo hunched his back and growled, ready to protect his prey. Branches snapped as a grizzly bear cub blundered out of the bushes. It was the cub he had rescued yesterday.

"You!" Toklo said.

"Yes," said the cub. "Thank you for the herb."

Toklo looked at the cub's shoulder. There was a greenish paste covering the wound. "Did the smooth-pelt put that on you?" he asked.

"You mean the human boy?" said the cub. "That was me. I'm Ujurak."

Toklo stared at him. "But you're a bear."

"I am now," the cub said, sitting down. He shook his head. "Just not all of the time. I don't know whether I'm really a bear or a boy, or something else."

His shoulders slumped. Toklo wondered what it was like to turn into something else. He didn't want to find out. A bear was clearly the best thing to be. "Well, you're a bear now," he said. He wasn't even sure if he believed the cub. Maybe he had seen the smooth-pelt, who had put the paste on his shoulder. And yet they had wounds in exactly the same place. And the same innocent, trusting brown eyes . . .

Toklo tore off half the salmon and offered it to the cub. Ujurak accepted gratefully. Toklo finished his half of the salmon and watched the cub gnawing away. He hadn't planned on meeting him again. The only thing Toklo had wanted was to make sure he didn't die, and obviously he was fine now.

"All right," Toklo said. "I'll be off, then."

"Wait," Ujurak said, scrambling to his paws. "Where are you traveling to?"

Toklo sank his claws into the soft earth. "As far away from other bears as possible," he growled. He pictured the bright star, alone and distant and apart from all the others. That's how he wanted to be, too.

"That's where I'm going, too," Ujurak said unexpectedly. "But I don't know how to get there. All I know is that the way will be marked by a path of fire in the sky."

Toklo tilted his head. Fire in the sky? More like the cub had bees in his brain. "Well, er . . . good luck, then," he said.

"No, don't you see?" Ujurak pressed. "We have to travel together. We can help each other find this place."

Toklo looked down at Ujurak. His shoulders were thin for a brown bear, and his paws did not look as if they'd been toughened by moons of climbing over rocks and snow. An image of Tobi flashed through Toklo's mind. If Ujurak was left on his own, he might not survive. But Toklo didn't want a traveling companion, one he had to look after, one who would slow him down. Especially not one who kept saying he could change into a flat-face.

"Where's your mother?" Toklo asked.

Ujurak shrugged. "I've been on my own for a long time," he answered. "Please help me find where I have to go."

Toklo thought about Tobi's body, covered in dirt and leaves. He thought about his mother, crazy with grief, who didn't love him enough to take care of him. Toklo knew he couldn't abandon Ujurak like that. "Okay," he said gruffly. "We can travel together for a while. But I'm not going all the way to a place where there is fire in the sky." That didn't sound like a place with sheltered valleys and rivers filled with salmon.

Ujurak sprang to his paws, wincing as he jarred his shoulder. "Let's go!" He bounded away up the river without waiting to see which way Toklo had been planning to go. He kicked up a flurry of pebbles behind him, and one of them bonked Toklo on the nose.

Toklo sighed, rubbing his muzzle. What had he gotten himself into?

CHAPTER TWENTY-FIVE

Kallik

The no-claw lowered his death stick and yelled something. Another no-claw—this one with fur growing from his muzzle—stepped forward and pointed a different stick at her. Kallik felt a sharp scratch in her side. She yelped and jumped back, pawing at the spot where she'd been scratched. She was surprised that it didn't hurt very much. Surely this wasn't the pain of the death sticks that the she-bear had warned her about?

Then she realized that the world around her was getting fuzzy. She felt as if her mind was melting like the ice. Everything around her was getting blurrier, like she was seeing it through a dense fog. Kallik blinked, trying to stay awake. Was this what dying felt like? She didn't want to die here, so far from the ice.

But she couldn't fight the weight pressing down on her mind. She slid to the ground, feeling her paws go limp. Slowly her eyes closed, and she sank into blackness.

* * *

When Kallik opened her eyes again, she was surrounded by white—bright, blistering white. Not snow. Something else that was cold and hard and didn't feel right. She rubbed her eyes with her paws. She could smell other bears. She shook her head to clear the buzzing from her ears. The bears were crying out to one another, calling names and pleading for help.

Kallik sat up, still feeling woozy. Now she could hear harsh clanging sounds, and there was a strong smell coming from somewhere very close by. She sniffed. The smell was coming from her! Something sticky had been daubed all over her fur. It made her eyes water. There was also a weird, sharp taste in her mouth.

Where was she?

Kallik stood up, her paws wobbling underneath her. She took a step forward and noticed that she was surrounded by hard gray columns, like tree branches but much straighter and smoother. Beyond the columns she could see a massive den. Her gaze traveled up the straight white walls to the roof looming far above her. She looked down again and saw that the other white bears were enclosed by gray columns as well.

No-claws were walking between the enclosures, looking at the bears. Some of them held long sticks, and Kallik flinched, putting her nose under her paws. She waited for the stick to sting her again.

The no-claws walked straight past, and Kallik peered up. An old male bear was pacing behind the columns opposite her. "We're all going to die!" he howled. "The ice will never return, and we'll all starve!"

"That's not true!" Kallik cried, feeling panic rise up in her. "The ice will come back. It always does. That's what my mother told me." Her voice faltered at the end, but he ignored her.

"Every bear in the world will starve!" he roared again.

"*The Endless Ice . . .*"

"*It never melts. . . .*"

"*That's where we need to go. . . .*"

Whispers ran through the bears, rustling like snow across the ice. Kallik scratched her ear. Were they talking about the place where the Pathway Star led—where the ice never melted?

"The Endless Ice?" Kallik yelped. "You mean the place with the dancing spirits? Where the Pathway Star leads?"

"*A long way . . .* " one bear murmured, but none of them answered Kallik's questions. She didn't think they even knew what they were saying. Most of them sounded half crazed and terrified, rambling to themselves instead of speaking to one another.

There was a *clang* close by, and Kallik saw that two of the no-claws were walking toward her. She backed into a corner, trying to make herself smaller. The cold, hard columns pressed into her back. There was no way to burrow out. She was completely trapped. The no-claws came closer and closer, then turned and went to the cage of the mangy old ranting bear. The male no-claw pointed something into the cage and there was a short hissing noise.

Kallik scrambled closer, trying to see what was happening. After a moment, the no-claws opened a door in the columns and pulled out the limp body of the old bear.

Kallik panicked. The no-claws had killed him! Maybe they were going to kill all of them! She threw herself at the bars, screaming. "Mother!" she howled, slamming her side into the bars with all her force. "Mother, help, please, help me!" She had to get out of here. Maybe she could knock down the columns, or break through them, or . . . Terror overwhelmed her and she threw herself against the bars again and again.

At last she collapsed to the ground, exhausted and gasping for breath. The bars hadn't budged even a clawslength.

"That's not going to get you anywhere," said a voice from the next enclosure. "You should save your energy if you want to get through this."

Kallik rolled over and looked up. A full-grown bear was watching her. She seemed to be the same age as Nisa, old enough for cubs, but her eyes were not gentle like Nisa's, and her voice sounded tired and cross.

"These cages are impossible to break," she went on. "Believe me, much bigger bears than you have tried."

"Who are you?" Kallik asked. She had a new word now: *cage*. She didn't like it.

There was a pause. "I'm Nanuk," said the other bear eventually.

"I'm Kallik. Where are we?"

"We're in a no-claw den. This is where they bring all the

bears who come too close to their dens."

"What are they going to do with us?" Kallik whimpered.

"Don't worry," Nanuk said. "I've been here before. They keep us for a while and then take us back to the ice. You'll be fine as long as you don't cause any trouble."

Kallik hesitated. "Have you seen any cubs like me, on their own? I'm looking for one called Taqqiq. He's a bit bigger than me and he walks with his paws splayed out like this." She spread her feet. "He—he's my brother. When our mother died he ran away, and I've been looking for him."

Nanuk shook her head. "You're the only cub I've seen this time. This burn-sky has been hungrier than any I can remember. Your brother is probably dead."

"No!" Kallik cried. "He isn't! I won't believe that. He's strong, much stronger than me! If I can survive this long, so can he."

The older bear studied Kallik for a moment. "I hope you're right," she said softly.

The clanging noise came again, and Kallik saw the two no-claws returning. She retreated to the back of her cage, feeling the hard stone scrape her fur. Her coat must be thinner than usual, because her bones stuck out now, rubbing against the wall. The no-claws came closer, opening her cage but blocking the way out.

"Nanuk!" Kallik howled. "What are they doing?"

"Keep still. There's no point fighting them," Nanuk growled.

The no-claw threw something flat and heavy over Kallik's

head. It felt slick, like the skin of a seal, and it was the color of the sky. It trapped her against the floor, and she struggled, yowling, as the no-claw wrapped his forepaws around her and held her still.

"What are they DOING?" Kallik yelled again. "Stop, STOP IT!" The other no-claw took something strong-smelling and started rubbing it all over Kallik's fur. It was the same sticky, horrible stuff that she'd noticed on her before. Some of it got in Kallik's eyes and made them water.

At last they let her go and left the cage, taking the skin-thing with them. Kallik crouched on the floor, shivering and smelling worse than ever. She gagged on the stench and tried to wipe it off her muzzle, but it was all over her paws, too.

"*Shhh*, Kallik, the no-claws are just doing stupid no-claw things," Nanuk said calmly. "They didn't hurt you, did they?"

Outside the cages, the female no-claw pulled a stick on the wall, and slowly the bars between Kallik's and Nanuk's cages rose into the air, until Kallik and Nanuk were in one big cage, with no bars between them.

Kallik could smell Nanuk more clearly now. She reeked of hunger and filth—nothing like the warm, gentle scent of Kallik's mother.

"Why did they put that stuff on my fur?" she whimpered.

"They're trying to hide your scent from me," Nanuk explained. "They're hoping I'll mistake you for one of my own cubs so that when we get to the ice, I'll look after you." Her voice was full of scorn. "No-claws. *Hmph!* They think they're the only ones who can talk to one another. I'd never think you were one of my own cubs!"

"What happened to your cubs?" Kallik asked.

Nanuk's eyes clouded, and she moved one paw restlessly over the ground. "I don't want to talk about that," she replied.

Kallik knew from the slump of her shoulders that Nanuk was carrying as much sadness as she was. She could smell it, above the stench of the sticky green stuff. She crept over and stretched her muzzle up to Nanuk and they touched noses. Kallik closed her eyes, comforted by the feeling of Nanuk's fur brushing against hers.

Nanuk lay down, curling on her side to allow Kallik to rest against her. "I know you're not my cub," she murmured. "And I'm not your mother. But we're all we have, for now."

Kallik drifted off to sleep, feeling safe for the first time since her mother had died.

CHAPTER TWENTY-SIX

Lusa

Golden sunbeams drifted down through the leaves, casting dappled green shadows over the forest floor. A gentle wind swayed the trees with a murmur like voices in the distance. Somewhere not too far away, Lusa could hear the trickle of a stream and smell the tart sweetness of wild berries.

She padded through the forest, breathing in the fresh air and letting her paws sink into the damp earth. She hadn't been out in the sunlight in days, and the warmth in her fur made her realize how much she'd missed it.

The trees were not what she had expected. She stood on her hind legs and studied one of them closely. It was tall and solid, its roots buried deeply in the dirt while its branches soared far up into the sky. She had thought it would look more like a bear. Lusa wondered how much she should believe of what Stella had told her.

As she dropped onto all fours again, she noticed a tree unlike the others in a clearing nearby. Instead of towering over her, this tree was small and covered in beautiful white blossoms. It looked as if the stars in the sky had been turned into flowers and scattered all over the tree. Lusa hoped that, when she died, she turned into a tree like this. She didn't want to float down a river like Oka and Tobi. She wanted her spirit to end up in a spray of blossoms.

She reached up the trunk with her front paws and found some small red fruits dangling from the branches. Using her teeth, she managed to tug one free. As she crunched it, sweet juice flooded her mouth, and the sharp taste of the skin tingled on her tongue. It was much tastier than the flat-face food she'd been scavenging for so long. She even liked it better than the salty potato sticks.

Suddenly she heard branches snapping behind her. Her heart sped up and she leaped into the tree, climbing in quick bounds the way King had taught her. Hidden among the soft blossoms, she clutched the trunk and peered down.

A large four-legged animal bounded into the clearing. Long branches grew from its head and its pelt was lots of different shades of brown, dappled like pebbles in a stream. It stood below the tree for a moment, sniffing the air. Lusa could have dropped straight onto its back. The creature looked around nervously, tension quivering through its fur. Lusa could feel the same nervousness making her own limbs tremble. A heartbeat later, the animal sprang away and raced into the trees.

Lusa stayed on her branch. She felt safe here. She reached for another fruit and ate it. The smell of the leaves and the blossoms and the tree sap mingled at the back of her throat. She reached again, then stopped, her paws still stretched out.

Another black bear was gazing at her from the tree trunk. Frozen with alarm, Lusa stared back. For a long moment, neither of them moved. At last, tentatively, Lusa reached out and pushed aside some leaves to see the face better. She let out a huff of embarrassed laughter. It wasn't a real bear—it was a series of knots and whorls in the bark that looked exactly like a black bear's face.

"Hello there," Lusa whispered, putting her face close to the trunk of the tree. "Were you once a bear?" Perhaps Stella was right after all. She liked the feeling that a spirit was this close to her, watching her. It made her feel less alone.

She stayed in the tree for a while, letting the sunlight and the smell of the blossoms soak through her. When sunhigh came, she whispered good-bye to the bear face and climbed down. She perked up her ears and went in search of the stream she had heard.

The glitter of water caught her eye through the trees, and soon she was splashing through the shallows, feeling the smooth, egg-shaped stones turn and tumble under her paws. She bent her head to lap up the water and felt the cool liquid ease the ache in her paws from so many days of walking on hard stone paths.

Lusa followed the stream. She was sure that it came from the top of the mountain. The ground sloped upward beside it, and the water tasted cold, like melted snow. If she followed it, she'd be traveling up the bear snout mountain toward the

Bear Watcher star, in the direction Oka had come from. She was going the right way—and yet the forest was so big, bigger than she'd ever imagined. If she climbed to the top of the tallest tree, she didn't think she could see to the ends of it. How would she ever find Toklo?

She stayed with the stream for the rest of that day and the next, traveling in daylight and keeping cool in the shadows under the trees. On her third day in the forest, the stream stopped going straight down the mountain. Now it flowed along the side of it, curving away into the forest. Lusa sat down on the bank, dabbing her paws in the water. The stream was going the wrong way now. She needed to go over the mountain to follow Oka's path back to Toklo. She would be sad to leave the stream—its bubbling chatter made her feel like she had a friend traveling with her. When she finally got up and walked away into the forest, she was lonelier than ever.

The days were getting longer and hotter, and the ground underpaw got steeper the farther she went up the mountain. She was grateful to the trees for their cool shade and also for their protection at night. As safe as she felt in the forest, she knew she mustn't stop being watchful. So at night she climbed up into the trees and slept in their branches, where no grizzlies or wolves or far-wandering flat-faces could find her.

Five days after she'd entered the forest, Lusa climbed onto a ledge that stuck out over some of the trees. It was a tough scramble up the rocks, but when she reached the ledge and turned around, she saw the world spread out below her. She sat down, awed. Far in the distance she could see the place where the sky met the ground, blurred by thin purple clouds. She could even see the edge of the forest, although it was a long, long way away. Beyond it she could just make out the shapes of flat-face dens and the sharp corners of firebeast paths. Lusa wondered if the Bear Bowl was down there, and if any of her family was looking up at the mountain at that moment, thinking about her.

Lusa felt a pang of guilt, and her loneliness rose up like a storm filling their water bowls. She hoped her family wasn't worried about her. She hoped they knew that she had escaped, and that they didn't think she'd died. She remembered how worried she had been about Ashia when the flat-faces took her away.

Her ears twitched, picking up an odd noise from nearby. It sounded like buzzing. Lusa got to her paws and lifted her muzzle to sniff the air. It smelled sweet, so sweet it made Lusa wrinkle her nose. A flash of memory came back to her: Stella telling her about something called a Buzzy Tree. "The tree buzzes and buzzes and stings you to keep you away," she'd said, "but if you keep trying, you can dig out the most delicious, sweet stuff, even better than blueberries."

Lusa followed the sound. To her surprise, the buzzing really was coming from a tree. It didn't look any different from the trees around it, except for a hole halfway up the trunk about the size of Lusa's head. Small furry bugs were flying in and out of the hole and crawling around the edges. They were bees—Lusa had seen them in the Bear Bowl, hopping from flower to flower. She scrambled up the tree and balanced herself on a thick branch so she could poke her head inside the hole. She reached out with her tongue and felt it touch something warm and sticky . . . and wonderfully, yummily sweet!

The buzzing grew louder, and Lusa wondered if the tree was angry with her. Suddenly a wave of bees poured out of the hole and dove at her face. It wasn't until she felt the first sting that she realized Stella was wrong—it wasn't the tree doing the buzzing or stinging. It was the bees! But the bees in the Bear Bowl had never buzzed like this or stabbed her with sharp points that she couldn't even see.

"Ow!" Lusa cried, swatting at them with her paws. "OW! Stop it!" But she couldn't resist the taste of the honey, so she stuck her muzzle back into the tree and lapped and lapped until her belly was full, trying to ignore the shocks of pain from the swarming bees.

When she had eaten enough, she swung herself down out of the tree and stumbled away. Her muzzle was burning from the bee stings and she kept shaking her head, trying to cool it off. But her stomach felt warm and full, and the melting golden sweetness of the honey stayed in her mouth for the rest of the day, so in the end she decided it was worth it.

Toward evening, as a light mist rolled down off the mountain, turning everything silvery, Lusa spotted a mark on one of the trees. She stood on her hind legs to examine it. It looked like scratches slashed in the bark at a point off the ground about twice her height. She was searching her memory for what her father had said about scratches on a tree when she was distracted by the scent of blueberries from a nearby bush.

She followed her nose over and pulled off as many berries as she could eat.

There were more berries on the next bush, and she kept going, eating whatever she could find. Soon she would need to find a place to sleep, since night was coming on quickly. Already she could see a few stars glimmering in the sky.

Lusa stopped to sniff a plant with sharp prickles on its leaves and branches. There was some interesting-looking fruit on it, but she would have to be very careful or else she'd be pricked, and her muzzle was still sore from the bee stings. She dabbed her paw at one of the leaves and pulled it back quickly. *Maybe if I—*

An aggressive huff interrupted her thoughts. Lusa spun around and came face-to-face with an enormous brown bear. Terror rooted her claws to the ground.

"You're in MY territory!" the bear snarled, cuffing her so hard that Lusa was knocked over. He raised himself up on his hind legs until he loomed over her. His teeth were long and fierce and his beady brown eyes glared at her through a tangle of dark brown fur.

"I'm sorry!" Lusa gasped, scrambling to her paws. "I didn't mean to—"

The bear growled and knocked her over again, this time pinning her to the ground. His weight pressed her into the dirt so she could barely breathe, and his claws dug into her skin. He leaned down and whispered in her ear, his foul-smelling breath hot on her muzzle.

"I guess that makes you my prey."

CHAPTER TWENTY-SEVEN

Toklo

A cool night breeze ruffled Toklo's fur, and he looked up at the lonely star, framed by the cliffs rising on either side of him. He wondered if it was laughing at him—tough, independent Toklo burdened with a salmon-headed companion like Ujurak.

The small cub had led the way out of the valley at a brisk pace, trotting on all day as if he knew exactly where he was going, even though he'd told Toklo he didn't. Now it was nearly moonhigh, and Ujurak was still scrambling along the ravine that led to the next valley. Toklo slipped on a stretch of loose pebbles and they clattered noisily down the slope. Irritated by his own clumsiness—and by the fact that he seemed to be following Ujurak instead of the other way around—he stopped and shook himself.

"What's wrong?" Ujurak asked, trotting back to join him. He ran in a circle around Toklo, his tongue lolling out as if he wanted to play. Toklo hunched his shoulders. He didn't know this cub well enough to play with him, and he was still confused by the shape-changing stories. What if he really was a smooth-pelt? Toklo didn't want to be rolling around with a grizzly only to find a slippery smooth-pelt in his paws.

"Where are you going?" he grumbled. "I think we should head up the mountain farther before we get to the next valley. There's better hunting up the mountains and fewer flat-faces than there are in the valleys."

"Sure," Ujurak said. "I've been following that star, but we can keep doing that by going straight up the mountain."

He pointed his muzzle at the sky, and Toklo realized with an unpleasant jolt that the cub was talking about the lonely bear spirit star. "You're following that star?" he said. "Why that one?"

"I don't know," Ujurak admitted. "It's just a feeling I get. Of all the stars, that's the one showing me which way to go."

It unsettled Toklo that Ujurak was drawn to the same star he was. That was *his* star, and he didn't want to share it with another bear.

"Well, whatever we do," he said grumpily, "we should rest for the night. It looks like there's a shelter over there, between those two boulders."

"Good idea," Ujurak said, twitching his ears. Toklo led the way over to the boulders. One was long and flat, with one end resting on the ground and the other leaning up against the second boulder, which was fat and round. The space underneath was just big enough for the cubs to squeeze in. Toklo noticed as he squirmed into the dark hollow that he took up more space than he used to, when he'd shared spots like this with Tobi. He'd been getting bigger without noticing.

Ujurak curled onto his side and rested his chin on Toklo's foreleg, looking as comfortable as if they'd been born in the same BirthDen. Toklo didn't know whether to shove him off or let him stay there, but before he could decide, Ujurak's eyes closed and he started to snore faintly.

"Perfect," Toklo muttered. He peeked up at the sky, where the bear spirit was still shining. It would always be his star—lonely, proud, and fierce. It didn't need any other bears, and neither did he. As soon as he was sure Ujurak could survive on his own, Toklo would go back to taking care of himself.

Toklo felt the heat of the sun beating down through the rocks before he opened his eyes, and he rolled over, stretching. His mouth felt dry and his fur seemed too heavy, like he was carrying another cub on his back.

Another cub! His eyes flew open as he remembered Ujurak. The hollow beside him was empty. Where had the stupid cub gone now? Toklo sat up, scratching his nose. If he went outside and found that smooth-pelt sitting there, he was not going to be pleased.

Pebbles bounced against the rock behind his back, and he poked out his head, sniffing the air. Ujurak was scrabbling at the base of the boulder. At least he was still a bear cub. Toklo wondered if Ujurak was crazy and had only imagined turning into a smooth-pelt. He still found it hard to believe that the flat-face and the grizzly cub were the same creature.

"What are you doing?" Toklo snapped.

Ujurak jumped. "Looking for worms," he said. "Or grubs. Sometimes I find things under rocks."

"If you dug up too much dirt, this rock might have fallen over on top of me," Toklo scolded, emerging into the sun. *I sound like my mother,* he thought and felt a twinge of pain.

"Oh, no!" Ujurak said. He looked horrified at the thought of squashing Toklo under a rock. "I didn't think of that. Sorry!"

Toklo *harrumph*ed and set off along the ravine, heading up the mountain. He could see the green meadows of the next valley through the cleft at the end, and beyond that, more mountains, their shapes filling the edge of the sky like giant slumbering bears. His claws scrabbled against the dry earth and he started to pant. He wished there were a river nearby.

Ujurak scrambled up beside him, scattering tiny stones under his paws. "So why are you on your own?" he asked, trotting to keep up. "Where's your mother?"

Toklo hesitated. He didn't want to tell the whole tale of how his mother had abandoned him, or how his brother had died on top of a mountain. "It's a long story. Where did *you* come from?" he said.

"I don't know where exactly . . . but I kind of remember my mother," Ujurak said. "I remember she was big and kind, and I felt safe sleeping next to her."

"Then you probably are a bear," Toklo said. "I can't imagine a flat-face being like that."

"Maybe they are to other flat-faces," Ujurak pointed out.

They came to the end of the ravine, where the green valley

opened out in front of them. Trees dotted the slopes in either
direction, getting thicker farther up, with snow-covered
peaks above them. Toklo sniffed the air and detected a hint of
grizzly on the breeze. Cautiously he started to cross the slope
up to the trees in the opposite direction from the brown bear.

Ujurak lifted his head to the sky and began swinging it back
and forth with his eyes closed.

"*Now* what are you doing?" Toklo grunted.

"I'm feeling for the star," Ujurak said. "I'm just making sure
we're going the right way." He scrunched up his face.

Toklo swatted a large stick down the hill and watched it
bounce over the termite mounds. Ujurak could tell where *his*
star was? Even in daylight? That wasn't fair. And it was stupid,
too.

"All right!" Ujurak said, opening his eyes. "You're right, this
is the way to go."

"Of course it is," Toklo growled. Of course the butterfly-
brained cub would choose which way to go based on an invis-
ible star instead of something sensible like whether there
were big angry grizzlies in the way. He scrambled into the lead
again, determined not to let the little cub boss him around.
Thick grasses grew in tangled clumps here, some as high as his
ears so he was almost wading through them.

"Where was your BirthDen?" Ujurak asked, his voice muffled by the grass. "Did you have any brothers or sisters? Do
you like being on your own, or do you miss them?"

"You ask a lot of questions," Toklo growled.

"I like knowing stuff," Ujurak said.

Toklo decided to use the same trick as before—ask Ujurak a question instead of answering. "When did you start changing shape?" he said. They were getting closer to the tree line, and Toklo hoped there would be a stream or river in the woods where they could stop to drink and cool down.

"I can't remember," Ujurak said. "When I was very young, I guess."

Suddenly there was a clatter of wings in one of the bushes beside them. Toklo and Ujurak both leaped back in fright as a large black bird burst out of the bush and soared into the sky.

"Oh, weasel breath!" Toklo yelped. "If I'd known that was there, we could have eaten it!"

He turned to Ujurak, but the cub was shaking in a weird way, his whole body jerking from side to side.

"It's nothing to be scared of," Toklo said, puzzled.

The cub's paws slipped on the grass, splaying out to either side, and then Ujurak's fur started to melt into his skin, replaced by glossy black feathers that sprouted all across his back. The cub seemed to collapse, shrinking to the ground, his front paws widening into wings, his back paws shriveling into scrawny bird legs. In a matter of moments, Ujurak had disappeared, and in his place was a large black bird like the one that had startled them.

Toklo opened and closed his mouth in astonishment.

"*Bawk?*" said the bird, tilting its head at Toklo. "*Bwaak?*"

"Oh, for the love of salmon," Toklo muttered. "What did you go and do that for, you squirrel-head? Go on, change back."

"Kabaawk," the bird observed, hopping forward a few steps and pecking at the dirt.

"Ujurak, you're wasting time," Toklo said, nosing the bird with his muzzle. "Go back to being a cub. Come on, stop playing around."

"Bawkawkawk," the bird announced, and then lifted off into the sky, flapping its wings.

Toklo sighed. Now what? He shook his head with frustration. He supposed he would have to wait for Ujurak to come back. Maybe there would be food in the woods, at least. He padded over to the trees and tried scuffling around among the roots and dead leaves. He managed to dig up a few bulbs and nuts, and by the time the black bird came plummeting back down out of the sky, Toklo was lying on his side in the shade, his belly full.

The bird landed in an undignified tumble of wings, and as it rolled across the ground, those wings grew longer and fuzzier. The feathers fell off like the bird was molting, and Ujurak's bewildered face popped back out where the beak had been. He ended his roll in a heap at Toklo's paws, gasping for breath.

"Well?" Toklo growled. "Are you done squirreling around?"

"That . . . was . . . terrifying," Ujurak panted. "I've never been a bird before."

"Well, you have now. Can we keep moving?"

"I thought I was going to die!" Ujurak went on. He shoved himself upright, shaking out his fur. "I didn't know when I'd turn back into a bear again, or if I'd turn into something else, and if it might happen in the middle of the air, so I'd just fall right back down and crash to my death."

"It looks like you made it okay," Toklo remarked.

"I sensed it," Ujurak said. "I could feel my bearness coming back, and I knew I had to land quickly. *Brrrrrr.*" He shook himself again. "That was much too close for me."

"Then you shouldn't do stupid things like turn into a bird."

"I can't help it," Ujurak said, his eyes wide. "It just . . . happens. Usually when I'm frightened or excited."

Toklo snorted. "Sounds like a dumb idea to me. You should work on controlling it."

"I suppose I should," Ujurak said meekly. He started walking again, and Toklo had to hurry to catch up. After a few moments, Ujurak added, with a mischievous gleam in his eye, "Flying was pretty fantastic, though."

"Well, try not to do it again," Toklo said. "Just . . . concentrate harder, or something."

Ujurak didn't respond, and after a moment Toklo sighed. "All right, tell me about flying," he said.

"It was amazing! I could see forever—over these mountains to the valley we came from and the ones beyond that. And I felt so light, like a leaf blowing around in the wind. The wind is really strong up there! I can't believe I even made it back to the right spot. It felt like I could float through the air all the way to the ocean!"

Toklo only listened with half an ear, his attention focused on the landscape around them. How was he supposed to protect them from danger if Ujurak kept doing dumb stuff like this? He sniffed the air again and picked up a familiar scent.

"I smell a river," he barked, interrupting Ujurak's gabbling. "One with salmon in it, I think. Come on, let's get to it—this early in the day, we might even have it to ourselves." He put on a burst of speed and raced through the trees with Ujurak close on his paws.

The trees thinned out at the edge of the river, which was wide but shallow, with large muddy patches in the middle where the water was very low. Toklo could smell other bears, but he couldn't see any from the wet, sandy shore; he guessed the closest grizzlies were around the bend of the river, where the trees were thicker.

"You stay here," he told Ujurak. "I'm going to catch us a salmon." Ujurak sat down, blinking.

Toklo stalked into the center of the river and stuck his nose under the water, lapping up the fresh, cool taste. The current was slow, but he thought he saw a glimmer of silver farther upstream. Keeping his gaze on the water, he waded upriver, feeling the mud squelch between his claws.

A flash of scales, a body sliding over the pebbles: Toklo dove for it, remembering a moment too late that he needed to aim for where the fish was going, not directly at it. His paws closed over empty stones, spraying water in his face.

"Ooh, almost!" Ujurak called from the bank. "Can I try? Can I try?"

"Shush," Toklo snapped. He took up his position again, his back to the current, staring at the water. A long moment passed, and he felt his shoulders aching with tension. His eyes

were starting to sting, but he forced them to stay open, focused on the river bottom.

"Is that one there?" Ujurak's voice said in his ear.

Toklo jumped, roaring with surprise, and fell with a splash on his side in the river. He couldn't believe he hadn't heard the cub creeping up on him.

"Sorry!" Ujurak gasped. "I didn't mean to startle you! I just wanted to see what you were doing."

"Oh, by the Great Water Spirits!" Toklo spat. He shoved himself to all paws again, his belly fur dripping. "Fine, you can stay out here and watch me, but you have to BE QUIET."

"I will," Ujurak promised. "I really will." He sat up and clamped his paws over his muzzle.

Muttering to himself, Toklo looked back down at the water. They'd probably scared off any salmon with all that splashing and hollering. But wait—something silvery pink was gliding toward them. He crouched, gauging its speed, ready to pounce where it was *going* to be.

"AHA!" Ujurak yelled. He sprang forward with all paws, crashing into the river with an enormous splash. The salmon shot out from under him as a cascade of water poured over Toklo, filling his ears and momentarily blinding him.

"Ujurak!" Toklo shouted, batting at his muzzle. "You're as dopey as a black bear!" He shook his head and opened his eyes.

Ujurak was gone.

"WHAT?" Toklo growled. He spun around, searching the trees and the sky. "Ujurak, you turn back into a bear RIGHT NOW."

Something slithered by his paws and he nearly pounced instinctively. But he stopped himself before his claws sank into the fish, realizing that it could be Ujurak.

"Oh, I don't believe it," he muttered at the river. Well, now he was stuck. He couldn't keep fishing in case he caught Ujurak. "I *should* eat you!" he yelled. "That might teach you a lesson!"

He scrambled out onto shore and shook his head hard, trying to force the water out of his ears. As his hearing cleared, he caught the sound of voices from farther downstream.

Uh-oh. Other bears—and they were fishing.

"No!" he shouted, galloping along the bank. Just around a bend, the river widened into a small pool surrounded by spindly trees. Two grizzlies were standing in the water, looking up at him with startled expressions.

"Don't eat the salmon!" Toklo shouted. His fur burned with embarrassment. He must sound completely crazy.

"What on earth are you talking about?" said the female grizzly.

"I haven't eaten in days," growled the other grizzly. "If I catch a fish, I am *certainly* eating it."

"You can't keep the river to yourself. Get lost, cub," snarled the first bear. They both turned their attention back to the water.

Toklo tried to figure out how long it would take the Ujurak-salmon to get to the pool. The grizzlies were too big for him to fight. He had to think of something else. "They're poisoned!" he blurted out. "The salmon—they'll make you sick!"

The she-bear narrowed her eyes at him. "What do you mean? How do you know?"

Toklo shuffled his paws, trying to look pitiful. "Because that's what happened to my mother," he whimpered. "Why else would I be all alone? She ate the salmon from this river and then she *died*."

The male grizzly reared up on his hind legs with a growl. "Salmon from this river?" he demanded. "Are you sure?"

Toklo nodded earnestly. "It was awful," he said. "Her stomach got all hard and she smelled funny and then she threw up and then she lay down moaning and then she *died*."

The she-bear waded quickly out of the river, but the male looked back down at the water as if he wasn't sure Toklo was telling the truth.

"Maybe it wasn't the salmon," Toklo said innocently. "Although that was the only thing she'd eaten in days. But I guess you could try eating it and see what happens."

The bear let out a low rumbling growl and dropped to all fours, then shambled out of the river. "This better not be a trick," he snarled as he padded past Toklo. "If I turn around and find you eating one of these fish—"

"Trust me, you won't," Toklo said.

"Thanks for the warning, cub," the she-bear growled. The two grizzlies paced off into the trees. Toklo waited until they were gone, then collapsed on the sand. His heart was beating so fast, he thought it might come racing out of his chest. He'd just scared away two big grizzlies! He couldn't believe that they'd believed his wild story.

A fierce bubbling started in the water a short way out, and Toklo sat up. He watched as a furry muzzle suddenly poked out of the water, followed by bony shoulders and shimmering flippers melting into shaggy paws. A few moments later Ujurak dragged himself out of the pool, dripping wet and coughing up water. He slumped down next to Toklo, gasping for air.

Toklo just glared at him.

Ujurak's sides heaved. He looked up at Toklo, shivering. "I'm . . . *really* sorry," he said.

"You should be!" Toklo roared. "I nearly got mauled by two grizzlies trying to make sure you didn't get eaten!"

"Oh, wow," Ujurak said, his eyes enormous. "Thank you so much. See, I *knew* we'd be good traveling companions!"

"You really do have bees in your brain," Toklo said. "I don't know if you've spent too much time as a smooth-pelt or whatever, but you don't have the sense of a newborn cub. I can't go any farther with you, Ujurak. It's too dangerous and . . . and weird."

Ujurak's shoulders drooped. "But I thought we were friends."

"Friends don't turn into salmon and nearly get their friends killed," Toklo snapped, thinking how ridiculous he sounded. "You're on your own now."

He turned and stalked off into the trees. Ujurak's gaze felt like the sun scorching his shoulders, but Toklo kept walking. He was a lone bear. He didn't need to travel with anyone.

He followed the scent of the other grizzlies for a short

distance, until he was sure that they'd headed down into the valley. Then he circled back up into the trees, climbing higher as the sun slid slowly down the sky. He spotted the bear spirit star before it was fully dark, while the sky was still turning from light blue to deep purple. It shone brightly, and he wondered if Ujurak was looking up at it, bounding along cheerfully on his mysterious journey.

Maybe he should just check and make sure Ujurak hadn't crossed the path of the other two bears.

He turned back, weaving through the trees in a straight line toward the sound of the river. The mountains above him were black shapes fading into the night sky, and the trees around him glowed in the moonlight. Toklo found the river and padded along it toward the pool, keeping his nose down in search of Ujurak's scent. He hoped he would find it heading away from the river up the mountain.

But as he came around the bend of the river, he saw a small dark form huddled on the muddy bank of the pool. Toklo picked up speed, trotting faster until he was running through the sand. He skidded to a stop beside the cub.

Ujurak was sleeping. His sides rose and fell evenly, and a tiny buzzing sound came from his nose. Scattered through his fur were leaves that had fallen from the trees during the day, and patches of dirt from where he had dragged himself out of the river. Toklo looked down at him, remembering another small cub covered in dirt and leaves.

He couldn't leave Ujurak alone. It was a miracle the cub had survived this long—without Toklo, he would be killed or eaten or maybe even squashed; Toklo didn't know if Ujurak turned into bugs as well. But he was definitely helpless, and Toklo didn't want another bear spirit following him around like Tobi's seemed to.

With a sigh, he stretched out next to Ujurak and pressed his fur against the cub's, sharing his warmth. Ujurak murmured happily in his sleep and wriggled closer.

Toklo looked up at the star, glinting through the trees. "I know, I know," he muttered. "But it's only until he can take care of himself."

CHAPTER TWENTY-EIGHT

Kallik

Kallik half opened her eyes. She was pressed up against Nanuk, the older bear's fur brushing against her nose. It wasn't the same as being out on the ice, but it was nice not to be running away from things all the time, and at least her paws weren't so sore and battered. She just wished the no-claws would give them some food.

"Kallik," Nanuk murmured, nudging her. "Kallik, wake up. It's time to go."

Kallik blinked and pawed at her eyes. She could hear the pawsteps of the no-claws coming closer. She opened her eyes fully and sat up. There were more no-claws outside the cage than she'd ever seen before, and they carried sticks and webs and other strange things in their paws.

"Don't be scared," Nanuk whispered. "The no-claws are going to put us to sleep, but not forever. It's like what they did to get you here. You'll be asleep just while they take us to the place where the ice comes first."

"We're going back to the ice?" Kallik gasped, jumping to her paws.

Nanuk nodded. "They'll leave us close to the edge of the bay, far from here. When the ice returns, we'll be waiting."

Kallik tried to be brave, but as the no-claws approached, she pushed her nose into Nanuk's fur. "I'm scared," she whimpered. "What if we never wake up? Or what if they take us so far away that I'll never be able to find Taqqiq?" She looked up at Nanuk. "Do you think he'll be there, too?"

"I'm sure he will be," Nanuk said. She touched her nose to the top of Kallik's head, and Kallik curled up in the curve of her side. "Don't be scared. Just think about the ice. Think about eating seals, and running across shining white snow, and playing with your brother where the stars shine all night long."

Kallik held her breath, waiting to feel the sharp scratch in her side. It hurt, but not as much as last time. As she slipped into sleep, she thought of Taqqiq. Would he be there when she woke up, waiting for the ice to return, too?

Kallik opened her eyes with a start. A cold wind was rushing through her fur. She was curled up on Nanuk's belly, surrounded by a strong web. Something was not right; it was too windy, and there was a strange swaying sensation, a bit like the waves on the sea. Something was thudding and rumbling above her, making the web tremble. She looked up and saw the belly of an enormous metal bird above her, its wings whirring in a circle and letting out a high-pitched roaring sound, unlike any bird she'd ever seen before.

She peeked over Nanuk's side and her heart nearly stopped. The ground was skylengths and skylengths below her! She was flying in the air!

Kallik let out a panicked shriek and scrambled over the web, clawing at the thick tendrils. Sleet flew in her face, stinging her eyes.

"*Shh, shhhh,*" Nanuk's voice said. One of her paws encircled Kallik and drew her back onto Nanuk's belly. "Keep still," she said. "The bird is carrying us. It'll be all right."

"But we're flying!" Kallik whimpered. "Bears don't fly! It's so cold and we're so high and how is this happening?"

"*Shhhh,*" Nanuk said. "Keep still and breathe in. Can you smell that?"

Kallik lay quiet and let the air rush into her nose. "It smells like ice," she said. "It smells like home."

"That's right," Nanuk said. "We're going home. Everything will be all right, little one."

Kallik buried her head in Nanuk's fur, trying not to think about how far above the ground they were. The wind was getting stronger, making the web sway back and forth. The air was thick with the scent of an approaching storm, and freezing rain blew through the holes in the web, coating their fur with icy crystals.

"When we get there," Kallik whispered, "can I stay with you?"

Nanuk rested one paw on Kallik's flank, holding her still. "Yes, you can."

* * *

Somehow Kallik slipped into a doze. She was jolted awake again when the web lurched, nearly sending her sliding off Nanuk's belly. The wind had dropped, and they were surrounded by something thick and white and fluffy. They'd been eaten by a cloud!

"It's only fog," Nanuk said. "Just like you get on the ice."

Kallik peered over Nanuk's flank. She couldn't see the ground anymore. Just billowing fog, hanging in the air, muffling the sound of the metal bird above them. From the sound of it, the metal bird didn't like flying in the fog. It sounded distressed, its wings whining and clattering. Kallik looked up. Her fur was tingling. Something bad was happening.

As Kallik stared up through the cloud, the spinning wings began to tilt and sputter. Then they stopped completely, and the bird plunged straight down, howling louder than the wind.

Kallik could see the bare brown ground now, getting closer very quickly. Not even birds landed this fast! She shrieked and buried her head in Nanuk's fur as the ground rushed up toward them. Nanuk's paws clutched her closer, and she could hear the older bear's heart pounding beneath her ribs.

"What's happening?" Kallik shouted.

Nanuk didn't answer. All at once there was a sound like thunder and the sky flashed orange as the bird burst into flames, the heat scorching Kallik's fur. They slammed into the ground and everything went black.

* * *

When Kallik awoke, she was soaking wet, as if she'd been lying in the rain for a while. She blinked, feeling a heavy weight against her side, and for a moment the brush of the cold air and the warmth at her back made her think she was back in her BirthDen with Nisa and Taqqiq. Then she smelled the stench of burning metal, and she remembered where she was.

"Nanuk!" she cried, squirming free. "Nanuk, are you all right?" She tore at the web around them, shoving the tendrils aside as she clambered up to Nanuk's face. The older bear's eyes were closed, and she felt cold beneath her fur.

"Nanuk," Kallik whimpered. "Wake up. It's me, Kallik."

The other bear stirred. She turned her head and coughed, and a bright red spatter of blood hit the dirt beside her.

"Oh, Nanuk, you're hurt!" Kallik cried. "What should I do?"

Nanuk opened her eyes and looked at Kallik. "Find your brother," she said hoarsely. Another fit of coughing wracked her body and more blood splattered onto the muddy ground.

"But I want to stay with you. I thought we were going to look for him together."

"I can't come with you," Nanuk croaked. "You must be strong. You *are* strong, stronger than you know. You'll be all right."

"But what about you?"

"It is time for me to join the ice spirits," Nanuk whispered, laying her head back with a sigh. "You will have to go without me. Go to the place where the ice never melts and the bear spirits dance in many colors."

Kallik gasped. "Is that place real? I thought . . . perhaps it was just a story."

"It is real," Nanuk murmured, her eyes closing. "I know it is." Her voice faded, whisked away by the wind that had begun to howl around them.

"Wait!" Kallik cried. "How do you know? Please tell me more, please, Nanuk, please don't die!" She shook Nanuk with her paws, trying to push the older bear up. But Nanuk was heavy and cold, and her sides were still.

Kallik pressed her nose into Nanuk's fur. "I'll miss you," she whispered. "Thank you for taking care of me."

She backed away, untangling herself from the web. The air was thick with smoke from the wreck of the metal bird. It crackled and popped like a death stick, and flames were shooting out of it into the sky. Although it was dark, Kallik couldn't see the stars through the stinging smoke and sparks.

She started to run, not caring which direction she was going as long as she got away from the burning bird. She could feel the mud squishing under her paws and the wind blowing sleet in her face. As she reached the top of a long slope, she turned to look back at the flaming wreckage of the bird and the still white shape of Nanuk lying not far from it.

"Good-bye, Nanuk," she murmured. "I'll go to the place of Endless Ice, just like you said. And maybe, if that's where the spirits dance, I'll find you there as well."

CHAPTER TWENTY-NINE

Lusa

Lusa screamed so loud she startled the brown bear, making him lift his weight off her for a moment—but a moment was all she needed. Wrenching herself free, she scrabbled under the prickly bush, feeling the thorns tug and tear at her fur. She slid out the other side and raced to the nearest tree, scrambling up it so fast the branches and leaves were just a blur around her. She remembered King saying that grizzlies couldn't climb trees like black bears could, and she thanked the tree spirits that he'd taught her to climb so well.

"Come down here!" the brown bear roared. He paced around the bottom of the tree, huffing with fury. Lusa clutched the trunk and closed her eyes, praying to all the bear spirits in the forest that he would go away.

"I'm going to tear you apart, puny cub," the grizzly snarled. "You'll be sorry you ever came into this territory. I'll show you what a real bear can do. I'll rip your fur off and dig out your heart with my claws."

Lusa wished she could close her ears, too. She was trembling so hard the whole tree seemed to be shaking. Why couldn't he just leave her alone? *Maybe he's hungry, like Oka was,* a voice whispered in her mind. *Well, he can't eat me!* she retorted.

Darkness fell while Lusa was trapped up in the leaves, and still the grizzly paced below her, snarling. Deep shadows crawled across the forest, with only patches of moonlight breaking through the tree cover here and there. It was nearly moonhigh when the grizzly stood on his hind legs and roared, "Stay away from my territory!" one more time, then dropped down and stalked away.

Lusa was too scared to climb down the tree. The dark forest felt cold and unfriendly, and King hadn't told her what to do *after* she'd climbed a tree to escape another bear. She buried her face in the bark and stayed there for the rest of the night, shivering and too frightened to sleep.

In the morning light she was able to scan the forest floor below her. There was no sign of the grizzly, and she couldn't find his scent in the air, either. She would never forget the earthy smell of his fur. She crept carefully down the tree and ran in the opposite direction from where he'd gone. It meant going out of her way for a while, but she could find another path over the mountain—anything would be safer than staying in that bear's territory!

As she raced through the trees, she passed another one with long scratches on the bark. Now she remembered what King had told her: *Stay away from a grizzly's territory. You'll know where they are from clawmarks on the trees.* She'd been stupid to forget—and lucky to escape with her fur in one piece.

She decided it would be safer to go back to traveling at night. She hid in another tree, far from the grizzly's territory, for the rest of the day, and climbed down when the sun sank below the mountains. It was harder to find food in the darkness, and hunger gnawed at her belly, but she felt safer among the shadows, so she spent the days hiding in trees for a whole moon. She was steadily climbing higher and higher up the mountain, where the clouds seemed closer to the ground and sometimes it rained for days on end.

At last Lusa reached the top of the mountain, scrambling over a pile of large boulders to emerge onto a wide flat space where there was no more up—only ground sloping down in every direction. She took shelter in a cave just below the peak, looking down at the lights of the flat-face homes. They looked like a sky full of stars spread on the ground. The world was so big . . . so much bigger than she'd imagined. Why hadn't Oka warned her about that?

She missed Ashia's gentle warmth, Stella's funny stories, even King's grouchiness. She missed wrestling with Yogi and racing around the Bear Bowl for treats. She wondered if they ever looked up at the Bear Watcher at the same time as she did. She wondered if they ever thought of her. She would never know, because she'd never see them again. Resting her head on her paws, Lusa felt cold and sad and hollow while the moon floated across the sky far above her.

The next morning, she emerged from the cave and set out in daylight. She couldn't feel sad forever. She had made a promise to Oka, and she was going to keep it. There was no way she could go back to the Bear Bowl, so she may as well keep going. She was heading down the other side of the mountain now, far from the grizzly's territory, so she decided not to stay in the cave all day and wait for night to fall again. The daylight would help her watch out for bark scratches . . . there could easily be other brown bears wandering on this side.

She scrambled over a ridge of boulders and paused, her heart thumping. Far below her, she could see three small lakes laid out next to one another, just as Oka had said. She must be going the right way!

A weasel darted across her path, and in her excitement, Lusa sprang to her paws and chased it. It moved too quickly for her to catch, but racing through the grass with the wind in her fur helped to lift her spirits again.

Lusa was tired, hungry, and pawsore by the time she reached the first lake, but the smooth, glittering surface sparkled like starlight in a bowl and she'd been able to see it through the trees for a long time, calling to her. She plunged into the water with a happy yelp. Now *this* was a real lake—not like the one she'd found in the flat-face enclosure. She wallowed in the water, letting it soak through her fur, soothing her scratches. Tiny silver fish darted between her paws, and she chased after them playfully, woofing with joy.

A skinny long-legged animal was watching her from the bank. Its fur was shaggy and brown and a set of thick antlers

sprouted from its head. Lusa thought it might be a moose,
from the descriptions she'd heard from Stella and King. It was
nice to see another animal that wasn't trying to eat her.

"Hello!" she called. "Come on in, it's lovely!"

The moose tilted its head, looking down its nose at her.
Then it turned and ambled away.

Lusa dunked herself in the water again. When she reached
the point where it was too deep for her paws to reach the bottom, she tried waving them in the water and discovered that
she could swim. She wished Yogi were there to see. Playing
with him was more fun than playing on her own. But she was
going the way Oka had described, which meant she was getting closer to Toklo. And when she found him, she wouldn't
be lonely anymore. She wondered if he liked swimming, too.
Perhaps she could teach him.

Lusa stayed by the lakes for five sunrises, splashing in the
water and feasting on berries she found growing close to the
shore. It was a relief to stop traveling for a while, although she
knew she couldn't rest for long. If Toklo had been moving
ever since Oka abandoned him, he could still be a long way
away.

On the far side of the third lake, Lusa reached the dead forest that Oka had told her about. It was the scariest place she'd
been since the firebeast path. The trees were nothing but
black, hollow shells, and there were no leaves or berries on
any of them. Her paws crunched softly on the dead twigs and
ashes as she walked into it.

The strangest part was the silence. Lusa couldn't hear any birds or even the scrabbling of tiny animals in the dirt. There was nothing but the sound of her paws and the occasional hiss of the wind or a tree branch creaking. She shuddered, wondering what had happened to the bear spirits. It felt as if perhaps they were still here, clinging to the place where they had died for a second time. But not in a friendly way; instead, the brittle black trunks seemed to be watching her, waiting for her to get lost and stay there forever.

She didn't dare sleep in the dead forest. There were no bushes to shelter her, and the branches rattled and clacked noisily when the wind shook the dead trees. Lusa kept walking all night and far into the next day. She came to the dry riverbed, with the dead forest stretching around it on either side. Oka had been here. But would Toklo be anywhere nearby?

Lusa stepped into the riverbed and began to follow it. Her paws were sore and black with soot, but she kept going as night fell, determined to get out of that eerie place.

Halfway through the next day, as she was stumbling along on heavy, numb paws, she spotted green leaves growing on one of the trees. She pricked up her ears and trotted faster, searching for more signs of life. Sure enough, bits of green were peeking out of the bark on the next tree down, and the next, and ahead of her she spotted a tree with vines wound all the way around it. It felt as if the forest were waking up around her. As soon as she saw bushes covered in leaves, she scrambled up the riverbank to search for berries. But there didn't seem to be any on these bushes, as if they'd been eaten off already. She searched the trees for any scratch marks indicating this was another bear's territory, but she couldn't find any.

By nightfall Lusa was back in a living forest, with the whispers of the bear spirits once again murmuring in the breeze. She found a hollow below some tree roots and collapsed into it, too tired even to climb the tree. A group of whorls in the bark beside her looked a bit like Stella, and she pressed her paw to the face, whispering, "Good night, Stella." She hoped that most animals wouldn't come this close to the dead forest, and maybe that would keep her safe.

Lusa curled into a ball, feeling loneliness wash over her again. She had never thought it would take this long to find Toklo. Perhaps she would never find him. She remembered the vast landscape she could see from the top of the mountain, stretching all the way to the sky. The wild was just too big. Why did Lusa ever think she would be able to find the lost cub? She would have to learn to survive alone.

CHAPTER THIRTY

Toklo

A cold nose was poking into Toklo's fur. Toklo growled and opened his eyes.

"You came back!" Ujurak cried. The sun was pouring through the leaves and sparkling off the bubbles in the river beside them.

"Yeah, I did," Toklo said. "But promise me you'll try really hard to stay a bear from now on. I don't want any more flat-faces or salmon or birds to deal with."

Ujurak bounced on his paws. "I'll work on that," he promised.

I hope so, Toklo thought.

They climbed out of the forest into another meadow, dotted with flowers nodding in the rustling grass. The mountain loomed above them. There was hardly any snow left now, even at the top. As he stepped out of the trees, Toklo caught the smell of something musty. He glanced around and spotted a tuft of white hair snagged on a bush. He trotted over to examine it more closely. It smelled like mountain goat, and his mouth watered at the thought of fresh prey.

"Ujurak," he hissed. "This way."

The cub stopped digging for worms and followed him, scrambling over the scattered rocks that had tumbled into the meadow from farther up the mountain. Toklo sniffed carefully, tracking the scent he had found on the hair. It led in a winding path around some bushes, where Toklo found scraps of leaves that had been ripped off as the goat grazed. These signs led him up a steep trail to the base of the rocky peak.

Toklo paused, looking around. The mountain soared into the sky, sharp-edged against the bright blue sky. Far above, Toklo could see small clouds floating past, as white and fluffy as the goat hair. He focused his gaze back on the mountain, following the rocks down and down, looking for movement.

"There!" he whispered to Ujurak. A black-and-white shape flickered among the rocks not far above them. It was the mountain goat . . . and it hadn't noticed them. It was grazing peacefully on the stubby grasses that sprouted between the boulders.

Toklo edged along the rocky path, his claws slipping on loose stones. It was impossible to hide the sound of his approach. The mountain goat's head popped up. It stared straight at him with its beady black eyes, chewing thoughtfully. And then, with a startling burst of energy, it leaped away, bouncing over the rocks like a leaf on the wind. Toklo growled.

"Let's get it!" Ujurak cried.

Toklo dug his paws in and chased after the goat, determined not to let it get away. This was the first live prey they'd seen in days, and he was getting very bored with eating roots and berries. He raced after the goat, ignoring the flashes of pain as rocks stabbed the pads of his paws. Ujurak wasn't behind him anymore, and he wondered where the other cub had gone. Well, he'd look for him after he'd caught the goat.

The mountain goat sprang over a boulder and darted around a narrow ridge of stone. When Toklo followed it, he saw the goat standing at the edge of a cliff. The meadow was a long way below them, so far that the flowers and the grass blurred together in a hazy green mist. He hadn't realized they were up so high. It would be a long way to fall if he slipped, and he shuddered, thinking about the grisly result at the bottom.

He skidded to a halt about three bearlengths from the goat, his paws kicking up a cloud of tiny stones. The goat eyed him warily, its hooves scrabbling close to the edge. *Surely it's not crazy enough to jump,* Toklo thought. The goat was so close, he could smell the blood pumping in its neck. It would be so easy to sink his teeth in and rip the life out of the goat, feasting enough to keep him strong for days.

But he couldn't risk it. The goat was more sure-footed up here than he was. If he tried to lunge at it, it could easily sidestep and send him plummeting over the edge. Toklo glared at the goat. He was exhausted, hungry, and frustrated, and there was nothing he could do but walk away from the only meal they'd seen in days.

There was a piercing shriek from the sky. Toklo looked up and saw a huge golden eagle swooping down, aiming straight for the goat. It sank its claws into the goat's back and dragged the animal off the cliff. With a bray of terror, the goat toppled over the edge, bounced off a couple of large rocks, and crashed to the side of the mountain below, on a gentle slope that led into the meadow.

Toklo sprinted down the mountain toward the fallen goat, leaping from boulder to boulder. As he got closer, the eagle swooped in and landed on the goat, digging its talons into its flesh. With a caw of triumph, the eagle stabbed at the prey with its beak and tore off a strip of meat.

"Hey!" Toklo shouted. "That's my prey! Get away from it!" He galloped up to the goat and stood up on his hind legs, roaring.

The eagle shook itself, and suddenly there was a shower of golden feathers onto the ground at Toklo's paws. Black fur sprouted along the eagle's back and down its legs as its wings shrank into sturdy round paws. And then Ujurak was standing there, panting and looking very pleased with himself.

"Did you see that?" he cried. "I chose what I wanted to turn into! And it was something useful! And I killed some prey for us!"

"*Hmm,*" Toklo grunted. "Yes, all right, well done."

Ujurak turned back to the goat, using his claws to peel off the skin. "I can't believe I did that!" he babbled. "I was chasing after you, and then I thought, wouldn't it be great if I could turn into something that could catch this goat easily, and then I *did*! It was amazing!"

Toklo eyed Ujurak warily. "I still like you better as a bear."
It all seemed very unnatural to him, but he was too hungry to
care how they'd caught their first real meal in days. He
crouched beside Ujurak and tucked in.

A cool wind trailed through the dense forest, making the trees
murmur and the leaves dance. It was late in the day, close to
sunrest, and the air was heavy with the possibility of rain.
Toklo's skin prickled under his fur, as if the fire from the sky
was skittering along his whiskers. He kept his nose low to the
ground as he led Ujurak through the woods, searching for
food with half his attention while looking for shelter with the
other half. They would need a warm, dry place to spend the
night if a storm was coming.

He could smell something strange not far off, like burned
trees and wood ash. Luckily their path led away from the
scent; he didn't want to get closer to it unless he had to.

A small shape darted out from under a bush, and both
bears jumped. Toklo realized it was a hare as it raced away.
Ujurak let out a startled yelp, and Toklo turned around. Long
ears were sprouting from the top of Ujurak's head as the cub
shrank and his hind legs stretched and got skinnier, folding
under his body.

"No, no!" Toklo yelled, but it was too late. Ujurak had
turned into a hare—and not on purpose, Toklo was sure.

"Wait, stay there!" he commanded, but Ujurak-hare was
already off and running in the direction the first hare had

gone. Toklo sighed, watching him disappear into the shadows. Now he wouldn't be able to kill and eat any hares, just in case it was that butterfly-brained cub.

A roar sounded from somewhere close by, and Toklo's fur stood on end. There was another bear in the woods!

Toklo leaped to his paws and started running. He burst into a clearing and saw a hare trapped against a stand of thick bushes. Facing it, claws outstretched, was a scrawny black bear cub about half Toklo's size. Her fur was thin and her roar was weak from hunger. She was clearly starving—and ready to eat anything, including the Ujurak-hare.

"NO!" Toklo bellowed, launching himself across the clearing. He bundled into the black bear, knocking her over and pinning her to the ground. She fought back, biting and scratching more fiercely than he had expected. For such a skinny bear, she had surprising strength.

"You can't eat that hare!" Toklo roared at her.

"Yes I can!" she yelped. "I caught it!" One of her paws swiped his nose, leaving a stinging claw-scratch on his muzzle.

"Ow!" he growled. He shoved her paws down and held her in place with his weight.

"Wait! Stop!"

Toklo glanced over his shoulder and saw that the hare had changed back into a bear cub. Ujurak was standing on his hind legs, waving his paws at the fighting cubs.

"Don't hurt her," Ujurak pleaded. "Look at her. She's half starved—she's no threat to us. Let her go, Toklo."

The black bear stopped struggling. Toklo looked back

down at her. She was staring at him with enormous eyes.

"You're Toklo?" she said.

"Y-yes," he said.

The black bear scrambled out from underneath him and got to her paws. "I'm Lusa," she said. "I've been looking for you."

BOOK TWO
GREAT BEAR LAKE

Lusa

Lusa stared at the grizzly cub. He was twice her size; in the desperate struggle, trapped under his weight, she had thought he would kill her for sure. But she wasn't scared of him now, watching him crouched in front of her, panting, his flanks heaving. She had found Oka's missing cub. Red light from the setting sun trickled through the leaves, speckling Toklo's brown pelt with spots of burning russet.

I could have searched for him all my life and never found him. Did the spirits guide me?

For a moment she couldn't speak, as if a huge paw was clamped around her jaws.

Toklo glared at Lusa. "How do you know my name?"

"I—I've been looking for you." Lusa stumbled over the words. "I've come all the way from the Bear Bowl to tell you—"

"What's the Bear Bowl?"

"It's a place where bears live," Lusa explained. "Black bears like me, and grizzlies, and huge white bears. Flat-faces come and look at us. There are other animals, too," she added. "Tigers, and flamingoes, and animals with long, dangly noses."

Toklo interrupted her with a huff of contempt. "What has that got to do with me?"

Lusa looked at him. He seemed so angry about something; would he blame her for what she was about to tell him? She felt her belly go tight; she knew she wouldn't be able to fight him off a second time. But she had promised Oka. "The flat-faces brought your mother to the Bear Bowl. She . . . she died there." She had already decided there was no point making Toklo even more angry by telling him how Oka had been crazed with grief for her lost cubs, so deranged that she had attacked a flat-face. "Before she died she gave me a message for you. She said—"

"I don't want to hear it!" Toklo turned away.

Startled, Lusa took a pace toward him. "But I promised—"

"I said, I don't want to hear it! I don't want to hear any-thing about that bear. She abandoned me. She is *not* my mother." He stalked away, his paws crunching through the dried leaves until he stopped under a twisted fir tree.

"She was sorry," Lusa murmured.

She didn't think Toklo had heard her. Without looking at her, he snarled, "Go back to the Bear Bowl!"

Lusa blinked at him, puzzled. She had risked her life to find him and tell him what Oka had wanted him to know. She had expected that Toklo would be grateful to her. Maybe he would even become her friend, so she wouldn't be lonely anymore. He was a cub like her; she had never imagined he would be so fierce and angry. What had she done to make him so hostile?

She couldn't go back to the Bear Bowl. The wild was bigger than she had thought, and she didn't think she could find the way back. She clamped her jaws shut to stop a whimper from coming out. There was no way she'd show Toklo how scared she was.

Lusa's gaze drifted to the other brown bear cub, who was sitting watching her with bright interest. Her belly lurched as she remembered what she had glimpsed during her struggle with Toklo.

She had been chasing a hare, hadn't she? A growl from her belly reminded her that she was still hungrier than she'd ever been in her life. She'd been chasing a bear *and it had turned into this cub*.

Her mother hadn't said anything about hares that turned into bears, or any other animal for that matter. Was this a bear, or a hare? Would it change again? Lusa stared at it suspiciously, looking for long ears suddenly shooting up.

"Hello," the brown cub said, getting up and padding over to

her. He was smaller than Toklo, and his eyes were warm and curious. "My name's Ujurak. You're Lusa, right?"

Lusa nodded. "Are . . . are you a bear or a hare?" she burst out.

Ujurak lifted his shoulder in a shrug, rippling the shiny brown fur. "I don't know. I can be lots of other creatures, too. A salmon, an eagle . . . sometimes I'm a flat-face cub."

"A flat-face!" Lusa stiffened. Would Ujurak be a kind flat-face like the feeders in the Bear Bowl, or one of the dangerous ones who shouted and shot their metal sticks? "Why would you want to be a flat-face?"

"I don't exactly want to be anything," Ujurak replied. "Except a bear, of course. It just happens." He glanced at Toklo. "I'm trying to control it, but I'm not very good yet."

"So you're really a bear?" Lusa checked. His ears were definitely small and round right now, nothing like a hare's.

"I think so." Ujurak blinked. "I hope so."

Lusa looked around. The trees grew close together here, with little room for berry bushes underneath, but there was no scent of flat-faces or dogs. "Is this Toklo's territory?" The big grizzly cub looked quite strong enough to score his claws on the trees and defend his feeding ground from other bears.

"No, we're on a journey." An amber glow lit deep in Ujurak's eyes. "We're going to the place where the bear spirits dance in the sky."

"Where's that?"

Ujurak looked at his paws. *Definitely bear's paws,* Lusa thought. "We don't know exactly," he confessed. "We're following the stars." He looked up again. "But I *have* to get there. However long it takes."

Something in Lusa prompted her to stretch up and touch her nose to the cub's furry ear. "You'll find the place, I know you will."

Ujurak turned his head to stare at her. "You understand, don't you?" he said softly. "Because you kept going until you found Toklo."

Lusa nodded. "I promised Oka that I'd find him, and I did."

"Will you come with us?" Ujurak asked suddenly. "To the place where the bear spirits dance?"

Lusa wondered if Oka's spirit would be there, and if Oka would tell Toklo herself how much she loved him. Lusa wanted to see that happen more than anything. And she didn't have anywhere else to go. Besides, she'd been good at finding Toklo, hadn't she? Perhaps Ujurak would need her help to find the place he was looking for.

"I'll come," she announced.

"Great!" yelped Ujurak, bouncing on his front paws. Even though he was younger than Lusa, he was bigger than her, and she took a step back to avoid getting bounced on.

"Do you think Toklo will mind?" she asked, glancing at the brown bear cub who was still standing under the fir tree with his back to them. "He doesn't seem to like me very much."

Ujurak followed her gaze. "Toklo doesn't like anyone very much. Including himself," he remarked quietly.

Lusa glanced at him in surprise, but before she could say

anything Toklo had swung around and pushed his way out from under the spindly branches. He glared at Lusa. "You can't slow us down," he warned.

Lusa bit back a growl. It wasn't Toklo's journey, it was Ujurak's, so he shouldn't be bossing her around. But she just shook her head. "I'll keep up," she promised. Though she hoped they'd stop to eat soon, because her legs were feeling wobbly underneath her grumbling belly.

Toklo swung his head from side to side. "Why are we standing around here? We need to find shelter for the night." Without another word he headed off into the shadows under the trees. Ujurak trotted after him, his stumpy tail twitching.

Lusa stood still for a moment. Was this really what she wanted? Being a wild bear didn't mean traveling who-knew-where with two brown bears, did it? But the only other choice was staying here without them, and she had had enough of being on her own. *Even wild bears have company,* she reminded herself.

"Wait for me!" she called, and bounded off to catch up with her new companions.

Lusa shifted into a more comfortable position and parted her jaws in a huge yawn. Moonlight filtering through the leaves turned her paws to silver. She was curled up in a tree, where two thick branches met the trunk and made a bowl shape just big enough for a small black bear.

She knew she ought to go to sleep, but her pelt prickled with curiosity and every time she closed her eyes, excitement made them fly open again. She had found Toklo, but now she was on another journey—and none of them knew exactly where it would lead.

Toklo and Ujurak had squeezed themselves into a hollow beneath the roots of the tree. They weren't sleeping either; Lusa could hear them shifting about and snuffling below her.

She caught the deep growl of Toklo's voice, and craned her neck to hear him more clearly.

"This is ridiculous," he was saying. "She can't stay with us."

Lusa's belly clenched with fear. Was Toklo going to leave her behind after all?

I don't care! If they won't let me travel with them, I'll just follow them.

"You said she could come," Ujurak reminded Toklo.

"No I didn't!"

"Well, you didn't say she couldn't."

"I'm saying it now," Toklo replied irritably. "Why should we want a stupid black bear with us? She's not even a wild bear!"

Lusa wanted to jump down and confront Toklo. She might not have been born in the wild, but she had managed just fine for moons and moons. She *wanted* to be a wild bear, even if it meant never going back to the Bear Bowl, and her family. And black bears were as good as grizzlies any day! Her father had said that they were the kings of the forest.

She was bunching her muscles to leap down when Ujurak spoke. His voice was quiet, and he sounded older than before.

"I think I was meant to find Lusa. I think she is meant to come with us."

A scoffing noise came from Toklo.

"If she can't keep up, she won't want to stay with us anyway," Ujurak went on. "But I think the spirits of the bears are waiting for her, just as much as they are waiting for you and me."

Above them, Lusa shivered as she crouched on the edge of her sleeping place, staring down into the bear-scented darkness.

POWER OF THREE

WARRIORS

BOOK 1:

THE SIGHT

Muddied tree roots shaped a small opening. In the shadows beyond, the knotted tendrils cradled the smooth soil floor of a cave, hollowed out by moons of wind and water.

A cat padded up the steep path toward the opening, narrowing his eyes as he neared. His flame-colored pelt glowed in the moonlight. His ears twitched, and the bristling of his fur gave away his unease as he sat down at the mouth of the cave and curled his tail across his paws. "You asked me to come."

From the shadows, a pair of eyes blinked at him—eyes as blue as water reflecting the summer sky. A gray tom, scarred by time and battle, was waiting in the entrance.

"Firestar." The warrior stepped forward and brushed the ThunderClan leader's cheek with his white-flecked muzzle. "I have to thank you." His mew was hoarse with age. "You have rebuilt the lost Clan. No cat could have done better."

"There's no need for thanks." Firestar dipped his head. "I did only what I had to."

The old warrior nodded, blinking thoughtfully. "Do you think you have been a good leader for ThunderClan?"

Firestar tensed. "I don't know," he mewed. "It hasn't been easy, but I've always tried to do what is right for my Clan."

"No cat would doubt your loyalty," the old cat rasped. "But how far would it go?"

Firestar's eyes glittered uncertainly as he searched for the words to answer.

"There are difficult times ahead," the warrior went on before Firestar could reply. "And your loyalty will be tested to the utmost. Sometimes the destiny of one cat is not the destiny of the whole Clan."

Suddenly the old cat rose stiffly to his paws and stared past Firestar. It seemed he no longer saw the ThunderClan leader but gazed far beyond, to something Firestar could not see.

When he spoke again, the ancient rasp was smoothed from his voice, as though some other cat used his tongue.

"*There will be three, kin of your kin, who hold the power of the stars in their paws.*"

"I don't understand," Firestar meowed. "Kin of my kin? Why are you telling me this?"

The old warrior blinked, his gaze fixed once more on Firestar.

"You must tell me more!" Firestar demanded. "How can I decide what I ought to do if you don't explain?"

The old cat took a deep breath, but when he spoke it was only to say, "Farewell, Firestar. In seasons to come, remember me."

* * *

Firestar jerked awake, his belly tight with fear. He blinked with relief when he saw the familiar stone walls of his den in the hollow by the lake. Morning sunlight streamed through the split in the rock. The warmth on his fur soothed him.

He heaved himself to his paws and shook his head, trying to dislodge the dream. But this was no ordinary dream, for he remembered being in that cave as clearly as if it had happened a moon ago, rather than the many, many seasons he had lived since then. When the old warrior cast his strange prophecy, Firestar's daughters had not been born and the four Clans had still lived in the forest. The prophecy had followed him on the Great Journey over the mountains and settled with him in his new home by the lake; and every full moon, the memory of it returned to fill his dreams. Even Sandstorm, who slept beside him, knew nothing of the words he had shared with the ancient cat.

He gazed out from his den at the waking camp below. His deputy, Brambleclaw, was stretching in the center of the clearing, flexing his powerful shoulders as he clawed at the ground. Squirrelflight padded toward her mate, greeting him with a purr.

I pray that I am wrong, Firestar thought. And yet his heart felt hollow; he feared the prophecy was about to reveal itself.

The three have come. . . .